P9-CMT-852

RING OF GUILT

RING OF GUILT

Judith Cutler

This first world edition published 2010
in Great Britain and in 2011 in the USA by
SEVERN HOUSE PUBLISHERS LTD of
9–15 High Street, Sutton, Surrey, England, SM1 1DF.
Trade paperback edition first published
in Great Britain and the USA 2011 by
SEVERN HOUSE PUBLISHERS LTD.

British Library Cataloguing in Publication Data

Cutler, Judith.
   Ring of guilt. – (A Lina Townend mystery)
   1. Townend, Lina (Fictitious character)–Fiction.
   2. Antique dealers–Fiction. 3. Archaeological thefts–
   Fiction. 4. Murder victims–Fiction. 5. Detective and
   mystery stories.
   I. Title II. Series
   823.9'14-dc22

ISBN-13: 978-0-7278-6960-9   (cased)
ISBN-13: 978-1-84751-291-8   (trade paper)

All Severn House titles are printed on acid-free paper.

Severn House Publishers support The Forest Stewardship Council [FSC],
the leading international forest certification organisation. All our titles that
are printed on Greenpeace-approved FSC-certified paper carry the FSC logo.

Mixed Sources
Product group from well-managed
forests and other controlled sources
www.fsc.org Cert no. SA-COC-1565
© 1996 Forest Stewardship Council
FSC

Typeset by Palimpsest Book Production Ltd.,
Falkirk, Stirlingshire, Scotland.
Printed and bound in Great Britain by
MPG Books Ltd., Bodmin, Cornwall.

ONE

I've had it up to here with policemen. They're either bent or they go off and get married – to someone else. But there are times when you'd rather see one than anyone else.

And this was one of those times. There I was, in the middle of nowhere, with a van full of delicate china, a few precious pieces of jewellery and a box of assorted kitchen tat – and there was a body lying in a field fifty yards away.

Any decent human being would have leapt out of the van, somehow got over or through that nice brambly hedge, tangled with some of the most vicious barbed wire I'd ever seen, and attempted to revive the body. I knew there was a better, longer word for bringing people back to life, but at times like this my vocabulary always did a disappearing act. Griff, my business partner and sort of adopted grandfather said it wasn't just my lack of education but something to do with stress, and spent hours playing memory games with me.

Griff was waiting for me at home. He'd just got over a head cold he insisted was the flu. I knew he was wagging, but I love him so much I was happy to indulge him on a miserable wet autumn day like this. I'd been to an auction near Hythe, and bought several lots. Some I knew were good, though most of them would never find their way into the shop; we did much better with Internet sales and occasional antiques fairs these days. Some would probably be offloaded on mates lower down the food chain and some – well, goodness knows what their destiny was.

Anyway, here I was, with my antennae working overtime. *Antennae*. That was a good word: I must be calming down. Whether it was them or something else but all I felt was suspicion. The other day on a lonely road just like this one of my mates had stopped to help a girl with a flat tyre and next thing he knew he was laid out cold by the jack, and his van, full of antique silver, was heading briskly for a Channel port.

Was this the same sort of scam, or was the youngish man in the field, the drizzle licking his face, genuinely in distress? (For *in distress* read *dead*.)

A long burst on the horn didn't make him so much as twitch. Neither did my loudest yells. Now what?

It wasn't a very heroic thing to do, but I fished out my mobile and dialled nine nine nine. No network coverage! So should I leap out? Or drive on a little further?

What about all those goodies, so far uninsured because I needed Griff to value some of them? The auction prices I'd paid would be way, way below replacement costs. And I was on my own and dusk was falling. Leaning out of the window as far as I dared, I used my mobile to take an indistinct photo before shoving the van into gear and driving on. I stopped every few metres to see if I was getting any signal but it must have been three hundred metres or so before the little bar showed any growth.

At last! I was even able to give a map reference, this being one of the latest tricks Griff was teaching me, largely because he couldn't bear the voices on SatNav systems. 'He's in his twenties or thirties,' I told the man picking up my call. 'Well dressed. He's lying flat on his back, one arm stretched out. I didn't see any blood or anything.'

'You didn't go and check him over?' the man at the other end demanded, his voice stern as the one in my conscience.

'A woman on her own? At this time of day?' Even his silence was critical. 'Besides which,' I added, suddenly thinking of a term that I'd learned from that marrying boyfriend, 'I didn't want to corrupt the integrity of a possible crime scene.' Let him chew on that. 'But I'll go back to the spot and leave my lights on and wave when your colleagues arrive. Any idea how long they'll take?'

'Something like that's a blues and twos job. Say five minutes?'

That sounded pretty efficient to me. I turned the van and headed back – it'd never do to keep them waiting.

In fact I'd just parked, pointing in the opposite direction, of course, and popped on my hazard lights so I'd be noticeable when I heard them. Then I noticed a rather important fact. The body had gone. And I'd a nasty feeling the police would take a grim view of my wasting their time.

Having arrived, they weren't pleased, that was sure, and all I wanted to do was hop back in the van and drive hell for leather. Much good that would have done me, of course. At last my common sense popped back. 'Here's the photo I took,' I said, waving my mobile.

'It's not very clear,' said the older of the men – he'd be about forty, I'd guess.

The younger looked me up and down. A spectacular spot glowed in the middle of his chin, though I'd have thought him a little old for teenage acne. 'You're sure this isn't just you and a mate having a bit of fun?'

'Wouldn't be much fun lying like that with this lot sluicing down,' I pointed out. 'Actually, wouldn't whoever it was have left tracks when he legged it out of the field? He's the one you should be bollocking for messing you about.'

The younger man vaulted over the hedge – I gave him full marks for not tearing his trousers – and picked his way along the edge of the field. He stood and stared at something, and then came back. This time he got stuck on one of those brambles, and his mate, not very gently, pulled him free.

Backs towards me, they muttered and pointed at the woodland beside the field. Since the older one was still clutching my mobile, I had to hang around.

Eventually, one of them turned to me. 'Looks as if there may have been something there,' he said, as if he begrudged every syllable. 'We'll confirm your details and you can be on your way.'

I reeled off my name and address, confirming what I'd said with a flash of my driving licence and a flourish of my business card. Then I held out my hand for my mobile.

'We'll need to hang on to this – download the photo,' the older one said.

'Uh, uh. It's got all my business contacts on, not to mention photos of things that don't concern you at all,' I said firmly. 'Tell me your number and I'll send it to you.'

The mobile he produced might have been driven by a water wheel for all the features it had – or rather, didn't have. After a lot of chuntering, it was agreed I'd take PC Acne back to the nearest police station so he could download the photo there. I really wanted to phone Griff to explain why I was going to be late home, but since I'd wrung that concession out of them, it didn't seem the moment to ask for another one.

I turned the van as neatly as if I were taking a driving test, and set off, leaving the other policeman talking into his radio.

Conversation didn't seem to be in order, either. No amount of pumping would get him to reveal why he was taking my call seriously, not even when a whole stream of police vehicles came towards us, many of them with their lights flashing. It all looked very impressive.

In my head I was asking a lot of questions: should I have gone to help? What if he had recovered enough to crawl somewhere else? What if he was now hiding from someone – maybe the police? My cheeks burned with shame.

'Would it have been better if I'd gone and looked?' I asked, in a horrible thin voice.

He shrugged, and fingered his chin as if I wasn't there.

I tried again. 'Why do you think no one else called him in? My body?'

But all I got was a tightening of the jaw that must have made that zit hurt something shocking.

'Whatever you say, I think you were very public-spirited,' Griff declared, fussing round me as if I'd been exploring muddy fields myself. 'And I think a cup of tea is in order, although it will soon be supper time.'

'It certainly is,' I said, with an enthusiasm I didn't quite feel. I'd persuaded Griff to drink more green tea, on the grounds that it was some wonderful cure-all – or prevent-all, which was even better. The trouble was, he kept experimenting with new flavours – yuck, cranberry! 'And while we're drinking it, I'd really like you to cast your eyes over my booty.' I led the way to the van, safely locked in our yard. 'I'm pretty sure about most of it,' I added, as I passed him several plastic boxes of bubble-wrapped items. Then we shifted damp cardboard boxes filled with odds and sods wrapped in scraps of yellowing newspaper. 'But I went out on a limb with others.'

Soon the kitchen was filled with the musty smell you always seem to get with house-clearance items.

Griff abandoned his supper preparations, unable to resist starting to sort through the cardboard boxes. He knew the plastic storage boxes' contents would be good, and left those till last.

'It's like my boyhood Christmases, starting on the tiny things in my stocking,' he said. 'I had such indulgent parents I knew what some of the bigger presents under the tree were – it's hard to make a cricket bat look like anything except a cricket bat. Which reminds me, my love – would you object to having supper on trays tonight? There's a day-nighter on TV.'

To look at him picking through balls of yellowing newspaper and dropping them in a black bin-liner as if he couldn't bear to touch them, no one would associate Griff with hard bats and hard balls. But even though the weirder patterns of the cricketers' strips for the short forms of the game enraged and amused him in equal measure – Griff was a white flannels man – he was, as I was coming to realize, something of an expert. I was trying to equate this dear dapper elderly gentleman with the killer wicketkeeper he assured me he once was when he laid a hand gently on mine.

He must have taken my silence as a sign that I was unhappy. 'My sweet one, I'm so sorry. I keep forgetting that Christmas was not a good season for you.'

It wasn't, actually. In fact, it was pretty crap. While my mates, such as they were, were loaded with goodies, many pretty unsuitable, as I now see, my various foster mothers resorted to toiletries and sensible and useful clothes. God, those dreadful shoes . . . Even then I suppose I dimly realized they were doing their best, but that wasn't likely to cheer me up. It wasn't until I came into Griff's life that Christmas meant beautiful things for me too – some practical but many wonderfully frivolous.

I hugged him tightly. 'It is now,' I said truthfully. 'It really is. And that's the most important thing.'

'I'm glad to hear it. And I think it may have come early this year. Look at this.' Once again he plunged his hand into the yellowing crumpled mess, and came up with a ring. He looked at me, his eyes bright with excitement. 'Did you know this was here?'

I shook my head. 'It was just a load of tat – you can see the rest of it. Some EPNS spoons, an old mincer – see, you have to clamp it to a table top and there's a bit missing, I think. But I knew I had to have it. Had to. Despite the other bidders,' I said.

There wasn't much wool I could pull over Griff's eyes. 'You pushed the lot up to what?' he asked.

'A pound,' I admitted. 'A whole pound.'

While Griff fetched his jeweller's eyeglass, I peered at the ring. It was gold, really bright – not quite the colour of Indian gold, but far more intense than modern stuff. At some time it had been bent slightly out of shape. What looked like brightly coloured beads had been set into it. Everything about it said ordinary. In my heart, I knew it was special. Just don't ask why.

'What do you make of it?' Griff asked, eyepiece already in place.

I passed him the ring, but he didn't take it. As usual when I'd come up with something out of the ordinary, he was setting me a little test – in the kindest way, of course, not like school at all. And the more he wanted me to do well, the better I was.

'Very old? Really old? When you fished it out I thought it might be a piece of cheap tat. Crude. Especially where they've set these pretty beads.' I touched them. 'Or not beads? It's important, isn't it?' I said seriously. 'I can tell by the way you're looking at me, Griff – nothing to do with my being a divvy.' Rather like a water diviner finding water, sometimes I can pick up some valuable item really cheap because something inside tells me it's good, when no one else has realized it's a treasure.

'But something made you bid for the lot in the first place, my angel child. And risk a whole pound in the process,' he added, with his usual twinkle. 'And maybe a little of your gift has rubbed off on me.' He opened the fridge door with a flourish and produced a bottle of champagne. 'Somehow I just knew there'd be something to celebrate.'

I was happy to drink the fizz, but had to ask one thing. 'What are we celebrating?'

'Ah, I wish I knew exactly. Gold, of course. And I suspect those beads are actually uncut gems. Possibly it's medieval, but I can't be sure. It might be older. I'm afraid we shall have to ask an expert.' It wasn't often Griff admitted defeat.

'Your friend at the British Museum?'

'Why not? We could go up together and see a show. I believe there's a very good play on at the Old Vic. What on earth have I said, dear one?'

'We don't have to go to the War Museum again, do we?' I was horrified to hear a little-girl quiver in my voice. Last time we'd been to the Old Vic, on the grounds that the Imperial War Museum was in walking distance, Griff had thought it would be helpful to give me a practical history lesson, to start putting some of what I knew about everyday objects into some sort of context. I knew it was good for me, but it didn't stop me having nightmares for weeks afterwards. I alternated between seeing rats in the First World War trenches and being a Holocaust victim rounded up for the gas chambers. Poor Griff got quite used to hearing me scream my head off at three in the morning, and it wasn't good for him, not at his age, because he would insist on getting up and making me cocoa.

'Not if you don't want to. And perhaps we'd prefer a different theatre. Let me look into it. Meanwhile, you'll be able to see those gorgeous medieval tiles I was talking about . . .'

This time when I screamed my head off at three in the morning it was because I saw the body in the field get up, tuck its head under its arm, and run towards our van.

TWO

I half expected the police to come banging on our door to ask further questions about the disappearing body or to say it was all a hoax, and that I must be more careful about dialling 999 next time. But they didn't. I read the papers and watched the TV news with more interest than usual for a few days; I even Googled for unexplained incidents that might not have reached the national media. I had to accept that it was a false alarm. I should have been pleased, of course – and not just for the young man. I wouldn't have fancied being a witness at an Inquest, let alone in a trial.

All the same, I didn't like loose ends hanging around. I wanted to know the rest of the story. I managed to find the road on Google Earth, swooping in close enough to spot my lay-by. And Griff's map-reading lessons meant I could trace any convenient footpaths or bridleways the young man might have legged it down, until they all disappeared into thick woodland. There was one odd thing – I didn't recall a road where the OS said there was one. My memory had always been a bit weak, of course, though Griff's efforts to improve it had made a huge difference. But I might have been taking tap-dancing lessons for all the good any of this research did me.

All the time – every moment I wasn't really concentrating on something else, such as repairing the tusk on a Meissen elephant for one of our regular clients – I beat myself up. As I told the reproachful figure still frozen on my mobile phone, I should have stopped and gone to help. What if he'd really been ill or been hurt? What if I could have saved his life?

Griff kept on looking at me a little anxiously, and once or twice had his mouth open, as if he was going to ask me something. But he said nothing, and, knowing better than to interrupt me when I was on a really tough assignment, spent a lot of time ensuring that the new addition to our team, Mary Walker, knew everything there was to know about the new stock I'd bought on purpose – unlike the ring, of course. We kept quiet about that.

When she first started to help out in the shop, we'd been afraid Mrs Walker – somehow we never used her first name – might be over-anxious. After all, she'd been wrongly sacked from her last job, and it couldn't have been easy stepping into the shoes of a victim of an armed robbery. (I'd never actually liked poor Mrs Hatch, her predecessor, at all, but all the same being literally scared to death – she'd had a heart attack and never recovered – isn't nice.) As it was, Mrs Walker had taken to the work like the proverbial duck to water. While Mrs Hatch had given the impression she was begrudging us every second of her time when we were away at fairs or auctions, Mrs Walker pretty well shooed us off so she could take her place amongst all the goodies. She also knew her way around our mail order system, and helped out with that when she had time on her hands. She'd even helped wash and catalogue some of the stuff I'd bought at the auction, though she'd drawn the line at the smelly box of kitchen items.

'Mrs Walker reminds me of you, in a way,' Griff said over supper one evening.

I blinked. Much as we liked each other, I couldn't see a retired teacher having much in common with someone my age who'd systematically skived off school.

'She's always so keen to learn,' he explained. 'But where you make intuitive leaps and back them up afterwards, she's a book-learner first and appreciates things second. You did well to choose her, sweet one; you complement each other.'

I'd asked her to work for us because ages ago she'd been kind to me when a bit of kindness was just what I needed. Griff and I had fallen out over something, and I'd stormed out of his life for ever (as if!), though it was a couple of days neither of us ever referred to. The other reason was that before she'd been sacked from the job she loved, she'd been the victim of bullying, and I'd been so often on the receiving end of that, I knew it wasn't funny. Oh, and there was the small matter of desperately needing someone to look after the shop while Griff and I were doing other things. So I didn't really deserve Griff's praise.

'Anyway, she's more than happy to cover for us for a couple of days. And guess what the postie brought today! Two tickets for a show, my love. So next week we shall journey to London with as much pomp as whatever the rail company's called these days can manage. We shall have lunch with dear Douglas, and pick his impressive brain about your ring – yes, my sweet, your ring it is! You paid a whole pound for it, remember. And then we shall go and see *Priscilla, Queen of the Desert*. One of my old friends is in the ensemble, so it is possible that we shall go back stage afterwards, and meet some of the stars. I only hope that none of them will steal your heart and take you away from me. All those handsome young men . . .'

Sometimes when he said things like that he wrung my heart. This time I suspected a twinkle in his eye.

There was one in mine, too. 'Handsome young men? More likely to steal yours, aren't they?'

There was one man, handsome or otherwise, that Griff wouldn't let me meet. Not his choice, he insisted. Occasionally someone would knock on the door very early in the morning – apparently, in the days before Griff became security conscious, he'd just appear in the kitchen, and would sometimes be helping himself to breakfast before Griff realized there was anyone else in the house. Apparently he scraped an existence rooting round boot sales and selling likely items to people like Griff. Any profits went to keeping a small float for the next fair and buying rough cider. He relied for food on people like Griff, as well as the burgers and such the boot-fair punters discarded. I heard his tap early one morning; Griff slipped a little note under my door telling me to have a lie-in.

Since the mystery guest had once seen my bedroom curtains twitch and hadn't returned for six months, I simply had to do as Griff said and wait for Griff's call before coming downstairs.

This morning, despite the cold, when I was allowed down the kitchen window was wide open and the extractor fan whirring full-time.

'I'm sorry, angel.' Griff was rubbing the table with that surface cleaner that's supposed to kill all germs. 'Our friend X's personal hygiene leaves much to be desired.'

'You mean, he stinks,' I said in my head. But not aloud. If it hadn't been for Griff, I might have been a female X, without X's eye for a bargain. 'Has he brought anything interesting?'

'You tell me.'

He unwrapped a filthy newspaper, producing a pair of tiny bowls, both with a single silver foot. I didn't need to turn them over. 'Late-ish Ruskin,' I said. 'Very pretty. Hallmarked Birmingham 1929. A matched pair, so we get more than twice the individual value . . . Griff, you did pay him enough, didn't you?' I asked, doing sums in my head.

'Dear one, if I paid him enough, he'd die of alcoholic poisoning in a week. I pay what he asks, though we both – we all three – know it's not enough. But as he says, he knows if he has a problem, he can always come here.'

The obvious place to sell them was Detling Antiques Fair, our last fair before our trip to London. We might not like the site, one of the windiest in the country, but we couldn't miss the event itself. At least we had the privilege of an inside stall, but there were a lot of poor dealers who could only afford an outside pitch. Some had marquee-sized tents, plus heaters. Others just huddled like the roadside refugees you sometimes see on TV, selling stuff I honestly couldn't see why anyone should want to buy. But then, since punters collected all sorts of stuff I wouldn't have given houseroom to even when it was new and clean, I suppose they made a living.

One man who certainly made a living drifted by as I put the finishing touches to the lights on our stall. Titus Oates. Aged somewhere between forty and sixty, and so ordinary looking no one would ever manage to put together an e-fit

of him, he had a stall in the darkest corner, away from the
main drag. I wouldn't have described him as a mate, and
he barely acknowledged my existence, but we did each
other good turns occasionally. I kept schtum about his dead
dodgy business; he'd tip me the wink about things I might
find useful.

This time, as we nodded to each other, he touched the
side of his nose. 'Word on the street is you've lost your
touch, doll. Bought a load of tat at that house clearance last
week. And you're supposed to be a divvy.'

'On a fishing trip, are you, Titus? What fetched up in the
shop or in the rubbish bin is for me to know and you to
keep quiet about.'

He slapped his thigh. 'So you did get something good?
I laid a fiver you would.'

'To be honest – and I know it's a word we don't often
use, Titus – I don't know.'

He narrowed his eyes. 'Hey up, there's one of the filth
over there. Don't want him seeing you and me together and
doing the sums about me and your dad, do we?' He disappeared before I could agree. Master forger and Cheshire
Cat, our Titus. And employer of my disreputable father,
Lord Elham.

But this wasn't the moment to worry about him, though
he was due a visit. Any moment now dealers and the punters
who paid extra to get in early would be upon us, and I still
hadn't had time to drift round to check out other stalls.
Maybe some people looked at me a bit oddly now I was
getting known as a divvy, but since it was mostly folk with
a lot to hide, I took no notice. There were more cheery
waves than scowls, and a huge hug from Josie. She got
tinier by the week, and always insisted that the current fair
would be her last.

'No handsome boyfriend in tow?' she asked. And then
she took my hand. 'I'm sorry, luvvie – he didn't break your
heart, did he?'

'Which one?' Griff asked, appearing at my side. 'There
are so many, Josie, beating a path to my door.'

'I hope they ask your permission, Griff.'

'I insist,' he said.

'I'm afraid he does. And he checks up what time I get home. But only 'cos he's jealous,' I added, grinning at him.

She cackled with laughter. 'So you won't be coming to old Josie for a ring yet a while?'

Not while I had two beauties from the last boyfriend to sell when the market perked up, but I needn't tell her that. I just shook my head, mock-sadly. 'So you'll have to stay in business a good long time.'

I left the two discussing their symptoms, and headed back to our stall. Already there was a man hanging round. I recognized him at once. Harvey Sanditon. He was the an . . . anti . . . He was pretty well as far from X as it was possible to be. What he was doing at a middling fair like this goodness knew, since he was LAPADA through and through. But here he was, and at our stand, no less. He couldn't take his eyes off a piece of early twentieth century Royal Worcester. I was never quite sure how to deal with guys who couldn't manage to shove their arms down their coat sleeves – you know, like that president of Afghanistan. And this guy wore his very fine camel-hair coat perched on his expensively suited shoulders. If you ignored all that, he had a face that was handsome in a Forties film star sort of way. I ducked into place and produced my most professional smile – what a good job Griff insisted I applied my slap before I left the house.

'You'd do better to have your spotlight on that,' he said, pointing to the Worcester vase.

'Replace the Rockingham, you mean?' I'd have liked to greet him by name, but thought Harvey was a bit familiar, while Mr Sanditon came in at the toadying end of the scale.

He looked taken aback.

'Would you like a look at the Worcester? The James Stinton pheasant vase?'

Before he could blink, he had it in his hands. In ordinary punters it almost guaranteed a sale. Somehow the object became theirs, just because they were holding it. But he was a dealer, and I was expecting something else.

He turned it upside down to check the mark, and also,

I suspect, to work our price code – not exactly rocket science, of course. 'You should tell your boss he's underpriced this.'

I shook my head. 'You see that little mark next to the price? It means it's been restored. So I think the price is about right.'

He nearly dropped it, which would have ruined three days' work. 'Where?' He turned it this way and that.

At last I pointed to one of its funny little feet. 'I never sell anything I've repaired without warning the purchaser –' I nearly said punter, which wouldn't be right to a man with such an elegant signet ring – 'and I never attempt to sell at the perfect price. All the information goes on the receipt and into our computer records.'

He passed it back. 'Why are you working for such a tinpot firm as this?'

Tinpot? How bloody dare he? I said tartly, 'Because I'm the Townend half of Tripp and Townend.' His eyes said I was very young to be a partner. 'I also do a lot of restoration for private individuals,' I added, trying not to laugh at the way his jaw had dropped. Or perhaps I was trying not to be dead furious. 'Here's my card.'

He glanced at it, then at me. There were no letters after my name, of course.

'Where did you train?'

'I did an informal apprenticeship.'

'With?'

'Old friends of my partner's.' The couple in the Midlands who'd taught me had a national reputation. I dropped their name out casually.

It was quite clear he not only recognized it, he knew how good they were. When his eyebrows returned to normal, he said, 'What do you charge?'

'My time and sometimes a proportion of the original value. I always give estimates and written documentation, plus before and after photos.' Thank God Griff had rehearsed me for hours on end: I knew the words and how to deliver them in a cool professional voice. But I was glad I'd put the Worcester back in its place before I started to talk. I was so angry my hands were sweating and beginning to tremble.

'I may be in touch.' He produced his own card.

There was something about the way he flicked it on to the counter that riled me even more. 'I should warn you I have a waiting list several weeks' long.'

But even that didn't slap him down. 'In that case you should be working in your studio, not wasting time here.' He turned on his heel, on what Griff would have called a good exit line. Pity he spoiled it by turning round again. 'Did you say the Rockingham was perfect?'

Griff had told me how to respond to questions like that, too, and to take a deep calming breath without it being seen. 'Its provenance is excellent, and I can detect no sign at all of damage, or even wear. Circa 1835. The view in the cartouche is of Howick Hall, in Northumberland.'

I wrapped it and stowed it for him in one of the recycled card carriers we'd started to use for our most fragile objects, and he was on his way.

Griff mimed applause as he came back. 'I've been watching from the wings, my angel. Heavens, you should be selling sand to Arabs. A piece of Rockingham to Harvey Sanditon! And at full price, too?'

'I gave him trade discount,' I admitted. 'Not because he needed it, but because I thought he might be a useful contact. Restoration,' I explained. 'If you think we can trust him not to palm off restored stuff as perfect?'

'His reputation's pretty good. As it should be, the prices he asks. I'll ask around for you. Meanwhile, my love, the ravening hordes will be upon us in five minutes, and we have a horrid blank space on our display. How shall we fill it?'

'The Ruskin bowls,' I said, giving their pedestals a final polish.

We were pretty busy all day, quite an achievement these days, though I suppose some people – the sort we love – would rather put their money into something beautiful than trust it to a bank account offering what Griff called miserly interest. The eye-catching centre piece had to be replaced several times in the course of the day.

'Is this anything to do with Harvey Sanditon's patronage?' Griff pondered, as we packed up the most valuable things for the night. Of course the organizers provided tight security, but we knew of other fairs where people had been robbed, despite the presence of guards and CCTV, so we went in for belt and braces.

I shook my head. 'Would you mind finishing up here? I need to go for a stroll.' Something was calling me from somewhere.

I let myself drift along with the last of the punters. I wished I could tell a nice-looking couple not to buy anything from one guy: every stick of his furniture was dodgy. I yearned to tell a woman Mrs Walker's age that the plate she'd just turned down was worth twice the asking price. Knowledge, nothing to do with my weird instinct. But I kept my mouth shut and my hands in my pockets and strolled along, not particularly trying to catch anyone's eye. If a mate waved, I smiled back – though I didn't stop to talk. Not yet, not yet. Perhaps whatever it was had just been sold and was walking out right now. Shrugging, I headed back to Griff and picked up the heavy box the silly old dear was trying to lift.

It was outside, of course. This lovely Stourbridge lead crystal fruit bowl. Thomas Webb. Oh, not very old – perhaps forty years, that was all. But the weight, the colour, the depth of cut – what skills had been thrown away when the glass industry decamped to Europe or wherever! The guy selling it was so cold and wet he might have given it me. As it was, he grabbed my fiver as if it was the first money he'd touched all day.

'Cut glass is quite down at the moment,' Griff murmured.

'Are you telling me I won't get my money back? Well, if I don't, we can put fruit salad in it.' All the same, I was a tiny bit disappointed myself. What if by talking about my gift, I'd driven it away?

All through Saturday and right up to closing time on Sunday I had this niggle at the back of my mind. It was if someone was tugging me by one hair. But I ignored it. I was busy, for one thing, and really couldn't say that anything other than an eye for a bargain had led me to the bowl – though it was twice as lovely now I'd washed it, and Mrs Walker said someone had been looking for something similar and had left a phone number.

There were steady sales – the Ruskin went almost immediately – but nothing spectacular. A regular customer brought back a nice piece of early Loetz glass saying she couldn't find a place in her new house for the light to bring out the best in it; she went away with a credit note and a funny Minton cheese dish in the shape of a beehive I'd never have associated with her. The glassware wasn't our usual thing, of course; how Griff had come to stock it I'd no idea. Anyway, it looked good in the Ruskin's former position under the light, and Griff upped the price a bit. Another regular customer bought the Victorian silver spectacle case I knew she'd want even though it was a bit over her usual budget. And there were plenty of people who really just wanted free valuations, and others who pointed out they'd got better at home. Security drifted round with a warning that some teenage girls looked as if they might be trying to shoplift – in other words, steal.

Been there, done that – but found Griff.

The kids were larking round the jewellery at the far end of the hall, with lots of screams and giggles. Dilly Pargetter, the woman who ran the stall that seemed to be their target, wasn't the brightest gem in the setting, but she didn't deserve to have her stuff nicked by a load of kids who'd probably throw it away when they found it wasn't as shiny as Accessorize bling. Since they were miles away from us, I explained to Griff what I was up to and went to her rescue. It was no big deal: people covered each other's stalls during loo or lunch breaks. And of course I knew from experience the tricks the girls might pull.

Even as I approached, a ring went into a back pocket – silly, because you could see the shape through the denim. It was a long time since I'd picked pockets, and jeans were trickier because they were tight and the victim would feel unless I went for heavy distraction. But the mere glimpse of a security guard would have them going hell for leather, and probably tripping up punters and upturning displays as they went.

I wasn't the only one who'd seen what was going on. Titus just happened to be ambling by – as if he ever just happened to do anything – and we exchanged a glance. Before I knew it he'd jostled the girl and dropped a twenty pound note right by her feet. As he stumbled to pick it up, he put his hand down quite hard on the girl's foot. She arched back, so the pressure on her pocket was reduced. Which is where I came in. By the time he'd dusted himself down and produced an apology, the ring was on my finger.

The girl was screaming she'd been groped, everyone could see Titus was nowhere near her, security arrived and I melted away. Dilly swore quite truthfully to the guards she'd seen Titus' hands all the time, and the girls were herded away, their shrill complaints echoing through the hall. Titus did his disappearing act, and I returned the ring to Dilly. Only to find it was what had been calling me all weekend. A twin to the one we were taking to London. More a second cousin, really, I suppose. But the same rich gold and the same unpolished stones.

And it was mine for twenty pounds, give or take.

Griff and Josie had obviously watched the whole thing, realizing what Titus and I were up to.

'Hmmm,' Griff mused, still admiring the ring. 'I've never known Titus Oates do anything public-spirited before. He must have a soft spot for you, my angel.'

'Titus? Me? You're joking! At least,' I added, thoroughly alarmed, 'I hope you are.'

That night, the body in the field sat up, holding a ring for me to inspect. But he ran away before I could scream.

THREE

After what seemed a very quick encounter with Griff's British Museum friend, Sir Douglas Nelson, and a salad lunch without him, we spent the afternoon shopping for clothes: Griff has the most wonderful eye and makes me try on things I'd never have thought of even reaching off the rail. We had what he protested was a meagre afternoon tea – I obey doctor's orders for him, even when he grumbles – and then headed for the theatre for the most magical evening.

The costumes, the songs, the razzmatazz – I didn't want the evening to end. Ever. But it did.

At least it didn't quite end for us.

After the show we went backstage, as Griff had promised to meet another old friend. This one was charming, but quickly claimed by a fan – and as Griff pointed out, fans paid the rent. In any case, Griff too had other fish to fry. Only one of the principals, drop dead gorgeous in anyone's book. He didn't half make my heart beat faster. But then he saw Griff.

So there I was, fancying this young man with the most beautiful legs you've ever seen – only to have him start flirting with Griff! But I suppose I'd rather know where I stood with a bloke before I fell for him – I'd made a shed load of mistakes in the last few years, and Tim the Bear was getting sick of waking up with soggy fur. Tim is the bear Griff bought me, but not a collector's item – just a homely, take-to-bed teddy.

So I stood back, and tried to imagine Griff having been this dishy bloke forty-odd years ago, when he was still a juvie lead. Who would he have been flirting with then? His long-standing partner, Aidan Morley, perhaps? They were just a pair of dear old ducks these days – though Aidan was more of a rather snooty heron, come to think of it – talking about fine wine and the best biscuits. But when they were both young and handsome . . .

Anyway, at last we had to tear ourselves away, to catch the last train, reaching Victoria with a minute to spare, just like Cinderella, really. We nattered away as we always did. While there were other people within earshot we spoke about the show – the choreography, the special effects, all the technical things that looked so easy but were, Griff assured me, the very devil to get right.

Only when the carriage was empty did we talk about lunch with Douggie, the guy from the British Museum.

'I know you said you and Douggie were friends,' I said slowly, 'but how well do you two know each other?'

'Oh, we've known each other for ever,' he said, which wasn't, of course, an answer to my question at all.

'He didn't seem very . . . keen to see us.' I hadn't taken to him at all, nor him to me.

'Well, he's a very important man, far above the touch of a lowly pair like us. On a heritage quango or two; on at least two national committees. Remember – that's why he couldn't linger for lunch.' Maybe Griff convinced himself – he didn't convince me.

I nodded. No need to point out I don't think he'd have wanted to lunch with us even if he'd had a week to spare. 'He was a bit b—' I almost had the word, but then it went. 'Broo—?'

'Brusque? Yes, he wasn't his usual affable self, I suppose. But who knows why people are short-tempered. The good thing is he's gone off with your rings – you still have that receipt, sweet one? – and will let us know what they're worth. And it's quite something that he wants the British Museum to have first option on them should you choose to sell.'

'Or put them on permanent loan with my name against them. That'd be pretty cool, wouldn't it? I just wish he'd given off better vibes.'

'Caution is his middle name, my child. So when he gave that quiet smile and said, "Very interesting", it was his version of leaping in the air and yelling, "Eureka!"'

I pulled a face. 'I'd thought an expert would know instantly. Like you or me with Victorian china. Mostly, anyway,' I added.

'That's because you and I are journeymen dealers, angel heart, not Scholars.' He waited for me to absorb the capital letter. 'Scholars at his level aren't *Antiques Roadshow* performers. So try not to be too disappointed. Tomorrow is another day, as they say.'

'Except it's not,' I pointed out. 'It's today already.'

And even though it was actually the same day, tomorrow brought a visitor who wouldn't have been very welcome even if he'd rung the bell and hammered the door a bit less viciously at just past nine in the morning. Griff and I prided ourselves on being neat and tidy by the start of the working day: we allowed ourselves breakfast, occasionally, in our dressing gowns – his a spectacular stage affair and mine an embroidered silk kimono, rather sexy, come to think of it. Somehow Griff managed to sleep through the onslaught, and I'd had no time to do more than slip on the kimono. Not even my slippers.

Being barefoot and opening the door – still on the chain of course – to a youngish man who might have had policeman written all over him was not very professional, to say the least. He waggled his ID through the crack.

'Give me three minutes,' I said, closing the door on him and dealing with all the alarms. That included switching on the little CCTV camera – we'd have him on record if he turned out to be a fake. Then a minute to pull on jeans and a sweater, another to drag a brush through my hair and yet another to yell at Griff to stir himself. And even then I hadn't got any shoes on.

Remembering all Griff had said about breathing and posture, at last I opened the door.

'DS Will Kinnersley, Kent Police,' he said, flashing his ID again.

I took a good look. It seemed OK. So I stood back to let him in, closing the door behind him.

'You've come about my body, have you?' I asked. When he

looked completely blank, I said, very formally, 'Do sit down.' Then I added, because one of us was clearly missing something, 'Look, I've got to get my caffeine fix or you might as well talk Chinese. Fancy a cup?'

I brought through a papier mâché tray, loaded with a couple of pretty early nineteenth century coffee cans, and milk and sugar in all that was left of an 1810 Newhall tea service. Everything was good, of course, but not perfect – perfect would have had to go into the shop.

He did a bit of a double take when he saw the handleless cups, but said nothing. He almost turned the milk jug upside down to check the mark but realized it wasn't a good idea.

'Regency,' he managed.

'If you've got it, you might as well use it,' I pointed out. 'And antique dealers do have a lot of china. How can I help?'

'I'm Kent Police's Heritage Officer,' he said, reeling off what was obviously his usual spiel, 'with special responsibility for locating and identifying objects illegally removed from historical sites.'

So what was that to do with my body? But I ought to try to say something intelligent. 'Ah! You mean you catch these night hawk people, who use metal detectors without permission and dig up and ruin historical sites. Brilliant.' I smiled. Generally speaking, I did prefer people to be on the right side of the Law.

Griff would have known the right word to describe his expression. Non-something. Was it nonplussed? Could be. Anyway, he looked pretty puzzled, as if I'd wrong-footed him somehow.

'No one's offered us anything dodgy,' I continued, since he was still silent. 'But I promise that if they do, we'll get on to you straightaway.'

He swallowed, his Adam's apple doing a little bobble. 'It was more what you've been offering, Miss Townend – it's Evelina, isn't it?'

'Lina, like Lena Horne. Now you've lost me. What am I supposed to have offered? We did a pretty good trade at

Detling the other day, but apart from a bit of Loetz, which was actually a return, everything was our usual period – Victorian.' Feeling that he wanted something else, I added, 'Do you want to see the receipt book?'

He didn't say he didn't, but asked, 'Do you have the original receipts for the objects you offered the British Museum yesterday?'

At last it dawned on me what he was implying. Griff preferred me not to swear before seven in the evening, so I didn't say all the things I wanted. 'Hell's bells,' I managed, which was pretty lame, considering, 'I didn't think that Douggie – what's his name? Sir Douglas Nelson? – was very pleased to see us. But grassing us up for no reason! Bloody hell!'

'My dear one, I do wish you wouldn't soil your lips with such expressions! Ah, good morning.' Spruce as if he'd had half an hour to complete what he always called his *toilette* Griff looked expectantly at DS Kinnersley, shaking his hand as I performed the introductions.

Usually I'd have nipped out and brought him coffee too, but I didn't want to miss anything Kinnersley said. They were my rings, after all. Sighing, Griff took the hint, reappearing a moment later with his own favourite can, a once-lovely Derby one now desperately faded because some idiot had put it in their dishwasher.

'Sir Douglas alleges you passed him two items that haven't been recorded on our register of finds, Lina. And he was concerned enough to contact me.'

'And you were concerned enough to come straight here. So they are precious! Wow! They're not my period, you see, or I'd have known,' I added, though whether I was explaining or apologizing I wasn't sure.

'Which is why we took them to my old friend Douggie Nelson. Former friend,' Griff corrected himself bitterly. 'Why didn't he ask me?'

'He said he did, and that you were very vague about the provenance.'

'It's hard to be accurate about a load of tat from an auction – the whole lot set me back a pound, Will.' If he

could use my first name, I could use his. 'The other one
came dirt cheap too. I did a fellow dealer a favour and she
let me have it for eighteen quid. Cash. Her receipt was
pretty vague, though. "Foreign dress ring with beads", I
think it says.'

'Could I see the receipts?' He sounded almost eager, as
if he no longer wanted us to be criminals. I must say I was
quite pleased. Pleased enough to nip upstairs and apply a
tiny bit of slap before fetching the paperwork from the
office.

He took first Dilly's slip of paper, wrinkling his nose but
jotting down what she'd written, then the auction one. His
face hardened. 'This just says "Box of sundry kitchen items".
It doesn't mention a ring.'

'It wouldn't. I didn't know what I'd find when I bought
it. Sometimes at house clearances it's worth taking a punt,'
I explained. 'What might be absolute tat to you and me
could be just what a kitchenalia expert needs. I might canni-
balize some old mincer with a few bits missing so a friend
can make a killing on a rare item.'

'Forget mincers. Tell me about the ring.'

'It was in a screw of newspaper – shoved in to stop the
contents of the box rattling.'

'Did you put it in?'

'No. But when I found it I examined all the other scraps,
believe me! One by one, and then some. They're all in the
recycling bin – from papers going back years before I was
born.'

'So you didn't think of going back to the auctioneers
with it?'

'I bought a job lot in a box. Let me get it. It'll be in the
recycling bin too. Hell, that sounds like the bin boys now!'

To my amazement, Will sprinted after me – perhaps
he thought he could manage a better turn of speed if anyone
needed to chase the lorry. He didn't even get near me,
though, as I grabbed my tatty cardboard from the hands of
the lad about to shove the pile of collapsed boxes into the
crusher.

'There!' I said, unfolding it and pointing to the lot number and label. "Sundry kitchen items, etc." The receipt left out the "etc". Does that put me in the clear?'

Carrying the box and the shreds of yellowing paper I retrieved from our bin, he walked back to the cottage. 'Legally, yes, I suppose. If you're telling the truth. But morally – well, what do you think?'

Despite the cold, I stopped and scratched my head. 'I don't know. I think it might depend on how much the ring's worth. And if I'd known – and as I said, it's not my period – I wouldn't have had to go trailing off to Griff's so-called mate Douggie. Sir Bloody Douglas. Dilly, who knows more about jewellery than I ever will, thought the one I bought from her, which was very similar, was worth twenty. Less, possibly, since she gave me discount. And to be honest with you, I don't think I'd have gone dashing back to the auctioneer waving a twenty-pound note in my hand. Come on, you know how auctions work. At the same auction, someone paid about three times what a pretty little water colour was worth. Thought it was a David Cox. It wasn't,' I added, not explaining how I knew. 'If I've paid under the odds for the ring, then I'd have thought it balanced out. And perhaps His Nibs didn't tell you I said if the ring was really special I'd let them display it on permanent loan. And had my name in the British Museum! Well, they can stuff that, now.' I stomped back into the cottage, rigid with anger.

He parked the box on the kitchen table, and waited for me to dump the paper shreds in it. Then he systematically opened every screw of paper, using only the very tips of his fingers, though he'd pulled on rubber gloves he'd fished from his pocket. He sniffed. 'Mice?'

'Almost certainly. Hang on, I'll get a bin liner so we can get rid of everything next week. Don't want it stinking the place out.' I knotted the top into two rabbit ears and popped it outside. When I got back in, he was already washing his hands. I waited till he'd finished and did the same. As Will used the towel, Griff wiped the table and spread a linen cloth on it. He'd fished out of the freezer some of the crois-sants I only let him have as a special treat – certainly not on an ordinary working day. And there was some of that posh French butter on a dish, not the cholesterol-reducing spread he's supposed to have. Home-made jam, too.

Will took it all in, and produced a wry smile. 'It's OK, you don't have to bribe me. Everything Lina's said hangs together. But,' and I could see him wavering, 'I might need to pick your brains.'

Griff pulled back a chair for him and passed him a napkin. 'One thing Lina almost certainly hasn't told you about,' he said, sitting down himself, 'is her friendship with two senior policemen specializing in antiques. The Fine Art Squad. Oh, one of them's gone into the private sector, hasn't he, my love? But either will vouch for her, I'm sure.' He gave a courtly little bow. 'And by extension, me.'

Will flicked a glance at me and must have seen a deep and painful blush burning its way up my throat and across my face. And he'd have a pretty good guess at why I'd not chosen to mention my involvement with one of them in particular. All the same, I said, my voice just a little on the squeaky side, 'Yes, I'm godmother to DI Morris's new baby.' So there. Was that convincing? 'Actually,' I managed to add, 'I got to help choose Bruce Farfrae's wedding anniversary present, too. Told him how to get it cheap. Though that was before he left the police.'

'So you wouldn't have helped him now?' Will sounded amused.

'On what he's picking up? He can afford to pay full whack.'

Our first and Will's second breakfast over, I thought it was time to talk seriously again. 'Now you know I got hold of my rings legally, do I get them back? After friend Douggie's given them the once over, of course. And valued them.'

'He might prefer not to, given his initial suspicions,' Griff said quietly.

'You mean you'd prefer him not to? Well, I don't mind free information,' I said. 'And it might make up for his snitching so unjustly.'

'If his suspicions had been right, his snitching would

have been entirely justifiable,' Will said. He might not have been so pompous if he'd realized he'd got a smear of jam on his chin.

'But he and Griff are friends: surely he should have challenged him first? And isn't there a difference between just and justifiable?' I frowned, trying to remember, not just trying to make a point.

He probably thought I was cleverer than I am. He smiled, making the jam quiver. 'Absolutely.' But his face became very serious again.

'What else did Douggie say? Sir Douglas,' I corrected myself.

'He – he did make one or two allegations which I'm sure are also baseless.'

I pondered. 'He and Griff go back for years, so I'd guess they were about me.' He flushed. I was right. 'About my background? Can't really help that, can I? Or about my restoration work? Well, that's absolutely legit. Sometimes I even do it for museums. I can show you the files I keep on everything. No, it'd be the fact he thinks I'm leading Griff astray – a little gold-digger. Sorry. Only I mean –' I took a deep breath, and plunged in – 'metaphorically, not literally.'

Griff nodded across the table – I'd got the words right. 'Of course she's neither, Will. I couldn't love her more if she were my own flesh and blood, but she's a partner in this business, not least because of her restoration skills. In times like this, sales can be hard to come by, and she brings in a good steady income. And she's—' He stopped because I'd kicked him under the table. Whatever else he said about me, the last thing I wanted him boasting about was my being a divvy. I didn't think such an odd activity would raise me one centimetre in Will's eyes.

Which were getting steadily harder as Will waited.

'She's a genius at selling,' Griff continued as smoothly as if he'd intended to say that all the time.

Will nodded.

Usually in a situation like this if the phone rang we let the machine take it. But this time Griff decided to lift the receiver. From the edgy politeness he adopted, I knew at once who it must be. Probably the only man in the world he was deeply jealous of. Then he said, very clearly, so I knew Will was meant to clock it, 'Quite so, my lord. Just have any items you want her to value to hand, and I'm sure she'll oblige. You can expect her some time this afternoon, Lord Elham.' He almost bowed as he cut the call.

You should have seen Will's face.

Of course, Will wasn't to know that Lord Elham was my biological father, and one of the most disreputable men I know – well, anyone employed by Titus Oates had to be on the iffy side of dodgy. Despite being generally pretty much of a parasite, he'd actually done me a really good turn not so long ago, which explained why Griff was being polite. Or perhaps he thought Will would understand that I was a really pukka dealer if I was employed by what he might suppose was a noble lord.

And he would have been right. Will, who'd got round to wiping the jam away, had pretty well sat to attention. Griff resumed his place, and poured more coffee, remaking, just as Will tasted his, 'Dear one, your father rings at such unpredictable hours.'

So why had the old bugger undercut the whole charade? Because now he'd made Will first choke and then become rigid with politeness. 'I'm sorry, ma'am, I had no idea—'

'I prefer to stand or fall on my own reputation,' I responded, truthfully, though it sounded pretty pompous, come to think of it. 'Now, back to my rings, if you don't mind. It'd be better if you, not Griff, told Sir Douglas that they were genuine purchases and that I could have them back.'

'I'll do my best. But I think I should take the receipts with me.'

I was on my feet in a second. 'I'll photocopy them for you,' I said. I quite liked Will, but he was still a policeman, and as such still suspect.

As I returned from the office, he produced a little evidence bag. 'I'd prefer the originals.'

'In that case I shall need a receipt for the receipts,' I said, trying to sound a bit quirky but meaning it all the same. 'Make it out to Ms Lina Townend, please.'

'You don't use your title, ma'am?'

'That is my title.'

He wrote and then looked up at me. 'I – I hope you don't mind my asking, ma'am, but I wonder – I know it's a silly thing, but—'

'Look, Will, I'm the daughter of a lord: so what?' I dug round for one of Griff's useful quotations. '*Cut me, do I not bleed?*' I think it was a bit of Shakespeare. Whatever it was, Will looked impressed.

'OK. Look, earlier you said something very odd about wanting to talk about your body.'

Griff grinned. 'Beautiful as Lina is, she's not narcissistic, Will. She referred, I should imagine, to what appeared to be a corpse in a field. She called it in, but then the body disappeared.'

'Exactly,' I said, 'and I assumed you wanted to tell me what happened next. I don't like loose ends, you see.'

Still looking as if he was about to tug out all his hair, he made a note of the date and other details and promised to follow it up. 'I could pop round and update you,' he said, sounding almost as if he was asking permission.

'That would be excellent,' Griff told him. 'But you should phone ahead. We work away from home a great deal.' Why did he wink at me? And why, for goodness sake, did he somehow drift us both into the village street and say admiring things about Will's car? Hell, flirting with a pretty actor was one thing, but pretending to know about CO_2 emissions was quite another. But then he drifted away, leaving the two of us together. Blow me if Will didn't get all blushful again.

I was getting cold. 'I'll look forward to hearing from you then,' I said, a bit too crisply, as if he was a client I wanted to put the phone down on. So I added, 'If my father needs me, I'd better go. I always take him supplies, you see – food and drink.'

He was all concern. 'Is he housebound, then?'

'Not exactly. If you ask Griff, he'll say he likes being

waited on, and Griff's usually right.' Damn, now I was
talking too much.

'I – er, I'll see you, then.' He let himself into his car.

'Sure. See you soon,' I added, just because that's what
you say, isn't it?'

He smiled this huge smile. 'See you soon!' And drove
off, looking at me, not into his rear-view mirror. It's a good
job our village street's quiet, or he might have had some
explaining to do when he got back.

That night my three o'clock moment featured Will, in
shocking pink drag, kicking the body's head across a field
as if it was a rugby ball.

FOUR

My father's address was Bossingham Hall. Will Kinnersley would have been really impressed. But Lord Elham had been relegated to one wing, where he lived alone with loads of tat he'd managed to squirrel out of the main body of the building before the trustees brought in the valuers and their legal team. Much of the stuff hadn't been worth moving in the first place, but mixed in with the rubbish there were some really good pieces. Not that he knew the difference. The deal was that I sold some of these from time to time to keep him in champagne and other items his pension wouldn't rise to.

Although his default expression was cunning, this afternoon he was looking less shifty than usual. Almost trustworthy. And decidedly cleaner. I might have been worried – perhaps I ought to have been – but since I'd been managing his diet and compelling him to have his hair cut from time to time there was an all round improvement. More often than not he shaved and he remembered to change his shirts and trousers before they became items even the Oxfam shop would have shuddered at. He'd even learned to use the washing machine I'd organized for him, and though he'd never have admitted he liked anything except Pot Noodles, he seemed to enjoy the casseroles and curries I filled his freezer with. He certainly told me when he was running low.

But he was still a master forger, I had to remember that, and was possibly the most neglectful father on the planet, though I had to admit he'd never been actively bad – no abuse or anything like that, or I'd never have gone within ten miles of the place. In fact he never saw – never had seen – any of his thirty other children, as far as I knew. That didn't mean he didn't, of course. And there was no doubt that some might have been attracted by the trust I'd insisted he'd set up for us all with some decidedly ill-gotten gains – wasps as well as genuine bees, however, swarming round the family honey pot, if you could call it a family, of course.

Today he actually ventured outside to greet me as I pulled up outside his wing – it was approached by a truly dreadful lane from the hamlet of Bossingham. He claimed his trustees were supposed to maintain it, and would have liked me to stir them up a bit. But since my van's suspension was the only one regularly at risk, and since I knew how much he'd diddled them out of over the years, I refused to get involved.

Since I hadn't had time to cook, I'd stopped off for some supermarket Healthy Option meals, which I unloaded.

He peered at them. 'Your cooking tastes much better,' he bleated, but he cheered up when I lifted out a couple of boxes of champagne. The clouds came down when he saw all the packets of green tea, however. A loud dislike of the stuff was about the only thing he and Griff had in common. I actually shared it, but since I bullied them into consuming huge quantities, I couldn't really admit that it wasn't nectar in a cup.

'I found some jewellery you might like to look at,' he said, when I'd stowed the last ready meal in the freezer.

Had he indeed? And where might that have come from? I knew of at least two highly unofficial ways into the main hall, in addition to the authorized one covered by CCTV cameras – so the trustees knew how often he went into his ancestral hall. On the other hand, they didn't have any jewellery on display. There was always the Aladdin's cave of the huge attic space, of course – I'd never had a really good rummage up there because I wasn't sure where my father's section ended and the trustees' began. My father wouldn't have bothered, of course – what was his was his and what was theirs was his too, so long as it wasn't in a tightly locked cabinet with CCTV trained on it.

He reached into the fridge for a bottle of champagne.

'I'll just make us a cup of tea and then I'll take a look,' I said firmly. Although one of the very few things I'd inherited from him was a taste for bubbly, the last thing I wanted was to get fuddled with booze. I always needed my wits about me when it came to dealing with the old guy, not to mention the clean driving licence Griff and I depended on.

He pulled a face, but found a couple of cleanish cups and saucers: one of his funniosities was only drinking out of china cups, never thick mugs. He went so far as to carry the tray through to his living room, dominated by a widescreen HD TV set and a wonderful table which would have seated twenty. It bore the white rings of so many wet-bottomed glasses I'd given up trying to rescue it; it needed proper restoration from the furniture equivalent of me. It was on this table he'd put a couple of ancient shoe boxes, which he opened with a flourish.

'There you are,' he said. 'What do you think of them?'

I couldn't work out the tone of his voice. Was he asking for my professional opinion? Or seeing if I could detect some expert forgery? Or even giving them as a present?

I soon dismissed the last thought. My father didn't do presents, any more than he did affection. We never exchanged a hug or a kiss, any more than I called him Dad or Father, or whatever you should call a Lord. As for the second, if he and Titus were up to something – if Titus was trying to use me as a fence – I'd walk out of his life forever. So I'd best assume it was my usual job, choosing a saleable item or two, pop them on our stall and giving him the money, minus my commission, when I'd got rid of them.

I plunged a hand in and came up with some chains, all hallmarked – a good sign. As part of my partnership with Griff, I'd learned all the hallmarks, so I knew I was dealing with Victorian stuff made in Birmingham. It didn't look very exciting, design-wise, and some of it was very worn. Then there were some little boxes for individual pieces. Nestling in the bottle green velvet of the first was a worn man's signet ring. Birmingham 1894. A gold bangle came next. Bristol, 1887. And so on and so on. There was an engagement ring, touchingly worn on one side only by the wedding ring it had nestled against. It was pretty, but none of the pin head stones was big enough to give it wow factor a century and a bit later.

'What do you think?' he repeated.

'To be honest, the best thing might be to sell them as scrap gold – prices are pretty high these days. I know someone who'd give a fair price.'

'Try the other box,' he urged, sounding disappointed.

'Are these the family jewels? The odd tiara?'

He shook his head. 'As if the blasted trustees would let me anywhere within sniffing distance!'

The gold in that box was much later – 1930s, with some nice deco pieces. I always think rings look better against skin tones, so I shoved one in the form of a bow made up of baguette cut diamonds on to my right hand, tilting it backwards and forwards to catch the light.

'This is much better, though I'd have to clean it to get a better idea of value – it looks as if someone's been rolling it round in the cow shed. And this watch – wow, it's Cartier. That should bring in a few bottles for you.' When he still didn't speak, I asked, 'Where did you find them?'

'Oh, here.'

'Where here?'

'My wing.'

I stared at him, an eyebrow raised, as one of my foster mothers used to stare at me when she knew I wasn't telling the whole truth. Or indeed any of it.

'I thought they might be there.' Though of course he still didn't say where. 'When my nanny died, she didn't have a family and she hadn't a will. So the housekeeper put every-thing together behind a cupboard while the legal chappies hunted for someone to pass it on to. Then the war came so I suppose they forgot. It's a miracle the soldiers they plonked in here didn't find it.' It was an even greater miracle that my father had remembered it.

'You must have been pretty young when she died,' I prompted him.

'God, yes. Only a nipper. Ready for prep school and all that. But Nanny Baird turned up her toes and that was it.' My father didn't do emotion any more than he did affec-tion, but I'd have sworn there was a note of tenderness I'd never heard before.

'Was she old?'

'She looked old to me, of course – positively ancient. But I doubt if she'd be more than forty. Not one of those aged retainers you hear about. And this was hers.'

There was no doubt this time: his voice was definitely sad. Perhaps my father really had once been fond of someone.

I shook my head sympathetically. 'So you don't want it sold or melted down, then.' So why was he showing it to me?

'Thing is, Lina, you've been making me think, what with one thing and another. And then there's this TV programme about ancestors. You know, people finding out about relatives they've never met. I wouldn't mind finding out about Nanny Baird's family.'

'Not yours?'

'Can read all about them in the Muniment Room,' he said, scornfully. 'Just names, not real people. Not to me. Mother, now – she was beautiful, I remember that, decked out in all the diamonds she brought over from the States as her dowry.'

'Dowry?' I echoed.

'Oh, yes – it was pretty well an arranged marriage, just like these Asian kids are forced into. You remember – we saw it on the news the other day. She brought enough money to pay off the family mortgages, he gave her a title. And when she'd produced an heir and a spare, she skipped off to Paris or somewhere. And he went back to his boyfriends. Good job they had me as the spare – the heir dropped off his perch when he was still a nipper, of course. Don't remember him – just have this vague recollection of people being sad, and arguments and stuff.'

'How come you've never told me any of this before?' I asked – wondering, actually, why I'd never cared to look it all up. After all, I could easily have got access to the Muniment Room now everyone working at the Hall knew I was his daughter.

'Not really interested. A long time ago, after all. But – you know, since that business with that rotter you got

involved with – I've been thinking more about family. And
that led me to Nanny Baird. And finding out her family.
And giving them this stuff. Thing is,' he said, leaning closer,
as if afraid the ancestral walls would give him away, 'Nanny
Baird was a widow, not some Norland trained virgin. What
if she had children we didn't know about? They should
have this lot – even if it's not worth anything.'

I could have done with some of that champagne. My
head was all swirly and I felt quite sick. I should have been
glad I'd managed to awaken in him some long dead feelings, I suppose, but I wasn't. I just felt a huge, fierce anger
that he now cared enough to find someone else's children,
when he'd never cared a snap of the fingers for me.

'I don't supposed you could find – are you all right, old
girl? You're sure?'

I made myself nod.

'All a bit of a shock, I suppose, hearing about your
grandma. I wonder if you look like her. No portraits in the
Hall, of course – there were plans afoot, to get someone in,
but then what with the war and the divorce and everything
. . . And she'd be pretty well *persona non grata*, of course.
Tell you what, forget this stuff for a bit – unless you know
some chappie who would do a bit of private eye work, for
me – and we'll go and see if there are any photos anywhere.'

It slowly dawned on me that my father realized something had upset me and he was trying to make it better. I
made an effort too. 'We should pack it away first – that
ring and the watch deserve better than being shoved in with
the rest.'

He picked up the watch. 'You know, I have an idea this
was my mother's. I wonder if she gave it to Nanny Baird
– or if it was nicked. Same as the diamond ring. Not the
sort of thing you'd expect a nanny to have, eh?'

'You say your father was gay?' I knew from the family
line-up in the Portrait Gallery the other side of the dividing
wall that he'd been an exceptionally handsome man, with
no resemblance at all to his battered specimen of a son.

'Most miserable bugger I've ever met in my life. Oh, you
mean queer.'

I pulled a face.

'Don't tell me – it's one of those words I'm not supposed to use these days. Well, he liked boys. And he liked some women too. Dipped his wick in all sorts of places, I dare say. Like father, like son. Not that I've ever done boys or men, except at school, and that doesn't really count.' He passed me the watch. 'If this was my mother's you should have it. Not to sell. To keep. A bit vulgar for every day, of course.'

My head had all sorts of things whizzing round. My mouth said, 'Cartier! Vulgar?'

'Well, Nanny Baird would have said diamonds looked better by candlelight. Try it on,' he urged. 'No?'

'I don't want to fall in love with it only to find it's someone else's,' I thought, but actually said out loud, surprising myself as much as him, I think.

'Hmm.' He looked at me as hard as Griff did, sometimes. 'Very well. Let's pop it away for a bit, and tuck it behind that cupboard again. And then I'll see if I can find that photo album – I'll swear I knew where it was the other day . . . Tell you what, though – let's have a glass of fizz first.'

This time I didn't argue.

'There you are,' he declared half an hour later, jabbing a typically Thirties photograph album, leather bound with some unlikely tassels on the spine. 'She'll be in here, your grandmamma.'

She was, too. It was like looking at a beautiful version of myself on a really miserable day. She oozed unhappiness, whether she was patting a horse, surrounded by hounds or tentatively hugging a small boy who might have been either brother – you couldn't tell from their clothes. But from the tragic cast of her face, I assumed it was my father.

Most were snapshots, but there was a series of much better ones of her on her own that might have been preparation for a formal portrait. My father jabbed a finger.

'See – there's that watch. But that doesn't mean she didn't give it to Nanny Baird, of course – she gave away a lot of things, come to think of it, just as if she was dying. More like she as trying to make sure my father couldn't get his claws on them as part of the divorce settlement. Look at those earrings, now – you should have those. Or was it that ring? She told me that she wanted me to have something to give my bride as a present from her. Never had a bride, of course. So I reckon you should have them. If only I can remember where they were put. Hell, is that the time? We should be watching that Egg Head thing.'

I nodded. But just as he was cramming the photo album back into a really horrible lacquered writing desk, I stopped him. 'Do you think you could spare me a photo of her?'

'What? Look, here's a loose one.' Barely looking at it, he flipped it across to me. 'Are you coming down? No? Be a good girl and find a couple of pots or whatever to sell. Mustn't run short of shampoo.'

It was only a step to Stelling Minnis rectory, and Robin, an old friend of mine. Maybe it would make my nightmares go away if I could talk to him about the body. I could ask him if I could pray for whoever it was. Better still, if he would. But the rectory was locked, and the people at the village shop said he was retreating. Or something like that. I bought some lemon grass and a couple of aubergines anyway.

FIVE

Having a photo of my grandmother was one thing, but knowing what to do with it was quite another – especially as I didn't know how Griff would feel. He'd suspect, as he always did if my father gave me anything, he was trying to woo me over to Bossingham. What he'd say about the search for Nanny Baird I'd no idea, but I'd an idea it wouldn't be enthusiastic. And however bright and cheerful I'd try to be, Griff could read me like a book and know something was worrying me. At least if I stowed the photo deep in my knickers drawer and I shut myself in the work room to tackle my backlog of repairs he wouldn't get to see too much of my face.

I reckoned without a phone call, which brought him to the bottom of the stairs calling up to me, something quite against our house rules when I'm doing delicate work. As it happened, all I was doing was sitting with my chin in my hands staring at a broken jug, but all the same, I was ready to be ratty.

'Harvey Sanditon!' Griff mouthed, his hand covering the phone. 'For you!'

Well, it would hardly be for Mrs Walker, would it? But I never snapped at Griff, so I managed a wary smile and ran down to the office.

'Ms Townend, I wonder if I could ask you the most enormous favour. A contact has damaged an 1810 Barr, Flight and Barr vase and turned to me for advice. I thought of you immediately. I know you said you have a long waiting list, but this is absolutely urgent. If you can prioritize it, this will be reflected in your fee, I promise you.'

1810 Barr, Flight and Barr. I was very tempted.

'Could you email me a photo of the vase, so I can see how much work's involved? You'll need an estimate, after all.'

'Of course. I'll let you have all the details as soon as I can.'

* * *

'Do you think this is all right?' I asked Griff, anxiously, as
I washed up after supper. 'He won't try and palm it off
as perfect, will he?'

'Is that what's been worrying you, dear heart? You've
been looking subdued, shall we say, ever since you came
home. I thought it might be something to do with that
disreputable aristocrat whose only good deed in a dark career
was to beget you.'

'Two good deeds,' I corrected him, because I knew he'd
want me to.

'Oh, I know he saw off that rotter for you. So two good
deeds,' he conceded, still looking anxiously at me.

There wasn't much I could hide from Griff. But I just
didn't want to talk to him about Nanny Baird's legacy, or
the ring my father wanted to find for me. Not yet. Maybe
tomorrow.

I clenched my hands, but kept them by my sides: I wouldn't
hit my face till I bruised it, not this time. No more black
eyes to try to cover with make-up. Never, ever, not if I could
help it. I said, as lightly as I could, 'Sanditon was very high-
handed at Detling. I really didn't take to him.'

'There's no reason why you shouldn't take to his money,
though. It'd really establish your reputation if it became
known that you worked for him, even though I suspect the
name is fake. Does it not ring bells with you, my child?'

I frowned. Something lurked in my memory. Griff worked
so hard to improve both that and the range of things I ought
to have in it. My fingers clicked almost of their own accord:
'That book! The one I got cross with because it didn't have
an end!'

'I'm sure the author got cross because she couldn't finish
it, poor lady.'

Another click. 'Ah! Jane Austen. Because she died.'

'Well done. Now, what is it the man with the possibly
spurious name wants you to tackle?'

'He's emailed me some photos. Have you got time to
have a look?'

'As if you even had to ask, my love. Now, where are my
glasses?'

'Round your neck.'

'So they are. Dear one, it's not like you to leave the computer on! We're supposed to be green, remember.'

'I know. It left itself on, though. Some new antivirus programme was installing itself, and wouldn't let me switch off. Anyway, here you are.' I touched the mouse and the picture leapt into full glory.

Griff sat down heavily. 'Goodness me, I can see why he might want to pass it off as perfect,' he breathed. 'Last time one of those came up for auction it fetched something like five thousand pounds, if my memory doesn't deceive me. All that wonderful lifelike floral painting. All that gilding. Those darling little dolphin handles. Oh, dear. Just the one dolphin handle . . .'

Nodding, I clicked the mouse again: the next picture was of the base, with the puce script mark. 'All hunky-dory,' I said. 'He says he's afraid the handle fragments are too small to stick back together. If he's right, do you think I can manage a complete rebuild?'

'So that's what it's all about,' Griff said. 'Not whether he'll pass off a restored item as perfect, but whether you're skilled enough to do it! Of course you can do it. And maybe a rebuild would be easier than a jigsaw job,' he added reflectively.

'But it's so fine.'

'I don't know anyone with a steadier hand.'

'And the gilding?'

'Especially the gilding. Has he said how soon he wants it done?'

'Urgent. Drop everything else. Which is another problem. I've made people promises – people we know, Griff. People who encouraged me when I was starting.'

He stroked his chin. 'I don't think there's any harm in playing hard to get, my love. Obviously you must concentrate on restoration for a bit – I'm sure Mrs Walker would be happy to do extra hours. And you must tell Mr Sanditon just what you told me. How soon do you think you can do it – if you put back non-urgent work? Two, three weeks? Tell him four and see what he makes of that.'

* * *

The answer was, not a lot, as Sanditon said in person, when he appeared in our shop a day later, the vase under his arm. Well, almost. It was wrapped with as much care as the Rockingham vase I'd sold him. He carried its box in both hands. Fortunately he wasn't trying to balance a coat on his shoulders.

I was only behind the counter because Mrs Walker had phoned to say she was trapped in an almighty traffic jam on the M20, and because I'd sent Griff down to our doctor for his repeat prescription. It was nice gentle exercise and very good for him. Plus he got to talk with all our fellow villagers and topped up his gossip levels.

'I told you, you're wasting your time as a mere shop assistant,' Sanditon greeted me.

'Good morning, Mr Sanditon,' I said, since Griff had told me never to be rude unless I could land a really good insult. 'Ah, this is the Worcester, is it?'

I spread the extra thick baize on the counter. In the interests of our insurance, I didn't offer to unwrap the vase myself.

At last it stood there in all its glory. About thirty-five centimetres high, from the bottom of its little gilded paw feet to the gilded rim. As lovely as the original craftsmen and artists had left it. Almost. Poor smashed dolphin. He put down an envelope beside it, presumably with the handle shards in it.

He broke the silence. 'It's one of a pair, as I'm sure you'd guess.'

I whistled. Like those little Ruskin bowls, together they'd be worth much more than as two separate items.

'In that case I could really do with seeing its twin to make sure I get the dimensions spot on.' He did not respond. 'May I?' I picked it up and turned it in my hands. I wasn't just looking to see if I could repair it, I was checking for other damage I might later be accused of – it wouldn't be the first time. At last I put it down and pointed. 'You realize there's a fleck of marbling missing just under the rim?'

He stared, and I hunted for a really good word Griff had taught me. Aghast, that was it.

'Don't worry. The work of minutes rather than hours,' I said. Then I turned my attention to the site of the damage. I didn't touch: I didn't want to do anything that might make the damage worse or harder to repair. When I actually got round to the work, I'd wear fine surgeon's gloves. The pieces in the envelope were as bad as he'd said, and might well end up in the bin. Trying to sound reassuring, I said, 'I shall want to tackle this slowly, so the repair's absolutely seamless. An extra layer every day. However urgent it is, I can't do it tonight and give it back tomorrow. If you want that, find some other restorer.' I looked him straight in the eye.

When he wasn't looking so full of himself, and managed a bite of the lower lip, he looked altogether more human. Like a little boy caught nicking a couple of Mars bars, actually.

'You did this, didn't you? Not a client?' I must have sounded like his mum. No need to wait for an answer. 'No wonder you want a speedy job. But you have to promise me – absolutely promise – you'll tell whoever owns it what you've done. Because I've got my reputation, same as you've got yours.'

'Very well.'

'Maybe the fee I charge –' *fee* always sounded pretty professional, I thought – 'will convince them you've done your best. So when I print the invoice for you and your insurance company, I'll do a copy for them – so they can't claim on theirs, of course,' I added with a grin. You'd be amazed how people try to diddle anonymous companies in ways they wouldn't dream of if it was the guy next door.

'How long will it take?' he asked humbly.

'Allow a fortnight. That's the best I can offer. And I really ought to have the other in the pair. No? I shall just have to hope the both handles are exactly the same.'

'I'll check with a micrometer and let you know. You're sure you can do it?'

'As sure as I can be. But it has to be done at my own pace.'

'Thank you,' he said with something of a sigh. 'I take it you don't work here?'

'My workroom's in our cottage.' I nodded across the courtyard.

'So it had better travel in style.' He touched the vase and its box. 'Shall you do the honours or shall I?'

'Still your baby,' I said, letting him wrap the vase as tenderly as if it were really an infant. 'Have you come far?' I added chattily, as he swathed it in bubble wrap and laid it on little pads of scrunched up tissue.

'Wellington.'

Where the hell was that? It wouldn't be the New Zealand one, would it? Or was it the one we'd once been to a fair at and Griff had pointed out a shop sign – the Wellington Boot Company – in Somerset, I think? And wasn't there one in Shropshire? None of them close.

I raised my eyebrows in surprise that he'd come so far – from wherever it was.

'I drove overnight,' he said. 'I had this terror of an M25 pile-up.'

At this point Mrs Walker came trudging in, as if she'd journeyed from John O'Groats. By foot. 'M25? You're quite right. I've just been in this incredible M20 jam. I must have sat there an hour, seeing the junction I needed but not being able to get to it. And men peeing by the roadside and everything. You'd think they'd use a bottle, for goodness' sake,' she said, muscling in on the conversation as she always did, poor woman. One day I'd buy her a parrot to talk to – except she'd have to bring it with her, since it wouldn't be fair to leave it alone all day. No, not a good idea. 'Do you mind if I get the kettle on? Or . . .'

'Of course not. And Griff's topped up the biscuit barrel – the more you have the less for him. No, fewer,' I corrected myself. 'I was just going to show Mr Sanditon where I work, so don't worry about us. After you,' I said, ushering him out of the back door and across the courtyard garden into our cottage.

'Miss Bates,' he breathed as I closed the door behind us.

'So I've always thought, and would have sacked her,' Griff said, standing at the table unpacking the groceries he'd bought en route, 'only Lina said she owed her a debt of gratitude and you'd be surprised how well she gets on with our customers.'

'Griffith Tripp,' I said politely. 'Harvey Sanditon. I'll take that straight up to my work room, Mr Sanditon, as I said.' I held out my hands for the box.

He didn't let go. 'May I see it?'

Weird. But then, that was what I'd said to Mrs Walker. 'If you want.' It made no difference to me either way. There was never any need to apologize for its being untidy, for instance, because I always left it as immaculate as I could, so I could walk in at any time and start on the work in progress. Everything else was stacked neatly on shelves. I led the way upstairs, the vase in its box still in his hands.

'In here.' All the lights focused on the table came on at once.

'Good lord! It looks like an operating theatre.'

'Yes, a fine arts version of *Casualty*!' I grinned at him, liking him more because we'd had the same idea. 'Best put the patient on the operating table then.'

He unwrapped the vase as carefully as he'd packed it and placed it in the middle. He gave a rueful smile. 'It's lovely now, even with only one handle.'

I nodded happily. Soon it would be utterly beautiful.

'I've never before had a guest who fell asleep at our table, my love,' Griff said, as we waved Harvey Sanditon on his way. 'Remarkable.'

I thought of his half hour doze. 'Not really. Apparently he drove down overnight.'

'And presumably intended to make the return journey immediately. What a good job we offered him coffee.'

'And a good job we could offer him those cup cakes. What did you think you were doing, buying all those, Griff? You know you're not supposed to eat sugary things, and those are diabetes on a plate . . .'

This time, I dreamt I got out of the van and tried to lift the body. But his arm turned into a funny little dolphin and shattered as I dropped it.

SIX

With such an important piece of restoration work on my hands, not to mention all the other precious things I needed to reunite with their owners, I didn't argue when Griff said he'd go to the next house clearance auction by himself. It was only in Sandwich, so he didn't have too far to drive.

Mrs Walker would be in sole charge of the shop, I told her. Even if someone actually asked for me, I mustn't be disturbed, I insisted.

'I understand – it's like exam marking,' she agreed, nodding. 'But you won't work too long, will you, or you'll lose concentration. A break – not that I should use that word, in the circumstances – every half hour.'

With a grin at her little joke I nodded. Every five minutes, more like. Just to relax the hands and the neck. Just in case I really could use the original fragments, I put them on my table and arranged them. As far as I could tell there was nothing missing, but there'd be more glue than china, with the risk of visible joins. Griff had been right to say making a new handle from scratch would be easier than trying to patch together the broken one. As I picked the fragments over, however, I found something interesting – evidence of two bad cracks. So perhaps it wasn't altogether Sanditon's fault.

Using the other handle, plus Sanditon's emailed details of the other vase, I got the template as accurate as I could, every measurement verified with calipers. Then I mixed the first quantity of epoxy resin putty. I'd leave it a couple of hours to harden very slightly – I'd still have an hour before it became too hard to work. Time for a lunch break, then. I popped into the shop to join Mrs Walker for a sandwich and a cup of tea and with a couple of orders from our website for her to attend to: she'd pack the items, and nip down to the post office early enough to ensure they arrived next day.

And then it was back to my workroom. Pure pleasure. First I rolled the epoxy resin putty into a long thin sausage, which I formed as closely as I could to the template. Then I stood the vase in a sand box, to make it absolutely stable, then put a lump of plastic modelling clay in place. This would support the new handle, which I attached to the broken edges of the vase with some epoxy resin adhesive, with a little filling powder added. There. I stepped back to look at it. Things were going well.

Griff came back at four, with a couple of cardboard boxes for us to open and exclaim over together. He called Mrs Walker over from the shop – it was pretty well closing time – so she could share the treat.

He regaled us with the gossip – who'd been outbid, who'd paid through the nose for rubbish. 'And of course Titus Oates sends his love, my sweet one,' he added.

'I'm sure you sent mine,' I replied, equally straight-faced.

'Of course. Tell me, do you know anything of Dilly Pargetter's background? She sells often deeply regrettable tat she glamorizes with the description *costume jewellery*,' he explained to Mrs Walker.

I scratched my head. 'Nothing at all. Should I?'

'I don't think so. I only registered her because she sold you that dress ring – the one with pretty beads,' he added. Clearly there were some things he preferred Mrs Walker not to know.

I nodded.

'She was there today, scooping up Woolworths rubbish as if she'd bid for the Crown Jewels. It wasn't her dreadful taste I noticed, but her black eye. And I fancy she was short of a tooth.'

'An accident?' I asked sharply, with a particularly nasty vibe I couldn't begin to explain.

'Who knows? She'd done her best with concealer, but there was no disguising the swellings. The funny thing was she kept on looking at me, as if there was something she wanted to say. I gave her one or two of my encouraging smiles, but I must have lost my touch. She obviously took them for bared fangs, and took off pretty sharply at the end of the sale.'

'Titus would have known what was up,' I declared.

'Of course he would,' Griff agreed. 'But he didn't choose to entrust me with whatever secrets he knew. Here – I bought these for the village hall: I know they're running short.' He produced a load of thick Duraflex tumblers. 'I don't know that it's even worth unpacking them,' he added, as Mrs Walker reached out tumbler after tumbler.

'I'll give them a good wash before you take them over,' she said. Then she took what looked like another, rather taller drinking glass from the same box. She rubbed it with a scrap of newspaper, and six panels appeared. Her eyes and mouth rounded and she put it down rather too sharply on the table. 'Is that . . . no, it can't be . . . Is it—? No, surely not.'

'My goodness,' Griff said, beaming with pleasure. 'Lalique, if I'm any judge. Well done, dear lady. Is it signed?'

She picked it up and looked at the base. 'R. Lalique.' She grabbed some kitchen towel and rubbed some of the dirt off. 'Look at these pretty blue figures. Heavens!'

'Who says you're not a divvy, Griff?' I chipped in.

'I actually was after the glasses, you know. May I look?' He turned the pretty goblet in his hands. 'It's a mite out of our period, of course.'

Mrs Walker responded with a grin of her own. 'One of our regulars collects glass. Do you think I should phone her?'

'Let me do my homework first, dear lady. I'd hate to overcharge her. Or worse still,' he added, apparently joking but, knowing him, dead serious, 'undercharge her . . .'

Griff tried to shoo me back upstairs to continue work on Sanditon's vase, but I refused to be shooed. The news about poor Dilly troubled me in a way I couldn't understand. I could understand anyone wanting to talk to Griff – the most approachable, kindest soul in the world – but why should she change her mind?

Griff and I had joked about Titus knowing everything. Maybe I should phone him. This wasn't just the ordinary, everyday thing you'd think. Titus objected to being phoned from landlines, for a start, though I'd tried to point out that mobile phone records were just as accessible to people who

might want to sniff round. Actually he objected to being
phoned at all. It was his pre . . . prerequ . . . pre-something
or other, anyway, to contact other people. Prerogative? Is
that it?

The other problem was that Griff didn't like Titus, and
really didn't like the weird relationship Titus and I didn't
so much enjoy as endure. So I said something about needing
a breath of fresh air and headed off towards the station,
where there was the best mobile coverage.

'Quick question, Titus,' I said, because he didn't do
flowery greetings and enquiries about health either. 'Dilly
Pargetter.'

'Got beat up by her old man. Husband. Partner. Whatever.
Does it sometimes. Bastard.'

And that was the end of the call.

Shoving the mobile and my hands in my pocket, I carried
on walking. Griff said it stimulated the phagocytes, whatever those might be; I just found it helped me to think.
Nothing doing between my ears this time, though.

Perhaps it was because I had this thing about domestic
violence. One of my carefully vetted foster mothers was
regularly beaten black and blue by her equally carefully
vetted husband Peter, a nice, well-spoken solicitor. And a
bastard. Actually I did my first ever bit of whistle-blowing,
even though I didn't know I was at the time. I drew pictures
for my social worker of where my foster mother had the
bruises – well out of sight, of course. Talk about volcanic
activity! What happened eventually I've no idea – people
say most women just put up with it, don't they? – because
I was whisked off somewhere else. I can't even remember
where, now, I was consigned to so many places.

I thought back to the triggers that had set Peter off.
They ranged from nothing at all to overcooked pasta. So
what might have provoked this attack on Dilly? *Does it
sometimes* didn't give me a lot to go on, of course. The
only clue might be that she was looking for me – and
the only connection I had with her was the ring currently
in the custody of Will Kinnersley.

It ought to be back in mine, now, surely, along with the

one I'd accidentally bought at the auction I'd been to. I could always call Will. Except I wasn't sure I'd be phoning about the rings.

Of course I was. I didn't do policemen, remember. Which brought me, in a very roundabout way, to my body. What had happened to it? I'd found it in Kent, so presumably Will would have access to any database it found its way on to. Why not?

Because I wanted to talk to someone about it first? Someone had once remarked that I needed friends my own age to hang out with, and gossip with. Well, much as I'd have liked that, I'd not found any yet. The antiques world, at least my corner of it, seemed to be populated almost entirely by old people. Of course there were some younger ones, but the women I'd met had said *yah* a lot, and tended to talk about their parents' place in France. As for the blokes, the less said about them the better.

Which left Griff, of course. Trouble was, once I started confiding in him I might just tell him all about my last trip to Bossingham Hall and all the confusion that had caused me. And that would upset him. He didn't like my father, any more than my father liked him – and would hate any legacy from him coming my way. Especially something as precious as my own grandmother's ring. He'd also probe away like a dentist at my feelings about my father's search for Nanny Baird's descendants, if there even were any.

Maybe I'd better get a sudden urge to continue the work on Sanditon's vase.

No, my head was jumping around too much for me to work on anything so special. I knew as soon as I switched on the lights. But at least I could look at what I'd done so far and decide how much to do the next day. At least I could talk about that when Griff called me down to supper, which he soon did.

'But I thought, dear heart, in view of her discovery, the very least we could do was invite Mrs Walker to join us. She plainly didn't fancy driving all the way over here and back again in the dark, and I didn't want to inflict the same on you. So I suggested that new place the far side of Charing. What do you think about that? We can go in tandem, and then come our separate ways home.'

'Excellent.' Griff never tried to talk while I was driving, and while we ate Mrs Walker wouldn't let us get a word in edgeways, especially if I encouraged her. Then Griff and I could talk about the meal all the way home. Brilliant. I was so pleased I gave Griff an extra big hug.

Usually if someone contacts me to find out if I'm making progress with a piece I'm either surprised or irritated. Or both. But when Harvey Sanditon emailed me, attaching a picture of the vase's mate with a label reading *LONELY* round its neck I found myself laughing, because it was somehow exactly what I'd have expected him to do if I'd thought about it.

I responded by tying a large piece of loo paper round the injured vase handle and sending a photo back, saying, 'Still in intensive care.'

For a while I toyed with sending a photo of my ringless finger to Will Kinnersley, but couldn't quite manage it – the idea, not the actual photo.

While I was at the computer, I surprised myself by doing another thing: I started looking up the websites of people who would hunt for missing people – folk missing out on legacies, for instance. I printed off contact details and put everything in an envelope to give my father next time I saw him. If he wanted information, let him find it himself. He wasn't very keen on making efforts; with luck he'd just give up.

Which left me feeling very ashamed of myself – I didn't just have my beadies on that Cartier watch, did I? Or – and this was even worse – did I want to keep all his pretty dilute affection for myself? The worst thing of all was that I knew there really was only one person I could rely on for advice: Griff himself. I shoved the envelope right to the bottom of my knickers drawer, with the photo of my grandmother.

SEVEN

At long last it was time to summon Griff to examine the vase. So he wouldn't know where to look for the damage, I turned it round several times so even I couldn't remember which handle I'd repaired. As for the tiny flake from the painted marble, I'd fixed that ages ago. I'd cook supper for a week if he spotted the scar.

Funnily enough, I didn't open the door to the workroom with my customary flourish and a loud *Da-dah*. I just ushered Griff inside.

He put a loving hand on my shoulder. 'I know, my sweet one – it's like finishing a long and exhausting run on the stage. You're bloody glad it's over, but you know you're going to miss it like hell.'

I glanced at him. It was against his house rule to use strong language before seven o'clock. And why had he sounded so regretful? He was so much of an antique dealer I'd actually forgotten how much of his life he'd spent as an actor, and how much he might miss the theatre.

Nonetheless it was a dealer's hands he ran over the handles and over the marbling. When they lingered over a slight defect I had a moment's panic – then I remembered there was a tiny flaw in the glaze, which had been present for nearly two hundred years – no trying to repair that.

He nodded slowly. 'I'm proud of you, my angel. Really, truly proud. And before you demur, think back to your concentration span when you first joined me. A goldfish would have been embarrassed. But now – how many hours have you spent on this?'

I shook my head. 'Hard to tell. Some of it was thinking and stretching and looking out of the window time. I tried keeping a time sheet, but it looked such a mess.'

'And he's not paying you for time, remember. He's paying you for your expertise, which is surely not to be counted

in hours and minutes. I think it's time to make the call,
don't you? Or email, or whatever you do.'
   'As a matter of fact,' I said, trying to sound casual, 'I
was wondering if I should make another call.'
   'To whom?'
   'To Will Kinnersley.'
   'What a good idea. Though I do implore you to find out
his marital status before you start getting fond of him.'
   'I'm only going to ask him about the rings!' I countered
more sharply than he deserved. 'Actually,' I added, much
more tentatively, 'there's another call or two I should maybe
make. On my father's behalf. And I truly don't want to.
Oh, Griff.'
   He pulled me to him. 'Why don't you tell me all about
it over a glass of something nice? Completing a task like
that deserves some sort of celebration.'

Despite clutching a glass of vintage wine – it was a gift
from one of our customers to thank us for locating a plate
to replace one from a Crown Derby service – I found that
I couldn't stop crying. This wasn't like me at all, unless a
mishap to my teddy bear was involved. Griff called me
stoical. But it all came pouring out – the relief of having
finished my most challenging job yet; the lack of news
about the body; the anxiety about the old rings; my lonely
and boyfriend-less state; and the fact that my father cared
enough about someone else to seek her descendants out.
   'And if you ask me, my love, it's that that upsets you most,'
Griff said, pressing a second linen handkerchief into my hand.
'But it's only since he had you in his life that he's realized
the importance of other people. You've awakened a long
dormant tenderness. Once he had a nanny he assuredly loved,
and she left him on his own when she died. And then there
was the trauma of being sent to school, and not being able to
go home because the Hall was requisitioned. A little cod
psychology would tell us that losing her helped turn him into
the damaged creature he undoubtedly is. And he was in denial
about all this until you showed him love. Tough love, but love.'
   'Hmm,' I hiccuped. 'So you're saying that it's a good

sign? The trouble is,' I admitted, unable to raise my voice above a whisper, 'I don't want to find them. I really do covet that Cartier watch.'

'That's strange: you never really engage with artefacts for their own sake, do you?' He stroked my hair. 'I don't mean you don't love beautiful things, and enjoy owning them, but you seem to know the difference between loving and admiring them and needing to keep them.'

'And there's something else I really, really want – his mother's engagement ring. He said he'd try to find it. But I shouldn't want it, not if it's going to upset you.'

'Why on earth should it upset me?' He sounded really puzzled.

'Because you don't like it when he gives me things.'

To my horror, as if his knees had given way, he sat down, covering his face with his hands.

I knelt in front of him. 'I'm sorry. I didn't mean it.' I don't know how many times I said it.

At long, long last he leant forward and stroked my face. 'You did mean it – and I'm afraid you're right. I can't give you my genes or my name. Just my love. And – just like you and the nanny's descendants – I don't want anyone else in the relationship. What a bright pair we are,' he concluded, with a pale smile. He took a long sip of wine. 'Is that why you've not been to Bossingham recently? Because you couldn't tell him you didn't want to try?'

'Well, I have been busy, haven't I?' I began. And thought better of it. 'Yes, you're right. And I haven't phoned Harvey because I'm afraid he'll find something wrong, and I'm scared of phoning Will – for all sorts of reasons.'

'He's not gay, I can tell you that,' he said.

I was gobsmacked.

'No vibes, angel heart. No vibes at all. Not to mention the fact he only had eyes for you. Go on, phone him. It's more than time he returned the rings. Or at least gave you an update. In fact, he's been decidedly remiss.' It was such a relief to have Griff sounding bossy and businesslike again I told him off for drinking too much wine.

*　　*　　*

Over supper, we worked out – or rather, I worked out and Griff nodded – the order in which I'd contact the various people we'd discussed. The first must be Harvey Sanditon, so that the vase could rejoin its twin and go back to its owner. I'd go and see my father with the information the following day. But he wasn't one for early rising, so before I left home I'd phone Will Kinnersley on his office phone. That felt good. A whole day planned. And then there was the doubtful treat of an antiques fair the day after that – a village hall affair Griff only went to out of kindness to the organizers. I felt so relieved I even allowed Griff a thimbleful of whisky after dinner.

Then I popped into the office to phone Harvey. Or would email be more professional? I'd have asked Griff, only he was listening to a Radio Three concert, his eyes firmly closed and his mouth decidedly open. Even as I stared at the desk, it dawned on me the best way would be to send a photo, which meant – given the lack of network coverage – a bit of a palaver with cameras and downloading. But within seconds of my having sent the email, while I was trying to work out a wordy order from an American collector, the corner of the screen flashed to show the arrival of a message.

Had Harvey been sitting glued to his computer?

And blow me if the phone didn't ring, even before I checked the message.

'When can I come and collect the patient?' Harvey demanded, his voice sounding much younger than I remembered – not stuffy at all. 'I could be with you by midnight.'

The guy was clearly even crazier about antiques than I was. I was about to get all flustered and gabble on about Griff's bed time, when I realized he'd given me the opening I needed. 'I think the patient would benefit from another good night's sleep,' I said firmly. I pushed my luck even further. 'And given the ward sister's schedule, a couple of days' conv—' Hell and damnation, I'd only lost the bloody word.

Thank goodness he chipped in so fast he might not have noticed my hesitation. 'Two more days? Lina, please!'

I felt tempted to reply as I'd heard other dealers reply: 'I do appreciate your concern but I do have other clients who have an equal right to my time.' It would have sounded very professional. But my mouth found it hard to say things like that. 'I'm absolutely tied up tomorrow, all day, and I'm committed the day after. Things I really can't get out of. I'm sorry.' What I found I could not do was tell him I'd leave the vase with Mrs Walker. I wanted to see his face as I switched on the whole battery of lights and revealed the vase it all its glory. That, now I came to think of it, was almost what I liked best – seeing the expressions on owners' faces as I returned much loved items to their care.

'Tomorrow evening,' he said. 'And I'll take you out to dinner afterwards. Six thirty?'

Sometimes an afternoon with my father required a long soak in the bath with some of Griff's cherished herbal oils.

'Seven thirty.'

'Seven. Please. Lina, you really mustn't make me wait a minute longer. Please.'

'Seven. But please come to the cottage, not the shop. Or you'll set off CCTV cameras and all sorts of alarms.' I didn't tell him, however, about the cameras that would register his arrival on our front door step.

'I can't make it out,' I told Griff later. 'I mean, what's half an hour here or there if he's got to take the vase back to its owner? Doesn't make sense. And all this business about taking me out to dinner . . .'

Griff frowned, but said nothing.

His silences always worried me.

Had I told him how insulting Sanditon had been about our little firm? How he'd sneered about me being a mere shop assistant? Surely not.

Griff took my hand. 'I know you're streetwise, my child, but sometimes your innocence alarms me.'

My turn to frown. 'You mean he's trying to . . . what do they call it when other clubs are after footballers? Tap me up?'

The idea seemed to surprise him and he let go my hand.

'Employ you full-time, you mean? I know he's a major player, but I can't see even him requiring his own restorer.'

'Even if he does, he can't have this one,' I said firmly.

'Well, we shall just have to wait and see.'

As planned, I phoned Will Kinnersley the next morning. His direct line. I had a vague idea that plain clothes officers didn't necessarily work the same hours as those in uniform, but nine seems a pretty universal start of business. While I cleaned my teeth, I'd practised what I wanted to say, and had even mentally prepared a voicemail option – when you're uncertain with words you want to cover all bases. I even wrote down one or two of the words that I was afraid might disappear wherever the wretched things insist on going when I try to use them.

In the bathroom it was easy enough. When I came to dial I was furious with myself – my hand was shaking. Hell, he might have been attractive, I might have fancied him like hell – though I'd never admit it to Griff – but he was a man holding on to property that was rightfully mine. There. Steel in spine time.

Voicemail of course. But I managed, without so much as a giveaway hesitation, to ask him to phone me so that we could arrange the return of my rings. There might have been a slight emphasis on the word *my*, come to think of it.

Right. And now to the business I was really dreading – the visit to Bossingham Hall.

EIGHT

You wouldn't have thought I'd need to phone my father to let him know I was on my way. After all, he hardly ever left Bossingham Hall unless I took him – before I'd come on the scene he'd had to make occasional excursions by taxi, but the track to his wing was now so bad most companies refused to risk their cars' suspension. But there was always the remote chance that I might find Titus Oates there, which would embarrass us all. At the moment I only suspected my father was deep into forgeries for Titus; the least hard evidence and they both knew I'd never visit the Hall again. Titus even suspected, I think, I might break our unwritten agreement never to mention him to the policemen I knew. I don't think I'd have shopped him, not unless I had proof positive that he was leading my father astray. But my father was more than willing to make a dishonest buck, so I couldn't have dropped one in it without the other.

Armed truce, then.

When my father suggested I might come via a supermarket – he usually left such ideas to me – I smelt a rat. Was the delay to give Titus plenty of time to get clear? Whatever the reason, I picked up green tea (my idea), champagne (his) and fresh fruit and vegetables (no prizes for guessing who thought of those). I would cook lunch for him, with plenty left over to freeze. Ah – he was short of naan bread. That was his favourite form of carb . . . carbon . . . Oh, whatever. He ate it with everything, Indian or not. From time to time he'd be really proud of himself because he'd prepared couscous. Well, if, microwave apart, the only kitchen item you ever use is a tea towel to hold over a champagne cork to stop it flying off, boiling water and pouring it over something you've had to empty into a pan is quite hi-tech. He'd only battle with rice if it came in sealed, ready-cooked packs.

He bounded out to meet me like an eager dog, helping me carry the bags of goodies into his kitchen. He'd not only washed up recently – there was foam round the plug hole – but had also dried up and put away, which was very suspicious. But I didn't ask any questions. No point – he'd only have lied.

Without even being asked, he made us tea and we went to his living room. He kept looking at me anxiously. Was it because he was feeling guilty about Titus? Or because he'd noticed I'd not been around for a while and was afraid he'd upset me? Unlikely – I don't think his conscience works like that, if at all. Or because he wanted to ask about my researches in Nanny Baird's family and knew I could be as cagey as he could?

I went for the last option, fishing the envelope of computer print outs from my bag. 'These are details of firms that would search for any family Nanny Baird might have left.'

'How would I get in touch with them? I don't want hordes of claimants bearing down on the Hall – think of that last oik.'

I could understand his shudder. 'Why not phone your solicitor and ask him to do it for you? It'd be easier than wading through this lot yourself. In fact, I can't think of it when you first raised the problem. Sorry.' I put the envelope on the table.

'I don't like these legal chappies. Charge you a grand for scratching your own arse. I suppose you couldn't—? No?'

At last I remembered his lawyer's name. 'Mr James is a bit of an old woman, but he's very met . . . met . . . thorough. Or if you didn't want to involve him, so long as these firms are *bona fide* –' that was one term Griff had made sure I knew and could use – 'then they wouldn't let anyone know who was asking. They'd take instructions from you about that.'

'But you could get in touch with them on my behalf. I wouldn't want them coming here.'

'People can't just tell a firm to find someone – there has to be a reason. It all gets too complicated if I try. I might even need power of attorney to do that,' I said, suddenly

realizing I might have to embark on an explanation. I knew
all about it because Griff and I had it for each other.
  'Matter of fact, I've been thinking of giving you that,
anyway. In case I lose my marbles. Or get ill. Don't want
any old idiot switching off the machine, you know.'
  I know I opened my mouth several times, but no sound
came out. It was a good job, really, because I couldn't think
of any adequate words to say.
  'Been looking into it,' he continued. 'Don't need any
legal training or anything. Lots of people have relatives to
do it. And you're my only family.'
  This time I did manage to croak, 'There are a lot more
out there.'
  'Who only crawl out of the woodwork if they think there's
money in it. And may not even be family anyway. Hmph.
Anyway, I know it's a lot for a little girl to take on, but
you could discuss it with that old queer of yours and see
what he thinks.'
  Little girl! *Queer*! I should have been down on him like
a ton of bricks.
  'Now, a little glass of something before lunch, eh? And
we'd better look for something else to sell. Can't find that
damned engagement ring of my mother's anywhere, by the
way. I think we should get you sniffing it out, you and your
instinct. God knows where you got that from . . .'
  I didn't sniff out the ring, probably because my instinct
doesn't work that way. If it did, I could make a living as
a bloodhound. But I did unearth some plates I'd put aside
for a rainy day for him.
  'Prices are just beginning to creep up again.' I said,
packing them carefully. 'But I think we shall have to rely
on two-for-one offers for non-vintage bubbly for a bit. I
always keep my eye open for good deals.'
  'I know you do. You're a good girl – and quite a taking
little thing.' For some reason he peered at my hand. 'Not
wearing that chap's ring? That socking great ruby – the
vulgar one? Of course not. Good job – good riddance. What
about that pretty sapphire? No? I suppose you'll be thinking
of selling them?'

I touched my finger to the side of my nose in a gesture he'd know from Titus. 'The market's still improving, and they won't go bad in my safe.'

He gave a crack of laughter. 'Good girl. Chip off the old block. You make a nice profit – that'll show the bastard.'

It would, of course, if I was ever likely to see the bastard again.

I made him another cup of tea and, letting him get on with his favourite afternoon TV programmes, I let myself out and locked up after myself. Only when he'd finished his day's viewing would he realize I'd left all the details of the tracing services on his table. Over to him.

It was a good job the drive home was straightforward, because I wasn't concentrating as hard as I should. I had quite a bit on my mind, after all it's not every day someone asks you to be the one to switch their machine off, as and when it is necessary, of course. That was bad enough, but to have him suggest I talked everything over with Griff suggested a good deal of understanding I'd never have imagined him capable of. It must be all that green tea sparking his brain into life.

It made me feel a bit bad about refusing to hunt for the Baird descendants, if any. But however I looked at it, it didn't seem to be my sort of job. All that paperwork for a start, and no doubt a lot of legal language. Plus I really was pretty busy on my own account. My father assumed my life revolved round visits to him, whereas sometimes it was as much as I could do to carve out the half day the trips involved. If I took on more work for Harvey Sanditon, then there'd be even less time to spare. Which gave me, if I thought about it, a very good reason to turn down any offers Sanditon made: I had to make enough time to care for my poor grey-haired old dad. Which meant, of course, staying in Kent, not moving to New Zealand or Devon or Shropshire or wherever.

I just had time to tell Griff my father's plans for me before he shooed me upstairs, where a bath was already running, complete with lovely soothing bath oils.

'And while you soak, consider what you should wear this evening – worrying about your father must take second place to that,' he called up the stairs.

If I knew Griff, he'd already have given the matter thought, which was a huge relief. It had to be an outfit that would tell him I was a professional to my rather battered finger-tips, when I showed off the vase. And then it had to transform into something I could wear for dinner – which didn't sound like a quick trip to the village chippie.

I was just about to sink down so that little more than my nose was above water when I heard voices. Surely Sanditon wasn't here already? Thank God I'd not got my hair wet. I leapt out of the water like a dolphin after an electric shock, towelled roughly and, swarming into my bathrobe, sprinted across the landing to my bedroom. My best trouser suit had mysteriously arrived on the bed, together with my really wickedly expensive boots (half price from Ashford Outlet) and a silk top that Griff's partner Aidan had given me – and his gifts always oozed quality. Hair? A glamorous pair of Art Deco combs, then. Slap. Thanks to Griff I could apply that in three minutes flat. And a whiff of light perfume. Phew.

It was hard to take the stairs two at a time in that partic-ular pair of boots, and in any case I didn't want to appear downright breathless, did I?

Especially when the person Griff was so artlessly chat-ting to was Will Kinnersley.

Will Kinnersley, and, just out of sight until I emerged fully into the room, another rather sallow young man, who all too clearly was another policeman.

Neither appeared to have a ring ready to press into my hand.

NINE

Then there was another sort of ring. On the door bell, this time. I looked in horror at Griff. Although they were crammed side by side on one of the sofas, the two tall young men made our cosy living room look cluttered. I also knew from bitter experience that people can get the wrong impression when they find you in the company of police officers.

Since I was on my feet, I did the logical thing – I stepped over the long legs, closing the living room door behind me, and answered it myself. Hell, it couldn't be Harvey Sanditon, could it?

It could. Harvey Sanditon and a very large bunch of flowers. I couldn't tell what colour they were because Will and his mate had stupidly left their car's blue lights flashing, as if they were on some televised raid.

Like the flowers, changing colour every time the lights pulsed, Sanditon looked puzzled. No, more like dead concerned. 'You've not been robbed, have you?' he gasped.

It wasn't hard to tell how his mind was working.

'No, and the vase is quite safe,' I said, all in one breath. 'The police are here about something else,' I added, ready to lead him upstairs to my work room. On the other hand, the flowers confused me – as did the box of something tied in ribbon he was also carrying. Did all this mean I should treat him as a guest rather than just a punter? After all, we were about to do dinner.

As I hesitated, Griff flung open the living room door, announcing, 'My angel, this young man wants to talk to you about your body.' His wink was probably supposed to help; it certainly made Will's colleague's face go the colour of the Royal Worcester egg-cup I'd used that morning. Mine went a much deeper shade, clashing horribly with my cerise top. Sanditon managed a tiny cough, and Will probably saved the day by throwing his gorgeous head back and laughing.

Whether he'd deign to explain might depend on how he viewed Sanditon. Was he just a punter, a besotted middle-aged beau, or a serious rival – always assuming Will fancied me half as much as I fancied him?

No point in hanging around to find out. 'I found a corpse the other day,' I said flatly. 'I expect he wants to talk about that. And, as you've probably already noticed, policemen tend to hunt in pairs.' Time to get more assertive, maybe. 'Sergeant Kinnersley, as you can see, this isn't a good time. Mr Sanditon's got a long-standing appointment to collect an item I repaired for him.' So I earned brownie points for authority, even though I was lying through my teeth.

Griff seized the gifts and did his best to spirit them away into the kitchen, as if all punters appeared with interesting payment in kind, not nice boring cheques. As he returned, he said, 'I'll make an appointment for you to see these gentlemen, shall I? In our business diary?' he added, in case I wished my mobile phone on him. Griff shuddered with horror at the thought of anything except a paper diary.

'Yes, please. I think tomorrow afternoon's free. Mr Sanditon, do you want to see the patient?' I gestured to the stairs, praying that despite my haste I'd shut my bedroom door so he wouldn't see the chaos on my bed and dressing table.

I think some of Griff's love of the theatre must have rubbed off on me. As before, I'd placed the vase dead centre of the work table. Things like the packing case and invoices were tucked out of sight.

I switched on all the lights at once.

Sanditon's face was all I could have asked for.

At last, when he'd turned his baby in his hands and examined it from every angle, he put it back and turned to me, eyes glowing. Then he did something that really took me by surprise – he kissed my hands. It's a gesture I always found really sexy, and I blushed all over again.

And then yet again, because I had to ask him for payment

before the vase left the building. It was one thing Griff was absolutely adamant about, I explained, so pleased I remembered the word I almost dropped the envelope with the invoice in it. Better that than the vase, I suppose.

There was a tap on the door.

Will popped his head round. 'Griff says you've worked a miracle and I ought to see it.'

'So long as you look, not touch, young man,' Sanditon rapped out. 'Unless your insurance still covers it, Ms Townend?'

I didn't think he was joking. Keeping the vase base firmly on the table, I turned it gently. 'That's the handle I repaired,' I said. 'Or was it this one?'

'Wow,' Will said, with what sounded like reverence. 'You built it up from nothing?'

'Yes. I was just about to hand over the fragments of the original to Mr Sanditon, Will. See you tomorrow afternoon? Make sure Griff puts the appointment in the diary, won't you?' Did that sound flirtatious or if I was just helping the police with their enquiries?

He didn't budge. 'Why does he need to see the fragments?'

'A little detective work I've been doing,' I said. I added, 'If you don't mind, that is, Mr Sanditon?'

I'd put the shards in a box on the shelves. 'Here,' I said, fishing one out, and showing one end to both men, 'you can see that this surface is dirty. The one it matched on the vase was the same colour.' I picked out another. 'This also has one dirty end, which also matched a dirty patch on the vase. So what you had was two major cracks running almost all the way through – but not quite. It was an accident waiting to happen.' Sanditon pulled a face – he didn't like the expression any more than Griff did. 'I've made a note of it in my statement of original damage.' Although I spoke to Sanditon, I flicked an eye to make sure Will was registering it too. 'Maybe it ex . . . exon . . . lets you off the hook.'

'Let's not worry about that now,' he said quickly. 'You've done the job as well as I could have hoped for. Better. Congratulations.'

I slipped our credit card terminal discreetly on to the table; even though there were only three of us in the room he covered the pad and tapped with great secrecy. It was all the same to the terminal, which chuntered a bit and produced a slip.

I didn't know Will well enough – hell, I didn't know Will at all! – to hint him away tactfully, and in a sense Sanditon was still paying for my time. He was certainly paying for me to wrap his property. So I said bluntly, 'OK, Will – show's over. See you tomorrow, then? Here?'

He frowned. For an awful moment I thought he was going to tell me to present myself at Maidstone nick for DNA and fingerprinting. Instead he just nodded once and went back downstairs.

'You wouldn't like to stand where he was standing, would you?' I asked.

'Why?'

'Because you're between me and the wrapping paper and bubble wrap.'

For some reason or other, now Sanditon had his vase back, all the kissing hands and gifts tailed off. That was fine by me, so long as the choccies were as good as the meal we were eating.

Because Griff was such a good cook, and we ate so many meals on the road, we tended not to go to local restaurants, even when they were getting a reputation for fine dining. So although it was only five minutes from the cottage, I'd never eaten at the Two Bays at Bredeham before – trees, not seaside, incidentally. Maybe I'd have preferred a jolly brasserie, but I was a sucker for widely spaced tables, lots of white linen I didn't have to wash and iron and waiters who knew their way around the menu. I was a little bit worried when Sanditon charged the pre-dinner champagne to his room number. He wasn't the sort of guy who expected payment in kind for a nice meal, was he? But there was no sign that this was anything but a business meeting. In fact, if he hadn't been so much a man of the world I'd have had him down as shyer than Will.

For conversation, he went into so many details of my restoration work I felt tempted to offer him an apprenticeship. But the food – although it was introduced on the menu by such terms as *To Commence*, *To Follow* and *Starches and Greens* – was too good to cut short with a silly quip, so I answered politely and occasionally ventured questions of my own about his stock and how he found it. The object that had brought us together, the vase, sat in its box where a third place setting would have been put. It was only when he excused himself between courses that he picked it up and presumably locked it in his room. I'd had enough champagne to speculate privately on the sort of sexual antics that might break it all over again.

So what was this all about? It sure as hell wasn't the usual way of celebrating a good repair. Otherwise I'd be on a constant diet. As it was, maybe I should give the *To Finish* course a miss.

It was only over coffee that he made the proposition I'd feared. No, not the bedroom one. The one I'd already dismissed without a thought. That I might leave Tripp and Townend and become a junior partner in Sanditon Moyles, Moyles being no more than a ghost on the letter heading. Even if he'd wanted me as senior partner my response would have been the same.

'I'm more than happy to do any restoration work for you, Harvey. And, if necessary, prioritize it like I did your vase. But my home's here, with Griff, and there's nothing that could drag me away from him.'

He gave a rueful smile. 'I suppose I should have expected that. But you must think of your own future, Lina. A woman like you shouldn't be tucked away in a sleepy village in an unfashionable part of Kent. Any part of Kent, actually,' he added bitterly.

'Ah, the M25 trapped you, did it? It does that to everyone. And you should see the M20 during Operation Stack, when they park all the lorries on it,' I added helpfully.

'I didn't mean just that – though yes, being cut off from the civilized world is a problem. But you must think in the longer term. Mr Tripp is hardly in the first flush of youth.'

It was a good job I'd declined the *To Finish* offerings, or he might have had a plateful of something sweet and sticky in his face. 'So you want me to abandon my dearest friend just as he's likely to need me most? I don't think so, Harvey.'

'He could move too,' he said, but there was something about his voice I couldn't work out.

'Abandon his old cronies?' Not to mention his lover, but that was none of anyone else's business. I delivered – what was the term? Griff had taught it to me only the other day – I delivered the *coup de grace* in a slightly sickly tone: 'In any case, I couldn't leave my father.'

He pulled a face. 'I thought that that was Arthur Habgood—'

'Mr Habgood thinks he might be my *grand*father, and has been pressing me very publicly to take a DNA test,' I said, deciding rather late that he didn't need to know all about Lord Elham. 'But who'd want a grandfather who sells restored goods as perfect?'

'Does he?' For the first time he really sat up and took notice. 'Really? Are you sure? I bought a pretty majolica plate from him the other day – a commission,' he added, as if he didn't normally soil his hands with items that far down the food chain. 'What have I said?'

I managed to choke back my laughter to polite levels. 'I hope you checked it very carefully. Because one of my apprentice pieces was a majolica plate. I sold it as restored. And Arthur Habgood, the man who wants to claim me as his own flesh and blood, put it on his stall as perfect. Have you still got it? Then maybe you want to take another look at it.'

TEN

Griff and I have a pact that neither pesters the other for details of their dates. But I knew that he'd have given anything to be a fly on the wall at the Two Bays, because he must have been as intrigued by the flowers and chocolates as I was.

So as I popped our breakfast eggs into their pretty Worcester basket weave egg cups the colour of the anonymous policeman's blush, I said truthfully, 'I wish you'd been there last night. I had this endless stream of questions about my work, followed by a spiel about how I'd do better working for him.' I tried to slip that in so casually he wouldn't notice. 'And then he told me he'd bought a plate from Arthur Habgood.'

Griff's eyes twinkled as I'd hoped they would. 'Not *the* plate!'

'Who knows? But it scared him rigid. He could scarcely bundle me into a taxi quickly enough. And I couldn't stop giggling – the driver must have thought I was pissed.' Griff – and to do him justice, Harvey – had insisted on a cab even though the restaurant was only fifteen minutes' walk away. OK, twenty minutes, in those boots.

He frowned – he hadn't missed the bit about leaving him after all. 'I think you'll find, sweet one, that at this time of the day the word is *drunk*.'

I shook my head. 'That makes it sound as if I was rolling round completely legless. There must be another word, Griff, surely. Merry? Yes, very merry . . .' While he cracked his egg, I continued, 'And since I can't ever imagine a discussion with Harvey Sanditon about English words, I have to say I told him I'd never consider leaving you.' *Or my father*, I added under my breath. Those were words Griff wouldn't want to hear any time of the day or night. They rather surprised me, actually. 'In any circumstances.'

'Unless young Will sweeps you off your feet. Or that rather strangely coloured young man he brought with him. Was it a liver problem? Or an excess of badly faded fake suntan?'

So Griff was happy again. He always got waspish when he was afraid, and was his usual gossipy self when his mind was at rest.

'I could ask him? Or Will, of course? What time are they coming round, by the way? No? Is there a problem?'

'I suspect they wished to discuss something in more official surroundings. But I persuaded young Will you'd be more forthcoming in a room you were familiar with – I fear I had to hint at traumatic experiences in your younger days, my love, when the police were inclined to intimidate and bully you. So here it will be, round about eleven – but don't expect the friendly flirtation to continue, especially if the liverish lad is present.'

I reached the bottom of the egg before I asked, 'Do they really suspect I've done something wrong? I don't want to dob in poor Dilly—'

'Another deeply unpleasant word, sweetheart! But I suppose it's no worse than *grass up* or *snitch on*. In any case, how can it be in any sense a betrayal? You've handed over the receipt so they know exactly where it came from.'

I fished out the empty shell and turned it upside down so that it looked new. 'I was actually going to say, *poor Dilly's husband*. Titus says he beats her. And I'm just wondering if he beat her because she sold the ring so cheaply.'

Griff slopped coffee. 'Wherever did that idea come from? I'm used to your being a divvy when it comes to objets d'art, my love – but not your coming out with strange theories about people. Without any evidence, I have to say.'

'Sorry. But it figures, Griff.'

He shook his head. 'It may well. But you can hardly quote Titus Oates' opinion.'

'Not if I want to stay on speaking terms with him,' I agreed. 'So I'll say nothing but do a bit of sniffing around at the next auction or fair.'

'You will be careful, dear one? For while I might pooh-pooh your theory, it doesn't mean it's wrong. And you're more precious to me than any number of rings.' He watched as I speared my spoon through the empty shell, and then leant over to smooth my hair. He didn't need to say what he was afraid of, did he?

The demure and quietly coloured top under my everyday suit told the two policemen that I meant business, not possible flirtation. I also wore my less threatening boots, the sort that I can wear all day at a fair and never notice. Apart from that, I was as neat as Griff could make me: after vetoing lip gloss, he'd fluffed my hair a bit, and wiped off almost all my blusher. 'Pale and interesting, that's the look. Someone they could rely on in the witness box.'

I clasped his hand. 'I don't want to go through that again, Griff.'

'Last time you spoke with as much authority as Counsel could have asked. Just think of it as stage fright, though in truth that's bad enough. But with luck, it may not come to that – in either enquiry. Now, your eye shadow's just a little heavy.' He tissued the spare away, and kissed my forehead. 'There – let battle commence.' He peered out of the window. 'At least they've had the sense to turn off those fairground lights they polluted the village with last night.'

Touching his finger to his nose, he set the surveillance system. The policemen might not know it, but even though he disappeared smartly as soon as he'd let them in, shutting the living room door with a sharp click, he'd be able to see if I got upset, and stage a miraculous invasion with a tray of tea things.

I managed to get the men sitting facing the window, so they were better lit than I was. As before they sat shoulder to shoulder. I looked from one to the other – which of them wanted to speak first?

Will.

Did this mean I had a good-cop-bad-cop routine? Because I definitely had Will down as a good cop. But he only spoke to introduce his mate – at last! – as DC Winters. 'Known to his friends as Bernie or Bleak,' Will said, nicely unofficial again.

'And what about to people like me? I asked.

'Dave would be fine,' DC Winters said, with another huge, deep blush, which didn't go at all well with the bruise-like smudges under his eyes.

'OK. Right: whose questions do I answer first?' All this sounded very competent, as if I dealt with the police every day. But it was the result of an hour's coaching from Griff: 'If they think you're rattled, they'll do their best to rattle you some more. So make sure they're the ones on edge – but not enough to make them hostile.'

Winters smiled without much amusement. 'Your body – the body you *found*, Ms Townend.'

I nodded. 'I'm happy to be Lina. All I did was see this young man in a field. As I said to your colleagues at the time, I should have done the right thing – gone to see what I could do. But I was on my own, with my firm's name blazoned all over the van, which was full of uninsured items, and I was afraid it was a scam. One of my friends was the victim of a similar one not so long ago. He lost his van and everything in it, which was a bit of problem, as you can imagine. Especially since he dealt in silver.' Was I talking too much? It sounded fine, but was it a bit too pat?

He nibbled a fingernail. 'Did you see any other vehicles in the vicinity?' He peered anxiously at me as if it really mattered.

'If I had, I'd have flagged one down. There was no network coverage for my mobile, but someone else might have had better luck.'

'So no cars, no vans, no lorries?'

'A pretty quiet road on a pretty nasty day. But I can't work out why no one saw him earlier and called him in.' Neither could they, it seemed. 'I know I should have done more. But to tell you the truth, I was – scared. For my safety.' I lowered my eyes as if ashamed, and didn't tell him that I reckon with the dirty skills learned during my street days I could deal with most individuals who attacked me. To be fair, not two at once. Not now I was out of practice.

He jabbed in my direction with another, badly bitten finger. 'But you took a photo.'

'Just in case. Because I could. I don't know.'

'Did you expect him to disappear? So you wanted proof of your story?'

'Put it another way,' I said, getting irritated, 'I was afraid that if I stopped another driver they wouldn't believe me. And I don't think your mates from Folkestone would have done, when they turned up and found him gone. But when they saw the photo they got all serious. And they found something to interest them – enough to want to keep my phone.'

'I gather you wouldn't let them.'

'Would you let them keep yours? All those phone numbers and appointments? Quite.' I smiled. 'In any case, they had the photo – surely that was all they needed.' I paused. 'Why are we going over all this again?' By now I didn't want to call him Bernie, Bleak or Dave. I think my voice might have told him that.

Suddenly he was Mr Nice, all apologies and fluttery movements of those poor hands. 'I just wanted to get everything straight in my mind. And to hope that talking about the incident might just help you to remember another detail or two. Can we just go back to how he was lying?'

Was one of us being dense? 'The same as in the photo. On his back. One arm across his chest. One behind his head, but not cushioning it.' I demonstrated.

'And it couldn't have been a cow or a sheep?'

'Not according to the photo.'

'I'm more interested in the photo in your head, so to speak.'

'Are you trying to ask if he moved between the time I first spotted him and the time I took the photo?' I closed my eyes as if trying to relive the scene. Funnily enough, I saw the body as if in the photo, rather than as I'd first seen it. I tried to see myself catching sight of it, pulling over, deciding not to get out – and then taking the photo. 'No, I'm fairly sure he didn't. And I didn't see anyone hanging around ready to carry him away, either. Though there could

have been – there was a bridleway on the left as I headed
north. That would have lead in roughly the right direction.
But I didn't see anyone driving up or down it. Or riding,
come to think of it.'

That had surprised Will at least. 'Riding?'

'Well, it was a bridle path. It said so on the sign. No
access for cars or something.' Not for anyone was I going
to attempt the word *vehicular*.

'That's very strange,' Winters said, accusingly.

'Are you saying there isn't a bridle path there?'

'Not at all. Or rather, there's a perfectly good road there,
leading exactly where you said. But it doesn't have any
signs like those you've described.'

'So I've done what that American politician did –
misremembered? Sorry.'

Winters shook his head. 'Not necessarily.'

'Someone changed the signs?'

'Not necessarily.' This time he said it with menace. 'Was
there something you wanted to say?' He managed to make
this into an accusation.

'Ye–es.' Quite a lot, actually. 'It's weeks since I saw this,
and made my statement. I'm a sucker for stories. I want to
know what happens next. And yet this story seems no further
forward than when your colleagues first asked me these
questions. If it was a body, aren't things going a bit – well,
slowly? And if the man was alive, won't he have left tracks
your clever forensic scientists could have picked up? And
if he was dead, someone else must have picked him up –
lots of tracks there.'

'We're exploring a number of possibilities,' he said, as
if that was the end of the matter.

'I'm sure you are. And here's another possibility. What
if you and Will didn't share the same car just because you
wanted to save petrol? What if my body and my rings are
connected?' Should I have said *the body* and *the rings*?
Probably.

Will flicked a swift glance at his colleague. 'Lina, you
know we can't tell you.'

'In that case they are. Are we talking night hawks here?'

I'd already used this term to Will, the very first time we met, but it hadn't provoked a response like this. I seemed to have pressed a button somewhere in Winters' brain. 'Night hawks! A fine romantic name for people who plunder and ruin historical sites all in the name of money!' It might have been he who was the Heritage Officer, not Will. To my amazement he got to his feet and smashed a fist into the palm of the other hand.

'They trespass on valuable farm land and risk livestock. They ruin the archaeology! And they're made to sound like *Boys' Own* heroes! Vandals who desecrate graves!'

Perhaps it was a good job he got nowhere near them – he'd have shoved them in one of those deep doorless dungeons and not bothered with minor details like a trial and a verdict. An oubliette. But goodness knows why I should remember a useless word like that, when I kept forgetting ones I needed.

I risked a glance at Will, who quite clearly didn't know what to do. Neither did I. So I did something, even if it was a bit girly. I nipped into the kitchen and put the kettle on. Griff had already laid the tray with pretty Victorian cups and saucers and a plate of his favourite Waitrose biscuits. All I had to do was fill the cafetière.

When I returned, they'd sat down again, though Dave had moved to Griff's favourite armchair. 'People with metal detectors, then,' I prompted, pressing down the cafetière plunger. They both stared at my hand, like other men stare at Page Three pics.

'Detectorists,' Will said at last.

'Weird word,' I said, wondering what Griff would make of it. 'But *metal detectives* isn't right, and *metal detectors* means the things they use. Sorry!'

Both men were blinking, first at me, then at each other. They might have thought I was just chuntering, but I was giving myself time to think about other things. Like the connection between my rings and my body.

I jumped into their silence. 'So am I wrong to think that there is a connection between the enquiries?' In my head I sounded as pompous as Harvey Sanditon. But they didn't seem to mind. Perhaps it reminded them of police station language.

'It's not impossible,' Will said slowly.

'So Dave's detectorist might have dug up one or both of the rings that came into my possession and got Sir Douglas all het up?' Not to mention Winters, of course.

'Possibly. Very well, likely. Several farmers claim that people have been going on to their land without permission. Holes have appeared. A human ulna turned up the other day. Anything to do with this sort of activity comes to me.'

'Anything?'

'From English Heritage – they've got an officer with responsibility for liaising with me; from members of the public; from experts like Sir Douglas; from detectorist clubs who suspect one of their members isn't playing it straight. From you, with luck.'

'I've told you all I know. You have the rings. Still.' I managed what I hoped was a winning smile. 'I gather the one I bought from Dilly wasn't a foreign dress ring with beads?'

'Saxon, we think. Possibly imported from Europe. So in part the information on the receipt might be correct. But the so-called beads are uncut gemstones. All the same, it isn't the intrinsic value that's important – it's their historical value—'

'In particular, their value as part of a complete site, for God's sake,' Dave chipped in.

'And someone's been digging near the place I saw the body? That's why you're both so concerned!'

Dave's sore, jabbing finger came into action again. 'We can neither confirm nor deny that.'

Ignoring him, I turned to Will. 'Is that why there's been no publicity? Because there's something important there?'

Will's face was serious. 'If we'd told you that from the outset, would you have been more cooperative?'

Anger brought me to my feet. 'I don't think I could have been more cooperative. I've told you all I know.' There was a heavy silence behind me. 'What?' I demanded, looking at Winters. 'Do you really think I'm holding something back?'

His calm smile unnerved me. 'Oh, yes. You haven't told us about your grandfather, have you?'

'My grandfather? I haven't got a grandfather as far as I know.'

Winters looked at me with a mixture of triumph and reproach. 'Come, Lina, the truth, please.'

He couldn't mean Griff. Couldn't. Not the man who'd single-handedly transformed me from a feral teenager to a respectable businesswoman. I wouldn't even breathe his name out loud in case that gave Dave someone else to accuse. At last, as I made myself sit down and breathe quietly, something started to swim through my brain. 'You don't mean the man who *wants* to be my grandfather, do you? Runs a downmarket version of our firm? Devon Cottage Antiques?'

'Arthur Habgood. Your grandfather.'

'Uh, uh. Nothing to do with me. He trails round antiques fairs with a gob-swab in a little tube, but that's as far as it gets. Can't stand the man.' No need to explain about the dodgy plate – they weren't in the business and about to be fleeced.

'He says you have a reputation for handling stolen goods and—'

'How dare he! And how dare you come round here and question me without doing your homework. Me handle stolen goods? Get real. And get on the phone to Inspector Morris, of the Met Fine Art Squad.'

He reached inside his pocket.

I was on my feet again, pointing at the door. 'No, not here. Not in my space. Go back to your office and check. Both of you. And when you're ready to apologize, you can warn my so-called grandfather that there are laws in this country against slander.'

ELEVEN

The moment I'd slammed the front door on them, kicking it for good measure, Griff was beside me, gripping my hands in one of his and pulling me to him in a healing hug.

I don't think he was worried about the door. He was afraid I'd hit myself this time.

What the therapist had told me to do was breathe slowly and try to work out what emotion I was feeling. Easier said than done. But I tried. Anger? Humiliation or rejection? Or what? I'd had plenty of all three to deal with in my past. Plus a few others.

This time there was no doubt I was angry. If I'd had Arthur Habgood handy, I'd have decked him, without turning a hair. And if he'd had a few plates with him, restored or not, they'd have ended in pieces on the floor beside him. Lots of pieces.

But the person I'd have loved to be my real grandfather was right in front of me. I pressed my face to his shoulder. My shuddering sobs made my teeth chatter at first. He didn't let go until I had enough breath to speak. 'Any chance of some hot chocolate?' I asked at last, with a really feeble little smile.

'I've reached the milk out already. Come with me, my dear one, and I'll brew up.' But he was careful to hold at least one hand as he led the way into the kitchen. I stuffed the other into my pocket. I mustn't let him down. I sat at the table, spreading both hands flat where we could both see them.

Sooner than I could have dreamt, there was a mug between them, comforting me with its heat and also with the smells of chocolate and cream which seemed to float straight into my brain.

Griff sat down opposite me. 'An official complaint might be in order.'

'To the police? They stick together like—' It was far too early in the day to say how closely they stuck. I pulled a face.

'Possibly. But let us not rule out the option entirely. And you might wish to send a solicitor's letter to that louse Habgood telling him that if he repeats his allegation again, you will seek legal redress. But above all, remember that revenge is a dish best eaten cold. Fume a little to me – fume a great deal, if you want – but don't do anything precipitate, especially something you may later regret.'

'Such as driving hell for leather down to Devon and putting a brick through my dear grandfather's window? Well,' I continued, shuddering as I recalled all the traffic jams we'd sat in, 'I suppose the A303 would put a stop to any hell-for-leathering.'

'That's my child. Now, indulge an old man in his whims, but I have a huge desire to find some sea and breathe in the ozone. Mrs Walker is more than competent to watch the shop. Why don't we take in lunch during our little jaunt?'

'Yeah. Why not?' But even as I smiled to please him, my mind was hunting for the term to describe what he was doing. Diver – digress – some sort of activity. That was it. Displacement activity. I'd got the words – a bonus point. Were they the right ones? They could be. But I couldn't ask Griff in case he realized I was on to what he was doing. 'It's a nice clear day, and you've got those nice new specs – do you want to drive?' That way he wouldn't be worried about my having an attack of road rage.

We found ourselves in Hythe, which shouldn't have been a surprise, given that there's a Waitrose in the middle of the town. We duly had a walk along the sea wall toward Folkestone, overtaken at intervals by Gurkhas running very fast despite backpacks that seemed bigger than they were. The shingle roared and sighed under the incoming tide; fishermen wielded huge rods from the shelter of canvas igloos; across the road golfers hit little balls that changed course in mid-air as the wind strengthened. It was time to turn back. Yes, I could have gone on forever, and at twice the pace, but Griff wasn't as young and still angry as I was, so I stopped.

'If I listen carefully,' I yelled above the wind, 'I can hear fish and chips calling. Can you? Back in Hythe?' This time I wasn't using my precious gift, either.

He cupped an ear. 'You know, I believe I can. I think they're calling from that nice restaurant overlooking the sea.'

They were. As was my mobile the moment two gorgeous platefuls arrived. Will. I switched him to voicemail. Bugger him and his excitable friend.

'It occurs to me, my love,' Griff said, as we left Waitrose with a bag of his favourite plunder – top of the range, end-date goodies, 'that our route home could take us past the place where you stopped to tell the police about your body. Would you care to retrace your steps?'

Nodding, I automatically went to the driver's door. Most of my anger had subsided – it was no more than simmering now. Griff probably needed a little doze after all that food – he reminded me that at least the fish gave us lots of useful omega oils – and all that shopping. So there was no way I was going to take my revenge on the human race by driving as if I'd just been let out of hell. Especially as I was still partly in it, if I was honest. So I drove extra carefully, watching out for Hythe's usual population of drivers who seemed to have parked by touch, to judge by the dents front and rear. There was a rumour amongst us dealers that at least one old dear regularly turned up to fairs at Folkestone in a nice Volvo despite being registered blind – anyone who knew her made sure they left their vans nowhere near.

I found my way to the road I'd taken back the day of the auction, and picked my way slowly along. Griff dozed quite noisily as soon as I switched on Classic FM. I'd got as far as the lay-by I'd pulled into to call the police before I realized I'd passed no police tape or anything to show there might have been a crime scene. On impulse, I found the road Winters had insisted was a real road, not a bridle way with no vehicular access. Vehicular. I said it out loud. There! If I took it really slowly I could manage the dreaded word. Weird. It was just an ordinary lane. So I turned down it, looking for goodness knew what.

And found nothing. Everything was dead quiet. So was it all wonderful inactivity, or was it all so secret they didn't want to draw attention to it? I pressed on towards Ottinge, which would take us eventually to Elham, and better roads? I sure as hell wasn't going to go left, because what should be occupying the road but a 4x4. Not for the first time wishing we had nice anonymous wheels, I carried on the way I was going. Maybe this car had also been heading that way all along. Or maybe the driver was just curious about why someone else should be on the road. Anyway, he sat behind me for mile after tedious mile. Why didn't he turn off? Very, very slowly – but then, I'd had a big lunch too – it dawned on me he might be tailing me. It'd be nice to be able to get his number, but it was covered with mud – and in any case, reading from a mirror never was my strong point, especially on a road that needed eyes-front attention. I pressed on. What else could I do? A little company might be nice. Elham? What about Lyminge?

If I turned west, I knew there was a garage, preferably with nice husky mechanics to protect me, if that was what was needed. And if the 4x4 shot straight past, I could simply get some fuel and get the number. The rattling and shaking as I pushed the van as fast as I dared woke Griff.

'Dear child, where on earth are we? What are we doing?'

'Just heading for Stone Street,' I said, through gritted teeth.

I didn't want to slow, but I knew I'd have to. The next section was narrow, with an awkward corner, and the last thing I wanted was to run full tilt into a car on the school run. Or any other run.

He was five or six metres from me.

I swung on to the forecourt without signalling. Far too fast: I nearly hit a pillar box. He slewed to a stop at the halt sign and turned right, for Canterbury, also without signalling. The rear number plate was just as filthy as the front one. But I did get a glimpse of his profile as he turned. Just an ordinary, common or garden profile. Did I know it from somewhere?

By now Griff had got out, heading for the little shop. He stopped dead. Was it something to do with the notice telling customers there were no public loos on the site?

I needed some fuel anyway, so he'd just have to wait.

'That's just it, dear one. I can't. Maybe your friend Robin might be in?'

Hell for leather to Stelling Minnis, then. But the rectory was in darkness, and there was no sign of Robin's clerical car, either. Still retreating.

I took a risk. 'We're only about two miles from Bossingham Hall.'

'The devil we are!'

'That's probably exactly what my father will say, if it's any consolation. It's pretty well time for his favourite TV programme and he won't be pleased to see me, let alone you. But at least he'll have a loo you can use. Tell you what – if you can spare a packet of those end-date bikkies and that cake, then at least it will make afternoon tea less like the Mad Hatter's tea party.' Or more . . .

I might have joked, but I actually felt sick with dread as I parked. At least there was no sign of Titus' van – not out in the open here, nothing like so risky, but tucked away in its usual hidey-hole. I fished out my mobile – a bit more polite to warn my father than simply to swan in, though I had my key with me. And somehow I'd never quite managed just to ring the front door bell.

'Mr Tripp too?' my father observed. 'Well, well.'

It didn't take him long to get to the front door and open it, with a bit of a mocking bow.

'Through there to the left, Griff!' I said, pointing, by way of greeting.

'Ah,' my father said. 'I quite understand.'

'I'll get the kettle on,' I said.

'Do that, Lina. And then hunt for a couple of your miracles. Mr Tripp and I can have a nice little chat while we wait.'

It was clear what they'd been talking about, because as I carried the tea tray in, Lord Elham was busy exploding with

rage. 'A man who claims to be her grandfather tells that
sort of tale about her? How dare he! And what would his
daughter have said? She must have been a nice filly, Tripp.
Wouldn't have laid her otherwise. More to the point, she
must have been nice, or she wouldn't have had such a decent
offspring, would she? Nothing to do with me, Lina's brains.'
    I wasn't so sure about that. My father could finish a
fiendish-level Sudoku in the time it took me to work out
the instructions. And the fact he'd escaped the notice of the
law all these years suggested something about his cunning,
at very least. But I wasn't about to interrupt, because he
and Griff, a glass of better champagne apiece, were sitting
side by side happily shredding Arthur Habgood's reputation. Well, everything about him really. Nothing for it but
to park the tea things, leave them to it, and go for my usual
wander round the place. Griff would have loved to come
too, if he'd known what I was up to. But the sight of all
those unwanted, unloved items, whose only function would
be to provide Lord Elham with more champagne, might
have given him a heart attack. Joking! Griff would have
admired some, coveted others, but would have been able
to price everything to the nearest pound. What he wouldn't
have been able to do was stand stock still in the corridor
and feel something calling silently but clearly. I waited. No,
it wasn't in the kitchen. It was in one of the rooms on the
first floor. In a cardboard box. I had to get at it even though
it meant heaving half a dozen other boxes off it. Logically
I knew that any one of these might have held half a dozen
more valuable or saleable items, but my divvy's instinct
told me it had to be that one. The first thing I touched felt
like a skull, and since this was a bit of a jumpy day, I nearly
screamed and dropped it. But then I realized it was
stoneware, not bone – a phrenological head. Why on earth
I could remember a term like that, not an everyday one,
goodness knows – especially when really useful ones flew
out of my mental window. So what was the head lying on?
I burrowed in the old newspaper. A chamber pot! What on
earth did my divvy's instinct think it was doing?
    Another burrow. A lid? A lid. A lid for the chamber pot.

Which suddenly doubled or trebled it in value. Staffordshire, I thought. A polish with a bit of newspaper brought up amazing bright colours – why something you'd want to sneak down the backstairs should be so bright was beyond me. But this had a broad blue stripe round most of the body, hung around with swags of pink and green garland. Then there were more stripes, and even more on the lid, which had a matching garland looping round the centre. Griff would take one look and declare it vulgar. My father would look and ask how much bubbly it would bring in.

Well, if the head brought in what I thought, and this pot turned out to be what I thought it was, the answer was quite a lot.

Which was a good job, because when I got downstairs, they'd started on a second bottle and were yelling the answers at *Countdown*. Griff was looking rattled – I should have warned him my father would have to win.

At last the programme was over. They looked at me expectantly.

First of all I held up the head. Lord Elham shrugged.

Griff nodded. 'A couple of hundred pounds' worth there,' he said, though whether to me or to my father was hard to say. Like me, Griff never used my father's name – apart from when he'd wanted to impress Will, he certainly never *My Lord*-ed him, and yet deep down, I guess, felt it was somehow disrespectful – to whom or what, for goodness' sake? – to use his first name.

Then I produced my find. Pot and lid separately.

'Do I see Mochaware, my angel? I thought so,' Griff said, taking the lid and examining it. 'Well done.'

My father peered at it without enthusiasm. 'Just a po,' he declared.

'A po worth well over a thousand pounds,' Griff said. 'With the lid, of course.'

'A thousand quid's worth of shampoo! Well,' my father said with a grin, 'bottoms up!'

TWELVE

I might have driven back to Bredeham very soberly – unlike my father and with Griff, who was now snoring gently, I was stone cold sober – but I did so with anger still seething away in my heart.

I didn't like being tailed. Or at least, being para-something or other enough to think I was being tailed. What if he was just a bad driver? There were enough of those about, many, but not all, of course, in 4x4s. But it did seem to be a bit of a coincidence to come across someone in that particular spot who might want to follow me. Paranoid, that was the word I was looking for.

Of course it was a coincidence. No one could have known I'd be going that way. I didn't even know I was going that way myself. Impulse, that was all.

But he could have chosen another route. More direct. Could have driven in a less threatening way.

If Will ever spoke to me again, I might just mention it. Big if.

Better to think about something else: what we should have for tea; how I could have a tactful word with Dilly (imagine it: 'Does your husband beat you, especially if you sell precious rings so cheaply?'); what to do about Arthur Habgood. He seemed to be popping up in all sorts of places; the police and Harvey Sanditon – all it needed was Griff's so-called mate Sir Douggie to mention him and we'd have a full house. And why was he so malicious? You'd have thought a man would want to keep his supposed granddaughter's name nice and clean, not imply she was a criminal.

As for our possible relationship, Habgood had the idea that his daughter, who'd stayed with her mother when they divorced and changed her name when her mother remarried to that of her new father, was my mother. There were two obvious ways of testing his theory – the DNA test he was always pressing on me and a short interview between him and my father. In view of this afternoon, I ruled that out as firmly as I'd ruled out the gob swab. After all, my father kept a swagger stick beside him to repel any intruders who'd penetrated his new security system, and might have been tempted to use it on someone casting aspersions on me.

Unfortunately the person whose advice I really wanted would be torn in two if I raised the matter – Griff. So I needed to think of someone else whose opinion I valued. Or at least someone who could be guaranteed to have the low down on him.

Titus Oates.

Actually there was another person I could speak to about him, as I realized when an email from Harvey Sanditon popped up.

> *Good evening, Lina,*
>
> *An inspection of the plate we discussed shows it to have been repaired – though not as expertly as my vase. Could it have been your handiwork? I think you mentioned that you tackled it early in your career. Did you say that you had paperwork detailing the work you had done, similar to the documentation you provided for me?*
>
> *Incidentally, the Worcester has now returned to its owner, who is extremely impressed by the quality of your workmanship, and even more so with the detective work you undertook. He has exonerated me from most of the blame, and we are on speaking terms again.*
>
> *Sincerely,*
> *Harvey Sanditon*

I wasn't quite sure about sending information about what might be a completely different item so I asked him to send me a photo of the plate. I'd have liked to send a crude enquiry asking what he knew about Habgood, but for some reason pulled back. Perhaps, like talking to Dilly, it was best done face to face. Although it took me a good half hour to check the rest of my mail – there were several orders that needed proper attention – he didn't respond, so I logged off and went down to play Scrabble with Griff. If I allowed my mind to wander even for a minute or two, he'd beat me hollow, so I put Habgood firmly to the back of my mind. And still got beaten hollow.

Early the next morning a little note appeared under my bedroom door. All it said was, *Have a lie in*. His anonymous friend was back.

This time the conversation didn't take long, and as soon as I heard footsteps in the hall and the click of the front door, I shot down to the kitchen. The windows were wide open and the extractor on.

Griff didn't bother with an explanation. 'My love, what do you think of this?'

He handed me what was basically a cylinder, about five inches long. The longer bottom section was white, with tiny sprays of flowers. The top was in the shape of a human head.

'Oh, Griff – isn't she lovely? With her lace cap and her mask and – are those diamonds in her eyes?' I pulled gently. Inside the little body were all the needles an eighteenth century lady would have needed for her fine embroidery.

'Can you say anything more? What do we call this sort of needle case?'

'An étui,' I said promptly. I put her down carefully. 'Is she from that little factory with a funny name?'

He smiled. 'You're nearly there. What do you fancy for breakfast? Some smoked salmon with our scrambled eggs?'

So it was a really good find.

'I know you won't allow me any Buck's Fizz,' he continued, turning his mouth down at the corners in the way that always made me laugh.

'Certainly not. Charles something. London?'

'Go on. At least we should have freshly squeezed juice.'

'Charles whose name I can never spell.'

'G-o-u-y-n. Floreat 1749–59.'

'*Floreat* . . . Working from–to?' I wrinkled my nose.
English was bad enough, but Latin really stretched my brain.
'Girl in a Swing!' I don't know whether the guy ever called
his factory that, but the experts did, like the people at top
museums.

'My darling, you never cease to delight me. What do you
think we should do with her?'

I took her apart – everything inside was just as it should
be. 'As far as I can tell, she just needs a good clean.'

'I meant about selling her. Our friend Harvey has the
right sort of well-heeled clientele – if I'm not mistaken,
she should fetch at least five thousand pounds,' he added.

'But you've only given X peanuts.' Having so nearly
been an X myself I still worried about the justice of the
situation.

'You'd have him drink himself to death? Really, my love,
you mustn't get sentimental about the man. Now, shall we
contact Sanditon or an auction house?'

'So long as you don't consult your friend Douggie . . .'

The next fair, one day only, was in a village hall. It was
the sort that Harvey Sanditon, who still hadn't sent a photo
of the dodgy Majolica plate, would never patronize, but at
which Dilly might have a stall. Titus, who didn't like
anything as fixed as a display stand in a place like this,
with no dark corners, might just float in, to buy cheap and
later on sell dear somewhere else. Just like the rest of us,
come to think of it.

But I'd rather talk to them both without Griff as an
audience.

As luck would have it, the next few days were really cold
and damp; if he thought I wasn't watching, Griff would rub
his arthritic knuckles and even take a painkiller or two. I
hated to see him suffer, but it suited me to have him laid
low for a bit. So I reminded him how cold and draughty
the hall had been last time – how he'd almost dropped a
Crown Derby plate his fingers were so numb. We'd not
done much trade, either, but it was worth taking a punt with

some of our cheaper stock. So why didn't he stay at home and deal with the recent orders and enquiries, and let me go on my own?

'My sweet, you work so hard.'

But I could see he was tempted.

'Not as hard as dealing with that guy from Argyll who always wants one more detail.' Or keeping Mrs Walker company, of course. 'And it's only an hour away. I'll leave after breakfast and be back in time for supper. A nice warming one, please.'

'It's a long time since I cooked one of my casseroles . . .'

Since I set up on my own, there was no time to do my usual drift round fellow dealers' outfits; I'd have to pick my moments for that. I put out quite a lot of restored china amongst the lustreware and Ironstone; if people had any money to spend, they had plenty of choice.

'Pocket money stuff,' Titus observed with a bit of a sneer, emerging from a shadowy corner as I unwrapped my sandwich lunch. I passed him a round. Griff's special cheese and home-made coleslaw on wholemeal, also home-made.

'Trouble is with pocket money, it seems to like it where it is,' I said. 'In pockets. With hands wrapped tightly round it.'

He chewed slowly – might have been waiting for something.

'Any idea why Habgood's spreading muck about me?' I prompted him.

'Can't say I have. Haven't even heard any.'

I explained. 'To the fuzz,' I added

'Fucking hell, that's out of order! I mean, person to person's one thing,' he continued, dropping his voice again. 'We all do a bit of that. But the filth . . . Anything to do with that gob-swab you won't do? All the same, seems a bit weird, mind, dissing someone you want as family.'

'Quite.'

He reached for another round, and nodded. 'Griff hasn't lost his touch, I'll say that. I'll get on to the other old bugger.' And was gone. For the rest of the afternoon, as far as I could make out.

For some reason, just as I'd wrapped my hands round a mug of coffee, there was a little rush, and I sold several things. None of them fetched more than twenty-five pounds, but since I'd probably not paid even a fiver for most, that was fine. And I more than covered the stall rental. At last, asking the next-door stallholder to keep an eye on things, I headed for the loo. It all looked very casual, I hoped, but in fact it was because I'd seen Dilly going that way, and on past experience I knew there'd be a queue – a good chance to fall into conversation with her.

Unless she was a brilliant make-up artist there weren't any bruises, recent or otherwise, on her face, but I noticed she carried her shoulder a bit awkwardly. Now I had the chance, I really didn't know what to say apart from the obvious things about business being slow and the weather being vile.

She nodded to both – didn't try to talk at all. Which did interest me. Broken teeth? While she used the cubicle, I tried to work on a Plan B. While I used the cubicle I tried to work on a Plan C. Useless.

At last I did the obvious, wondering why it hadn't been Plan A in the first place. I went over and rooted in some of the boxes on her stall. I came up with a heavy gold Victorian pendant, with two entwined locks of hair in it. Normally I'd have coughed up the fiver she asked and scuttled off, pleased with my booty. This time I said, 'Are you sure this is in the right box? I'd have thought you could get a few more quid for it, it's so pretty. Good clear hallmark too,' I added, with my dealer hat back on.

Her eyes widened. 'How much?' she whispered.

At this point it dawned on me that though it was cold, there might just be another reason for the scarf round her neck. Nothing to do with a sore throat, either. When I'd worn one for a few days, it was because someone had tried to throttle me and I wanted to hide the bruises. I hadn't had a voice much above a whisper, either.

I weighed the pendant in the palm of my hand. 'I'd have thought – look, this is more Griff's job than mine – but I'd have thought on the basis of the gold alone you might be

asking well over two hundred.' Which was a bit more than
a fiver.

So why didn't she look pleased? Just terrified? She
grabbed it, and shoved it in her coat pocket.

'If I tell you all about it, you could write down and reel
it off if anyone asks.'

She fished it out and stared first at it, then at me. I had
to bend close to hear what she said next. 'Will you sell it
for me? On commission, of course,' she added quickly. 'But
I'd want cash. Cash.'

'Of course.' It went into my trousers pocket. 'How do I
get in touch?'

'Keep it. Keep it till I tell you. And don't tell anyone –
promise! Anyone. Not even Griff,' she added.

'Can't promise that. He's senior partner. And my friend.
Can't pull wool over his eyes.'

She looked wildly over my shoulder. 'Give me a quid
and take this.' She thrust a viciously ugly green plastic frog
at me.

'What if I kiss it?' I asked, but by then she didn't want
to hear me. And I was too busy trying to see who had scared
her so much without obviously looking.

No luck. Just the back of a big guy in a hoodie. I kissed
the frog anyway.

In a final spurt, I sold a lustre jug, the sort with a mask for
a spout, and a piece of green Jasper ware. So I hadn't had
a bad day. But though I smiled and waved as people packed
up and went home, I felt as if the pendant was burning a
hole in my pocket. The sooner it was in a little jewellery
box the better – did I have one, in our odds and ends box,
along with the tape measure and bubble wrap? Of course
I did. Wrong decade, but it'd do. I stowed it with the rest
of the stock.

But I still felt – what was the word? Vulnerable. Yes, I
even remembered to say the 'l' in my head. No idea why.
I made sure I went backwards and forwards to the van with
other people around me, and chose the M20 route home –
further, but a lot more public than the little lanes that were

the alternative. The frog, quite a friendly character, now I
came to think about it, sat on the passenger seat.

'It seems to me that it would be much better all round if
we didn't sell it for her at a local fair,' Griff said, doling
out ladlefuls of goulash and dumplings spiked with caraway
seed. 'By the way, there's an email with an attachment from
Harvey Sanditon on the system.'

'Why didn't you open it?'

'It's not me he's trying to seduce from Tripp and Townend,
cherub. Or seduce full stop,' he added with an anxious-
looking twinkle that didn't fool me for a minute.

'Too far away; too old; too full of himself,' I said, sipping
a heady Hungarian wine which Griff had served in a tiny,
old-fashioned crystal glass.

'An enormous alcohol count,' he said, touching the bottle.
'So easy to quaff too many units. All right for an old bugger
like me—'

'Hmph. After what the doctor said about your liver?'

'He then said it had made a remarkable recovery, didn't
he? All the same, if it makes you happy . . .' He swapped
his glass for one my size. 'Cheers. Are you going to mention
the étui to Sanditon?'

'As a sale, or for him to sell on commission?'

'Either. It depends if he has a passion for Girl in a
Swing. Or if he has a passion for Girl in an Antique
Shop . . .'

Cracked and restored Harvey's Majolica plate might be, but
I'd never seen it before, as I told him, pleased that I hadn't
sent him a load of information he had no right to. Why
hadn't he checked the quality before he'd bought it? It
wasn't as if the damage wasn't pretty obvious. It didn't
make sense for a man of his experience.

Did a man who'd been caught out like that deserve the
étui? On the whole, I thought not. I was so unsure of what
– if any – our relationship might be, my email just said it
wasn't the same plate. Nothing more.

*   *   *

It was only at about three in the morning that I realized I hadn't followed our golden rule. I hadn't given Dilly a receipt for her pendant. I went hot and cold. Anyone else I could have phoned and asked for one. But clearly she wanted the matter kept quiet. Perhaps the money was part of an escape fund. In which case keeping quiet was the best, if not the only thing to do. On the other hand – and here my brain raced ahead so far and so fast I had difficulty keeping up with it myself – what if it, like the ring I'd bought from her, was dodgy?

It was hard to fake a clearly Victorian pendant. So . . . ?

All the same, apart from the étui and one or two other items Griff had bought from X – and a couple of things in our top secret safe, our rainy-day insurance – every single thing we dealt with had documentation. Provenance. Receipts. We had a reputation for absolute openness and honesty. Except when my so-called grandfather drew people's attention to a libellous piece about me. And we took historic rings to an expert.

The more I thought about it, the less I knew what to do. And although Tim the Bear told me nothing could be solved by worrying, and it would seem better in the morning, I found it very hard to believe him.

THIRTEEN

f I didn't do something, Griff would be on to my anxiety like a shot. So I did something I'd always tried to avoid – I involved a third party. Shrugging on my dressing gown, but missing one slipper, I tiptoed down to the office and emailed Morris, the policeman with whom I might, if he hadn't discovered his ex-partner was pregnant, have had a relationship. I told him what I'd done and why, and asked him to print off the email and keep it, just in case. I even sent a photo of the pendant. I didn't want or need a reply, except to acknowledge that he'd received it. In any case, since most people weren't checking their in-boxes at something before four in the morning, I didn't expect one.

That done, I returned to the comfort of Tim the Bear's paws and was dead to the world before I even realized my foot was thawing out.

Morris had once surprised me by saying I ought to have more friends my own age. Mostly I didn't need them, but today I really did. First of all I needed someone to pretend I was going for a girly day out with. Second I needed someone to go with me on a not very girly trip: I wanted to tramp through the woods near where I'd found the body and see what was going on. Taking Griff was absolutely not an option – he wouldn't have approved, and in any case I wasn't going to march someone his age out in the rain on to land where people would much rather not see us. Which ruled out my father, not that he was ever ruled in, and Mrs Walker, despite her surname.

I probably wasn't in Will's good books, because I'd not called him back immediately and had only left a couple of words on his voice mail when I'd eventually got round to it. In any case, breaking the law (possibly) wasn't something you could invite a policeman to do. As for the Rev Robin, he probably had his head in the Good Book, and it wasn't exactly an option for him, either.

So any exploring had to be done on my own. OK, it would be risky. But there was one thing I could do to reduce the risk a bit, if only I could get clear of Griff. Even that was difficult. He got it into his head I was looking peaky, and was inclined to fuss me, with offers of hot chocolate and comfortable chairs.

He wasn't pleased when I had a phone call from my father, claiming he'd run out of all sorts of essentials. He dictated a list of things he needed.

'Anything we want?' I asked Griff, as I gathered the hessian shopping bags we always used these days.

'Waitrose?'

'Sainsbury's.'

'In that case, I don't think so.'

The old snob. As for me, I actually liked the Sainsbury's run, and often ran bargains to earth. Today wasn't one of them, so I just bundled up the items on the list and headed to Bossingham Hall.

'No sign of the ring yet,' my father said by way of a greeting.

'Any news of Nanny Baird's descendants yet?' I asked foolishly.

Blocking my ears against his pleas that I should help with the search, I stowed the shopping.

'Lina, am I ever going to use all these lavatory rolls?'

'They were on offer. Twelve for the price of nine.'

'But recycled: does that mean—?'

'Recycled from newspapers or something,' I said, not wishing to go down that particular road, not with a man who thought you should be able to get full wine bottles out of bottle banks, not throw away empty ones.

I found a couple of items to sell for him, putting the receipts I always gave him in a folder I'd bought for the purpose, and left him glued to a new quiz.

Maybe I should nip down to Hythe – not all that far, after all – and buy Griff some Waitrose goodies as a little treat. But as I headed south, I realized I was going to be going very near the spot where my presence had so annoyed the 4x4 driver. I pulled over on the Minnis, the common land which gives Stelling Minnis its name.

'I'm going to do something daft, Titus,' I told him, down the phone. 'I'm going to go and look round where I found that body. And if I don't call you back by four, I want you to call the police.'

'Got the wrong man, doll. Me phone the filth? Hand'd drop off if I tried dialling 999. Besides, they'd ask questions.'

'You could call the AA – say you'd seen an abandoned van and thought you might have heard a scream.' For good measure I gave the map reference.

'And you don't think they might wonder why I wasn't phoning from near this here wood? They know all about where you make these calls, doll. Like you say, even mobiles,' he added with a sigh. 'I thought they couldn't track them, but you were right.'

'Well, I'm going in anyway. So if I die it's your fault.'

'It's bloody yours, doll. Nothing to do with me.' He cut the call.

He was right, wasn't he?

At least I could drive slowly past, as I'd done before. Just to see.

What did I see? I saw a mud-covered Fiesta, same as every other mud-covered Fiesta, parked deep under a droopy tree. The driver checked carefully in his mirrors before he emerged, cap down over his eyes, filthy Barbour collar turned up. He'd got a pair of wellies in one hand.

'Just got a few minutes to spare, doll. Your dad'd go doolally if anything happened to you. Not that he isn't, anyway. Now, shut up squeaking and get back in your car. We'll leave mine here. One doesn't attract attention, two might. Torch? Bloody hell, don't you know anything?'

Eventually Titus, with his wellies, two torches, some rope and a large scale OS map, joined me in the van. 'We're going round the far side, see. Then we walk through the woods, eyes peeled. And then you get in my car and I run you back to yours. Easy-peasy.'

'Easy-peasy it is,' I said, setting the van in motion. At least Titus wouldn't want mindless chatter. This was good, because I was actually quite scared. Very few people liked Titus; many feared him. All sorts of rumours sloshed round about his past, and I don't think he'd have hesitated to use violence if anyone crossed him. I dare say he'd taken every care not to be linked to the area in any way, and could have raped and/or murdered me – why did he want that rope, for goodness' sake? – and got away with it. But I trusted him. For one thing he needed my father's skills, and without me to keep an eye on him, Lord Elham would be back on the Pot Noodles and champagne diet and the shakes within a month. For another I think he quite liked the old reprobate, and wouldn't want to have him upset, as he would be if I disappeared. And maybe – this was a very shaky maybe – he quite liked having me around to spar with.

While I drove, he fastened the rope into a noose – quite a small one, certainly not big enough to go over my head.

'Anyone asks, lost our dog, see.'

'Bit of a basic lead,' I sniffed.

'Bit of a basic dog. Lot of mongrel in him.'

I didn't argue.

The rain might have eased a bit, but the light was poor. I parked under a convenient tree but with two wheels firmly on the road, and pulled on my wellies. He did the same. I zipped up my waterproof and pulled up the hood, shoving my hands in my pockets and wondering why I never thought to bring gloves.

Without speaking, we set off.

'I don't even know what I'm looking for,' I said, a couple of hundred yards down an almost liquid track.

'Me neither. But you wanted to look, so we're looking.' He stopped dead, and pointed with his torch at something. When I stood peering blindly, he switched it on, a fierce narrow beam picking out disturbed undergrowth.

'Thing is, badgers or night hawks?' He widened the beam. There were a lot of lumps and hollows. 'Badgers. Only

sometimes they dig things up. And sometimes they dig them
after the filth have been over the place with their fine tooth
combs.' He played the beam to and fro. At last, shaking his
head, he moved forward a few more yards.

'Ought to separate and zigzag, but not in this light. Have
you getting yourself lost, and then where would we be?
More badgers.' He narrowed the torch beam again.

'Looks like an old milk bottle top.' I pointed.

'And since when did the milkman deliver out here?' He
headed off; I followed.

'Lucky old badger,' he said, picking up a bright disc and
wiping it on his trousers. 'Late Roman. Anything else?
Apart from a nice dose of bovine TB?'

Swallowing a suggestion that something as precious as
a gold coin should be reported to the Coroner, I shone my
torch into the sett, proud I'd remembered a word I don't
have much call for. And screamed.

'For God's sake, doll – just a few roots!'

'Looked like a hand. Skeleton of a hand.'

'Or do you mean hand of a skeleton? Come on. Shift
yourself.'

It was hard to move quickly, but Titus set a cracking
pace, especially when we picked up a track reinforced by
some hard core.

'Recent, if you ask me. Needed to get people in here
without getting bogged down.' He waved his torch backwards and forwards.

I did the same. No idea what we were looking for, but
it looked good. And it lit something up. I'd seen enough
blue and white tape in my life to recognize police activity
when I saw it.

Titus stopped short. 'OK, that's it, doll. We take that path
over there and go back to my car that way. Don't want to
tangle with the Old Bill.'

No derring do there, then. But I shouldn't have expected
it. Titus didn't do drugs, never drank while driving, observed
speed signs as if they were Holy Writ and was generally
so damned law-abiding you'd never have dreamed he spent
his whole life committing serious fraud.

I nodded and fell into step. 'At least we know they're treating where I found my body – or near enough – as a crime scene,' I said. 'Hang on, what's that lot over there? Looks like a building site or something.'

We struck off on a feeble track leading towards it. At last we came upon another, much better path, again reinforced with hard core.

'Knew this old bird once. Had to get rid of a lot of rubble from her old outhouse. Advertised it in the local rag as hard core. Had all the pervs in the county beating a path to her door.'

We took the track. Titus started fiddling with his rope. If I'd been scared before, now I was terrified.

My mouth was too dry to say anything. Why should he be playing with the end, fraying it and picking at it? Why should he be looking at the trees, which now loomed over us?

He went right up to one and seemed to wipe it with the rope. And then he set off down what was really only a rabbit run, dabbing trees at intervals.

'Want to get left behind, doll? Going the right way about it.'

My legs didn't want to move. At all.

But his weird route led us round to chained up gates, festooned with barbed and razor wire. We played our torches over high stakes covered in thick plastic-covered wire mesh. A nice impenetrable fence. For good measure it was lined with more mesh, the fine plastic sort, like they put round the village tennis courts to reduce the wind.

'Bloody gulag. All it needs is a few high towers, a search-light and an Alsatian or two.'

I didn't argue.

Titus shone his torch in great arcs in front. 'Looking for the Welcome mat. No? Someone must have nicked it. And see that sign there, doll? Private security? That means dog patrols, and I for one can't abide the creatures.'

'Not even mongrels?'

'Especially fucking mongrels.'

'It also means cameras. Those are the people who do our security. Cameras where you don't expect to see them.'

'So pull your hood down a bit more.' He set off for a brisk walk round the fence.

'Gap there.' I pointed. His eye-height, not mine.

He peered. 'Bloody hell. Looks like a load of Eskimos have landed. Plastic igloos everywhere,' he explained.

'Like police put over crime scenes?'

'Here.' He put a key in the tear and dragged it downwards. 'Nothing like a spot of vandalism.'

'I wonder if it's an archaeological site . . . I'd expected it to look like the Somme, all flooded trenches. But I suppose they have to protect something from all this rain.'

'Question is, what?'

'We've been spotted – camera on your left.' I turned right and hunched my shoulders. 'And do I hear—?'

'You do. Fucking run. Now. No, that way!'

I ran. And fell.

I caught male voices. No baying, no barking. But that didn't mean –

Titus grabbed me as I tripped. 'Stupid bitch. Got to keep up, got to keep quiet. Get it?'

I got it. Couldn't do otherwise since he'd got a hand clamped over my mouth and was using the other to lever me up. Then I was dragged along, willy-nilly. We reached the trees he'd dabbed with the rope and veered off sharply. I suppose there might have been a path – I certainly couldn't see it.

We stopped suddenly. I didn't so much as squeak this time. Like him I listened for – goodness knows what. At last he pointed. 'Road's that way.'

By now it was almost dark. He stopped suddenly, used a craft knife to slice the end off the rope and threw the cut piece as high as he could into a tree. He stowed the knife, and wrapped the remaining rope round his waist. Then he grabbed my wrist and ran hard back not towards his car but to the van.

I think.

I'd never been colder or wetter or more scared. Not since I was a kid, at any rate. I was about to fall into the van as if it were Griff's arms when Titus grabbed me.

'On any DNA database?'

'No.'

'Course not, or bloody Habgood wouldn't be on to you for a gob-swab, would he?'

'But—'

'Easily bend a policeman, get what he wants. Give me your foot. Oh, sit down if you must.' He grabbed my wellies, one by one, filled them to the brim with mud and rolled them in more mud. Then he slung them, hard as he could, into the deepest, thickest bit of hedge. He did the same for his own on the other side of the road.

'What are you waiting for? Get your heater on, woman. And get moving.'

Slipping shoes on to numb feet, I obeyed.

'Pity about all the stuff on the sides of your van. Never thought of being more discreet? Nice anonymous set of wheels like mine is what you want. How you going to explain all this to Griff then?'

'I've been wondering about that myself.'

'Flat tyre. Had to get it sorted. My mate back end of Ashford'll alibi you if needs be.'

'But I never lie to Griff.'

'So you'll tell him you spend the afternoon strolling hand in hand with me? I don't think so. Here's my wheels. No, don't stop close by, silly cow. Up the road a couple of hundred yards.'

I obeyed. As I pulled up, I ventured one question. 'What was all that with the rope?'

'Never heard of patterans? Gypsies leave clues for their mates to track them.'

'But I didn't think we wanted to be tracked.'

''Course we didn't. That's why we came back the same way.'

'So why did you cut of the end and throw it up the tree?'

'Because it was all soaked in aniseed, see.'

'Aniseed?'

'Give the little doggies something to sniff at and go that way. God, don't you know nothing?'

'Not a lot.' I must have sounded as dismal as I felt.

Suddenly he grabbed my chin and turned my face towards him. 'None of that, doll – d'you hear me? You might not have your GSCEs and stuff, and you'd get lost in a wood, but you're as bright as they come. Got your dad's genes, and that old bugger Griff's polished them up something lovely. Understand?' He shook my head slightly. 'All you want to worry about now is not going wandering about the woods with some old bastard you hardly know. Fucking stupid.'

I put my chin up. 'Not as fucking stupid as wandering around on my own.'

'As it happens, no. But you want to ask yourself what you've achieved. You've lost a pair of wellies and missed an afternoon's work. You've found a police crime scene and something no one wanted you to get into and you didn't get into.'

'What do you think it was?'

'From all this stuff about the rings, not to mention my little souvenir, I'd say you're right. It's an archaeological site. But I don't know, any more than you do.'

People raiding a site like that would be total menaces.

'So, all in all, not a good afternoon's work, doll. Plus you've got to invent some cock and bull story for Griff. So I tell you something for nothing – don't do this again. OK? 'Cos I might not be there to look out for you.'

'At least I know the aniseed trick,' I said.

This time he squeezed my cheeks, quite lightly. 'So you do, doll, so you do.'

With that he was gone.

'We had yet another hunt for his mother's engagement ring,' I told Griff. 'And he tipped over boxes – piano music – and made so much mess I had to tidy up a bit.' It was all true, more or less. 'And he talked a bit more about Granny Baird.'

'Nanny, sweet one. A granny is quite different. Has he run her family to earth yet?'

'He still wants me to try. But I can't, Griff, I can't.' For some reason I put my hands over my face and cried. Real tears, too. Mostly caused by trying to pull wool over his eyes, actually. But we had a hug, and a nice drop of some home made cherry brandy one of his clients had given him for Christmas and everything seemed better. Mostly, at least.

At three in the morning, it wasn't roots in the badger's sett, but a hand, and the rest of the body too. And it changed before my eyes into the one I'd found and never tried to rescue.

FOURTEEN

Titus had been right. I was left with a slimy conscience and nothing more. In fact, the more I thought about it, the less I wanted to think about it. Particularly as I'd bet the whole shop that Titus wouldn't hand over to Will or anyone like him the coin he'd trousered.

Then, the following day, something weird happened. A woman near Dover phoned, telling me she wanted me to look at an epergne, to see if I could repair it. Since it was too large to bring to the shop simply on the off chance, she would pay me for a house call. Her address was Mattock Farm, which suggested a pair of wellies might be in order. I'd have to stop and buy some more – probably that wonderful village shop would oblige. I took some first aid items; not the human sort (we had a box in both vans), but for ornaments, so I could do an immediate repair. If the patient needed hospitalization, then I had a large plastic box and plenty of tissue and bubble wrap to hand.

Before I could agree with Griff that dancing attendance on a client at her home was not part of my job description I set off. I didn't like high-handed folk who brayed instructions at me, and would normally have told her so. But since I'd shopped for my father the day before, I could offer to do a Waitrose shop for Griff, which cheered him up considerably.

It took me almost as long to get into the Broad-Ticeman residence – after a heart to heart with their entry phone – as it had to get from Bredeham to the estate near Dover. The firm providing the security was the same one that looked after our premises and also that archaeological site, so I knew that somewhere there was a camera to smile at – and probably another not meant to be seen.

At the end of a metalled road at least a mile long, I saw the farm. It was very grand indeed for a mere farm; part medieval hall, I thought, part Elizabethan (even I knew that) and a bit of early Georgian thrown in. I don't suppose it would have pleased someone who knew about architecture, but I rather fell for its haphazard roofline and random windows. If someone at junior school had told me to draw a place for Cinderella to hang out in, I would have come up with the same sort of thing.

I wasn't sure whether I should ring the front door or hunt for a servants' entrance, so tried my luck with the front. I was admitted by a sallow wisp of a woman whose English was limited to the word, 'Sit.' She pointed to a chair. I sat.

The entrance hall – Georgian – was full of pillars and niches for statues. They were mostly empty. But the walls were full – pictures from ceiling to wainscot. It was like a jumbled art gallery. You could see patches of different colour on the silk-hung walls where large pictures had been replaced by smaller ones. There was nothing in particular that grabbed my attention: I've never gone for the self-conscious and self-satisfied family portrait.

At last the museum-like calm was destroyed by the patter and skid of feet on marble, and I was surrounded by dogs, all intent on jumping up at my throat. I cowered in the chair.

'Don't be so silly!' came one of those voices that you know cost £20k-plus a year in school fees.

Me or the dogs? It was hard to tell. But the dogs – it turned out that there were only two – fell back and sat down. I managed to stand.

'Phoebe Broad-Ticeman,' the voice said.

Its owner was about five eight, size ten and in her early thirties. She also had a really nice smile and held out a friendly hand.

I stood and took it. Suddenly I was charmed into liking her. Maybe they teach that at posh schools too. With lots of giggles at the absurdity of one of the pictures, suppos-edly of a woman but clearly posed by a man, she took me through to a cave-like dining room, with a low Elizabethan ceiling (the plasterwork was no more than average) and tiny windows pretty well covered with ivy and other creepers.

The wind was lashing them so fiercely I feared for the old brittle glass. On an oak refectory table with a sheen that must have given generations of housemaids tennis elbow to maintain, stood the most hideous early Victorian epergne. It was as bad as if Mrs B-T's perfect smile had a gold tooth right in the middle.

Why she couldn't simply have unhooked the broken part and brought it to the shop in Bredeham, I don't know. It was all that was necessary. One easy movement. I swathed it in bubble wrap, and explained the repair procedure, and how long it would take. All very professional, especially as I had those dogs bounding round me as if they had springs on their legs.

Actually, in spite of everything, I quite took to Mrs B-T. She might have indulged the dogs but, taking me to her private sitting room, with what looked like a Romney over the fire, she was generous with apologies, cake, excellent coffee and a deposit on the repair (her idea, not mine). She even pressed me to see some of the other glass about the place, every single piece a hundred times better than that epergne. Then the china, including a full early Worcester dinner service. I had to stop myself dribbling.

I think she was as bored as I'd have been in her situation, in her thirties, stuck three miles up a drive you could only get into when you'd charmed an entry phone. No near neighbours, obviously. No children. No job. She even looked wistfully at the silver-gilt clock and said it was awfully near lunch time and did I fancy some soup.

I almost said yes. But some words came out of my mouth I hadn't known were there. 'I'm so sorry, but much as I'd love to I've got another job to go to.' I hope I sounded politely regretful. Actually I couldn't wait to get to my feet and be off. Looking at my watch, I said, 'They'll think I'm never coming.'

Did I feel a cooling of the atmosphere? Hard to tell, because she shook my hand nicely enough, but handed me over to the maid to get rid of. At least it felt like that.

Wondering what had gone wrong took me all the way back to her gate and along the main road to Hythe. Why, when I'd loved the place and liked its owner, had I wanted to beat such a rapid retreat? *Been desperate to escape* would be another way of putting it.

All the way from the lemongrass to the sherry and then in the checkout queue I pondered. But none of my theories seemed to work.

I'd warned Phoebe Broad-Ticeman it would take time to do her repair to my satisfaction, but I did move it up the list a bit more than I should have, because it was simply fiddly, not hard. Without explaining to Griff, of course, I worked late several nights to make up for the hours I'd wasted in the woods. And then I phoned her, saying I'd bring it back when it was convenient.

'I'll collect it myself,' she said. And put down the phone.

She turned up an hour later. The moment she arrived, she looked at her watch (just for the record, it was Gucci, and not the sort you can get discounted on Amazon), and declared she must dash. There was no smile and she didn't so much as look over the contents of the shop. In her haste to go, she almost forgot what she'd come for. Even worse, I had to scuttle after her, reminding her she'd only paid a deposit on the repair, and owed the difference. When asked to be invoiced, I had to point out that our terms were strictly cash.

So the woman who'd wanted my company so much she had offered me soup for lunch had turned into a bored iceberg? Actually, a hostile iceberg. She made me stand, hand outstretched like Oliver Twist, in the pouring rain, while she counted out tenners, fivers and pound coins. I even had to nip back into the shop for a fifty-pence piece to get the change right. So much for a potential friend, I thought, not bothering to wave goodbye to her or her stinking dogs, which bayed at me from the back of her monstermobile.

Griff poured the first glass of the evening and sipped slowly. 'It's not often one snoops on clients, my angel, but I wonder if we should have a little exploration of Google. Mrs Broad-Ticeman, of course. We might find – who knows what we might find. You see, the name is decidedly familiar. The stage, maybe. '

So with Griff beside me, I Googled. And nearly squeezed the poor mouse to death.

Mrs Broad-Ticeman had a husband, Charles Broad-Ticeman. All the art that hung about Mattock Farm was probably the same as the china that decorated our home – goods that might one day go on sale.

'A top of the range art dealer! International, not little provincials like Tripp and Townend!' I gasped, moving about the very slick website, and then chased up other references. Not all were complimentary, but most simply fawned. 'All this might explain the security and the grand house,' I said, 'but it doesn't explain Mrs Thingy's strange behaviour. She showed me round that house as if I was about to buy it. Or something in it. Something eyewateringly expensive, of course – there was a camera on everything she pointed out.'

Something started to buzz in my brain.

Maybe it buzzed in Griff's, too. 'I wonder, my love, if we might ask Morris about him.'

'A nice impersonal email. Maybe from you, not me.'

'Very well. I'll see to it while you lay the table, shall I?'

Meanwhile, Griff and I had a fair coming up in Bath. Apart from the tussle with the traffic and the one-way system, it was a gig we enjoyed, because Griff had no end of theatrical friends down there, some of them also in the trade, whom he loved seeing. If he was happy, I was happy. So we had to decide which stock to take. As we sat over our breakfast coffee, we started on our list.

'What about Dilly Pargetter's pendant?' I asked. 'Bath's a long way from Kent, after all. We should be able to sell it there without anyone recognizing it and accusing me of nicking it.'

Griff looked at me. 'You don't sound convinced.'

'If I had my way, I'd shove it in a jiffy bag and send it back.'

'But you could have your way. We have the jiffy bags to hand, and Mrs Walker makes daily journeys to the post office.'

'What if Dilly needs the money to escape from her husband?'

'She doesn't need your assistance. There are plenty of refuges. She might call the police. She could get an injunction against him. That's if your supposition is correct.'

'If it isn't . . .'

'Dear one, who knows?' He looked at me closely. 'You're going to do something I don't like, aren't you? You're going to consult the nearest thing we have to a Kentish oracle: Titus Oates, and his gnomic utterances.'

Miserably I nodded. 'The thing is he's got his ear nearer the ground than anyone else I know. Next time I'm out and about, I'll phone him – he prefers mobiles, you know.'

'I'm not unaware that from time to time you claim you need a walk and go out with a bulge in your coat pocket. So I presume you're in contact with him. Unless, of course,' he added with a strange blend of wistfulness and hope, 'you have a secret admirer?'

I hugged him. 'I should be so lucky.'

'You liked young Will until you had that dust-up with him. Is it time to declare a truce and ask him for advice? Maybe over a quiet drink . . . ?'

'I'd rather talk to Titus first,' I said, hating myself. 'As soon as I've washed up . . .'

Griff was cross enough not to tell me he'd do it, although to be fair it was my turn.

'Crawling round the countryside all day,' Titus croaked, 'got the fucking flu.'

At least he'd got a gold coin, too. 'I was wondering about something even worse than flu. Dilly Pargetter.'

'Still getting beaten up. But won't leave the bugger. Or the bugger won't let her. Tell you what, doll, you ever get involved with a bloke that so much as touches you, you jump ship.'

'Can I trust her?'

'You trust a puppet with its strings pulled by someone else? Work it out.' He gave an enormous, but slightly unconvincing sneeze.

'Bless you,' I said automatically. 'You'll keep clear of my father until you're better, won't you?'

'Afraid you'd have to drop everything and go and nurse him? Makes sense, I suppose.'

'And Dilly?'

'Give her the flu, you mean?'

'I mean—' I poured out the whole story.

Another sneeze. 'No receipt? Then you're a bigger fool than I took you for.'

'But you don't deal in receipts and stuff,' I pointed out.

'You do. And there's the difference.'

FIFTEEN

I let myself in, cutting the alarm systems. Griff must be in the shop, still hurt and offended. A peace offering would be a nice cup of coffee, with one of the forbidden biscuits. I rang through for him.

Mrs Walker answered the phone. 'I'm on my own here, Lina. Mr Tripp's gone off somewhere in the van. In a bit of a hurry. Now, I wondered if I might help you with the preparations for Bath – I'm happy to polish and wrap, you know. And now I know your price code, I'd be happy to affix labels.'

Affix. She and Griff used words like that as if they were born with them.

'You've both been looking a bit peaky recently, so I'm more than happy to help.'

Griff would know how to shut her up without offending her. But Griff wasn't here.

I must have missed at least another paragraph of what she was saying while I worked out how to be tactful. Eventually I just cut in, not tactfully but truthfully: 'Ah! I've just seen a note propped up by the kettle.'

Not having you worried another minute. I'm taking action myself.

G xxx

He'd switched his phone off. Of course he had. I left a message. 'Just stop and turn round. Don't do it, Griff, please.'

Surely he'd check when he reached Winchelsea, where Dilly had her shop. It was a place that for some reason he didn't like at the best of times, though with all its history you'd have thought he was in heaven. Just for good measure, I left another message. 'I really don't want you doing this. Even Titus doesn't like Mr Dilly – thinks he's violent. It's bad enough him beating up Dilly – but you're not involved at all. The whole thing's my fault. Please Griff.'

That makes what I said sound almost coherent. It wasn't.

And then the doorbell rang. I flung the door open to find Morris silhouetted against a sudden burst of sun. I flung myself into his arms. 'Thank God you're here! I don't know what to do. Griff's—'

At this point I realized two things. He definitely wasn't hugging me back. And he was pulling forward a woman with a baby in her arms. His partner. Mother of Leda, to whom Griff and I had sent a coral teething rattle. From both of us, you understand.

'This is Penny,' he said, rather late. 'Penny, Griff Tripp's partner, Lina.'

We air-kissed, left-right.

'We were passing and I thought I might be able to find Penny a pretty ring here. When we got married we only had a wedding band, and I thought . . .'

My God, the man only wanted me to find him what in other circumstances would be an engagement ring. We were now supposed to be friends, no more, but that seemed to be pushing the boundaries of understanding a little far. Or maybe Penny had wanted to check out what she saw as the opposition.

My smile felt stiff. 'Of course. We don't carry many, as you know, but there might just be the right thing.' In fact, we'd only started to deal with them after we found someone selling imperfect ones at perfect prices. 'But come in and have a coffee first. I'm worried, as you might have gathered,' I said with a little nod at Penny. 'Griff's decided to do a knight errant thing and get me out of a hole I dug.' For once I thought on my feet. Though he obviously knew about Griff's email, I wouldn't mention the SOS email I'd sent unless Morris mentioned it first. Especially as I couldn't remember whether I'd sent it to his home or work computer.

But I was thinking too fast. I ought to be cooing over the baby. Babies didn't turn me on one bit, but this one seemed quite nice and even managed what seemed like a smile. What if Penny put her on the floor? Would she crawl and grab all Griff's precious things? Or stagger around and collapse fragile furniture? The only child-oriented things in the entire cottage were two collector's Steiff bears, not meant for children at all, and Tim, and she certainly wasn't chewing his ears.

Fortunately Morris had picked up the panic in my voice. Helping to peel layers of clothing off Leda, he looked at me under his eyebrows and asked very coolly, 'What's this about Griff? Is he in real trouble – his email didn't suggest anything too serious – or just something you're imagining?'

'Let me make you coffee – or would you prefer tea? I've got green, too.' If I sounded flustered it's because I was. All I wanted to do was leap into the other van and hurtle to the coast.

They asked for different things and than apologized and changed their minds. In the end, I gathered that she wanted peppermint tea – did we have any left? – and he'd like decaf instant coffee. In the kitchen I tried phoning Griff again – nothing. So then I turned to hostessy things. Biscuits. Tray. The right sized cups. Sugar and milk. I must have knocked everything over at least once. Still mopping the milk off the tray, I carried everything through and parked on Griff's favourite Regency occasional table. Bad idea. At least there was just room on the bookshelf for it.

As we all sat down, Penny grabbed Leda and to my horror put her nose to the back of her nappy. 'The smell test. And she's failed. Your turn, Morris. After all, you must know where the bathroom is.' Was that smile a bit on the acid side?

It was like having a conversation with someone in the dentist's waiting room. We must have talked about something, but I can't remember what. At last Morris returned with a clean baby and something unpleasant in a polythene bag. 'Dustbin?'

'Back yard,' I said. 'Shall I—'

'No, I'll find it.'

I had an idea that this was Morris's way of letting Penny and me get to see something of each other. I saw rather more of her than I'd expected. She suddenly lifted her T-shirt and started to breast feed. It seemed to me that Penny was making a lot of statements, the strongest of them without any words.

At long last Morris returned. 'So, tell me about Griff.'

'I agreed to sell something secretly for someone,' I said, as if he didn't know already. 'A pendant – I could probably sell it for two or three hundred. You know how meticulous Tripp and Townend are about receipts. Well, I didn't have any paperwork for it. And I – we both – had a nasty feeling I was being set up for something. Don't know what. But rumours are flying – most of them emo . . . emi . . . emanating from the guy who claims he's my grandfather.'

'Arthur Habgood, right?' Morris's smile was so swift it was hardly there but it told me I'd got the word right.

'Right. He's reminding everyone that I was once accused of handling stolen goods.' I said all this for Penny's benefit, since one of the people who'd accused me was none other than Morris. 'He's conveniently forgotten the fact that the woman who accused me is now doing time for handling stolen goods herself, and that I was completely exonerated.' I went at the word with a great rush and seemed to make it. 'And I just have this twitch in my bunion that Dilly Pargetter is going to spot the pendant on one of my displays and claim I've nicked it. Or her partner is. He's got a reputation for violence. Domestic violence.'

'And Griff's gone to sort him out?'

'I think he's just gone to return the pendant. But a word out of place—'

'Is far more likely to bring harm to Dilly than to Griff.'

'Do you think so?' For a moment, that seemed a better option. But then I recalled the black eyes after I'd bought the ring at rock bottom price and the throat concealed by a scarf.

'There's an awful lot of ifs and maybes to take in, Lina. Have you tried phoning him?'

Suppressing a tart answer, I set the phone on conference and pressed the redial button.

'OK, so he's not picking up. But he wouldn't if he was driving, would he?' Penny said, removing Leda from her breast.

Leda yelled in fury and then settled down on the other.

'Anything else I should know?' Morris asked.

'Someone else has accused me of the same thing – different items, though. Kent Heritage Officer's on my case. At least I had receipts to prove I'd actually bought the items – one of them from Dilly. Sorry, this is coming out all jumbled.'

'What sort of item?'

'A rare old ring. Old enough for it to be way out of our period. Old enough for Griff to take it to the British Museum. Rare enough for his mate there, Sir Douglas something or other, to contact you lot and accuse us of thieving.'

His eyebrow said he recognized the name. 'You said items.'

I'd forgotten how cold his eyes could be.

'Another ring. In a load of packing material – I'd bought a box of rubbish at an auction and there was this ring in a screw of paper right at the bottom.'

'And you're being framed?'

'It might all be coincidence. But—'

'But your immediate concern is Griff, right?' Penny summed up.

'I'll just make a call or two,' Morris said, without any warmth. He slipped into the hallway so we couldn't hear what he was saying.

Leda had stopped suckling and was falling asleep. I ought to say something. I ought to make an effort. 'Might I hold her?'

'I think she's just failed the smell test again. Could you point me to the bathroom?'

I can't say the experience was exciting, but since I'd never seen a nappy changed before in my life, it was educational. Penny and I managed a slightly better conversation, and we ended up in my bedroom where Tim the Bear took one look at Leda and smiled.

I was ready to help him into her arms, but Penny pushed him away.

'He's much too smart. You don't want milky dribble down him. Or sick, which she sometimes produces when she burps. God, this motherhood business is so hard.' She sat

on the bed. Staring at Leda's head, she said, 'He says . . .
he told me . . . he'd met someone. It wasn't you, was it?
Because he said whoever it was sent him back to me with
a flea in his ear. Said he had to love me as well as Leda.
Was it . . . ? It was, wasn't it? It was very generous of you,
Lina.'

I was surprised that a musician didn't hear the connection between Lina and Leda. And the version of events
wasn't quite as I remembered them. However, all I said
was, 'I think he always loved you, only with your jobs . . .
The thing is, I desperately needed someone to be there for
me. Bit of an Orphan Annie. But since my father was decidedly absentee,' I continued, more upbeat, 'I did point out
that any baby deserved a better start than I had. And I'm
glad he had the sense to see that. At least he's a hands-on
dad. Nappies and everything.'

'Better had be. Look, is it OK him looking for a ring
here? It's a bit . . . crass.'

'I won't cheat him. And none of my friends will. But it's
a very personal thing, isn't it, a ring? I mean, it has to be
your choice, not my recommendation. And if you don't see
anything you fall in love with, you just walk away.'

I thought of the two lovely rings in our secret safe – so
secret that apart from the guy who installed it, Griff, and
me, Morris was the only one who knew where it was. And
even he didn't know the combination. I'd had them both
repaired. And that ruby would look stunning with Penny's
dark hair.

'Lina! Lina? Are you there? Phone for you!'

Morris's voice brought me straight back to what I ought
to be worrying about – Griff.

'Maidstone? Police Headquarters? Griff, what the fucking
hell are you doing there?' I sat down hard on the stairs,
since my legs seemed to have gone woolly.

'My darling, your language! It's not yet seven o'clock.'

'What *on earth* are you doing there?'

'Having a word with young Will. What did you think?
Where did you think I was going? I get this barrage of

phone messages. My dear child, I wish you wouldn't worry so. We're going to have a cup of tea and a morsel of conversation, then I shall be on my way home.'

'In that case I'd better put lunch back,' I said, grasping for something neutral to say. 'We've got visitors. Morris and Penny, not to mention Leda.'

'Maybe I should forego that tea. And, I fear, the conversation.'

Mrs Walker was more than qualified to show Morris and Penny our stock, though if I knew anything she'd be too busy fussing over the baby to think about selling anything. I sat on the bed, nuzzling Tim's ear, and thought about the rings. There was no doubt that Morris would recognize them. What sort of signal would that send? Did I really care? At last, I fished them out of their hiding place, gave them a bit of a polish, and sneaked into our office for a couple of price labels. Now they wouldn't look out of place in the display cabinet.

Penny was too busy trying to shut up a howling Leda to be looking at anything. Mrs Walker had found a silver teaspoon and was busy waving it at the poor child, talking to her, talking nineteen to the dozen. Morris was looking at a lovely eggshell Ruskin trio that I'd set the spotlights on.

'Nice set Lina,' he said as I let myself in through the back door.

'Very nice. Who could resist something like that? Every time I come in the shop I wave to it. I don't really want to sell it. And that's the first rule of dealing, to let things go.'

He looked at the price tag, and worked out the price. 'But you would, if someone came along with a wad of cash. Quite a large wad of cash.'

'Some things you can sell, some you can't. Dealers can't keep everything they like. Or sell everything they dislike, I suppose,' I added, trying to be witty, but in my ears sounding a bit false. There was a lot of what Griff would call subtext. 'Want to look a bit more closely?' I unlocked the cabinet.

'I know that trick of yours, Lina, my girl. She's got this

wonderful ploy,' he said, raising his voice to explain to Penny, 'of letting punters handle something they quite like but can't afford. As soon as they do, they're hooked. Happens all the time,' he said, closing the door with a click.

By this time, the combined efforts of Mrs Walker and Penny had silenced Leda, who had probably gone to sleep in sheer self-defence, chomping on the wrong end of the spoon. While Morris wandered over to them, I opened the jewellery display case and slipped the rings inside. I left it wide open, as if I was hinting they could make their selection as soon as they felt like it. I also ran my mind over the contents of our fridge and freezer: did we have enough to feed us all? – there was no way we could exclude Mrs Walker, now holding the sleeping baby and still cooing over her, from our feast.

Actually, now it came to it, I didn't want to see them looking into each other's eyes as she tried on possibilities. So a quick exit to the kitchen was a good option. I just smiled at Penny and patted the display case. I suspect she understood.

I intercepted Griff, who looked quite cross as he let himself into the cottage. He was clutching a paper carrier bag from the local delicatessen. 'Lunch,' he said, handing it over.

'They're choosing an engagement ring. I've put the other two in the case too.'

He knew at once which I meant. 'My child, are you sure?'

'Yes. Time I got over myself, Griff.'

'Even so . . . I can't help hoping she selects something else.'

'At that price? Go and see to it that she doesn't!' I pushed him gently to the shop.

I laid the dining table quickly, with a matching service and silver cutlery. Five of us. Where to put Leda? Penny's problem. Griff had brought baguettes, a couple of flans and two bags of salad. The rest was up to me. And it had to be seamless. A quality show. More competent than Morris would expect.

The best butter. Dressing. Cheese. Fruit – time to make

it into a fruit salad? No. A cake from the freezer – I set it
to defrost in the microwave. Another thought – if they chose
a ring, champagne would be called for. But only wine if
they didn't. Griff kept a supply of both chilling. Glasses,
two sorts, both within reach but neither on show. Water
glasses on the table too, plus a lovely crystal water jug I'd
rescued from a skip a few months back.

Then I sat on the stairs again. All this was fine and dandy,
but why had Griff gone to see Will and what was the
outcome? And why had Morris come here when there were
a thousand places to buy a ring? Whatever the reason, I'd
pick his brain about Charles Broad-Ticeman. Paintings were
his area. I was still at the know-what-I-like stage, with not
a lot but my divvy instinct to back it. Fakes I could sniff
a mile off. But I couldn't have told one Renaissance artist
from another, except I did rather like that guy who did
lovely light and shadows and died on the way back home
after exile. Cara-something.

There was a lot of laughter – you could almost feel the
smiles and happiness. I braced myself. She came in waving
a pretty Edwardian ring, a centre diamond with strange
ribbon shaped gaps between it and the twelve stones
surrounding it, so the flesh of the wearer's finger showed
through. Penny was dark enough for there to be a real
contrast. It looked as if it had been made for her. It was
also a clear three thousand pounds cheaper than the ones
I'd just put in the case. That's business, I suppose. She was
also making a great show of some cufflinks she was trying
to insert in Morris's cuffs – a bit of subtext there, too. Still,
they put more money in our coffers, so I fished out the
champagne.

SIXTEEN

When we'd finished lunch, Mrs Walker and Penny took Leda for a walk round the village. I'm not sure Penny wanted to leave us, but it was hard to resist Mrs Walker in full flood. Bredeham's pavements are too narrow for three abreast, so I had a good excuse to stay put. Not that I'd have budged anyway.

Although Griff was fussing round clearing it, I plonked my elbows on the table and said, 'Charles Broad-Ticeman, Morris.'

'A bit out of your league, Lina.'

'You know him then.'

'Know as in we've met or know as in he's appeared on the Squad's radar?' It must be the champagne talking; Morris was usually even more discreet than Griff was about his visits from X.

'Either.'

'Or, I suppose, neither. Let's just say I've heard of him.'

'Same as I've heard of Caravaggio?' I gave myself a brownie point for remembering the name just when I needed it.

He looked at me, raising his eyebrow in the way I'd found so attractive. Resolutely, I didn't smile back. I wished he hadn't come here, wished his ringless wife had gone to H Samuel, wished she hadn't had to breastfeed Leda and most of all wished she wasn't such a nice woman.

'Not quite,' he said. 'Though I have come on both their names in fine arts magazines. As I'd have thought you would have, too.'

'Right magazines, wrong pages,' I said, with a bit of a glower. 'Stop messing about, Morris. Is he kosher or not? Why should his wife stick a tatty epergne on their price-less refectory table and break a piece off it? Why should she welcome me as if I was a spring flower—'

'*Were* a spring flower, my love,' Griff put in, producing coffee in three old Derby cans and sitting down between us, like a referee. 'One uses the subjunctive when there's no possibility of—'

'Quite,' Morris agreed, suddenly tetchy.

Maybe it was best if I continued blithely, 'And then, when she comes to collect the flower holder, does she treat me as if I'm less than the dirt on her shoe?'

'Are you asking about her or about him? She might just be a spoiled, rude poor little rich girl for all I know. He – well, like I said, he's a big player. I'll ask around for you.'

'Thank you. And see if you can find out why he should want my face on his security cameras? Not just one, a lot. And scattering my DNA all over the place. Even more, I suppose, if I'd had lunch with her.'

Morris nodded. 'And you say she conducted most of her business with you out in the street?'

'Paid cash, too. And wanted fifty pence change,' I added.

'Ooh, such venom,' put in Griff, very camply.

Morris ignored him. 'So will she be on your security system?'

'Of course. Even though I doubt if she realizes it.'

He nodded. 'Excellent. So what's your take on it?'

'If you take it in con . . . conjunction? . . . with Habgood's rumour machine and Dilly wishing this pendant on me, I feel like that goat they tether to a stake to attract other animals; something nasty's lurking that may turn out to be tigers. And when your Kent colleagues join in and keep remarkably schtum about things I feel quite vulnerable.' There – I'd pronounced that *l* again.

'Have you made any enemies?' Morris asked, just as if he was a brand new constable with a brand new pen interviewing a complete stranger.

'I shouldn't imagine Lady Petronella's my best friend,' I said.

'Perhaps not. But I can't imagine she's sitting in her prison cell organizing revenge. Can you?'

'Not unless someone's smuggled a mobile phone inside,' I said, cocking my head in challenge.

'Not, I accept, beyond the wit of man. Or woman. And it would explain one thing – why all this is focused on you, not Griff.'

'Anyone attacking Lina attacks me.' This time he didn't sound at all camp.

'I know that.' He smiled as he used to, but only at Griff. 'But do they? Whoever *they* are, of course.'

I frowned. 'So could all this be designed to separate me from Griff? Because someone I thought was pretty much a goody might have an interest in that, too.' I told him all about Harvey Sanditon, and his efforts to get me to join his firm. 'On the other hand, I can't see how he'd benefit if I was disgraced. Or Habgood, of course. Who'd want a con for a granddaughter?'

'He's still banging on about that, is he?' Then he surprised me. 'What does Lord Elham make of it?'

Griff answered for me. 'I think he'd consider horse-whipping an appropriate treatment. Much as I would, as it happens. We have spoken about it, Elham and I, as you'll have gathered.'

He was so pompous I wasn't surprised Morris hid a smile. He made an obvious effort to take control of the conversation again. 'You mentioned the Kent police. Tell me about them.'

I ran through the story about my body for what seemed the twentieth time. To boost my rather dented ego, I was tempted to imply there was rather more between Will and me than there was, but then thought better of it. After all, if I hadn't picked up the phone when he called, Will hadn't responded to my message either.

'Anything else?' he asked at last.

'Only that I know that the area I found the body is still considered a crime scene, and there seems to be some hush-hush archaeological site in the same area. Titus,' I mouthed at Griff, as if I'd learned about it from him, not with him.

'Been snooping?' Morris asked unkindly.

'I have my sources,' I said, with dignity.

'That old guy that drops off artefacts here?' Morris asked. Griff literally went pale. 'How do you know—?'

'He rapped on your window while I was here, very early one morning, before Lina was stirring. I don't know who was more surprised, him or me.'

'Lina's never met him,' he said quickly.

'I have a contact of my own, someone Griff loathes,' I said, just as quickly. I think we overlapped.

'And no, you're not going to tell me who. OK, doesn't matter for the time being. Look,' he said, getting to his feet, as we heard the ominous sound of Mrs Walker's voice doing baby talk, 'if I have a moment I'll do some sniffing around. One thing, though, Lina, I'd rather you only contacted me on my work phone or my work email address. I'm sure you understand.'

Until that moment I'd gone along with his decision about us. It was the right one, for heaven's sake. But just at that instant, I really hated him. Not just for starting the relationship in the first place, but for telling me off like that in front of Griff. My chin went up. 'I quite understand.'

All the same, I felt more alone at that moment than I had since I'd found the body.

Perhaps he sensed my anger. Or at least he knew he'd done something wrong. He sat down again. 'That body. If it moved, it might not have been dead.'

'Quick thinking,' I said, managing a bit of sarcasm. Though I should really have thought of that before. If only my brain wasn't like blancmange.

'And it might not have liked your drawing the attention of my colleagues to it,' he continued as if I hadn't spoken. 'So I think we should add him to the circle of people who might have a motive for harming you, don't you?'

'Harm her?' Griff got up and put his hands on my shoulders. 'Harm *her*? Not just her reputation?'

'Who knows? I don't suppose,' Morris said idly, 'you've ever seen him again, have you?'

I turned to Griff, my eyes rounding despite themselves. 'You remember the guy who tailgated us to Six Mile Garage? No, of course you wouldn't – you were asleep and then all you wanted was the loo. But when he turned his gas-guzzler

towards Canterbury, I caught sight of his profile. And I just
wondered if I recognized it.'

'E-fit?' Morris asked.

I shook my head. 'That'd make it way too official. It was
only a passing fancy.'

'*You* don't get that sort of fancy, Lina. But I won't hassle
you, because in my experience the more you try to "help"
a memory, the more it goes away. All the same, this Will
of yours might be interested.'

'If it means seeing her again, I'm sure he will be,' Griff
said, squeezing my shoulder lightly. 'Smitten is the word,
I fancy,' he added. Was it? Perhaps he was just trying to
boost my poor battered ego a bit. He continued, in a fake-
confidential tone, something else that was news to me, 'I
suspect from the way Lina blushes every time I mention
him that it might be reciprocated.'

This was the first sentence Penny heard as she stepped
into the room, which was either Griff's perfect timing or –
less likely – good luck. While she was fiddling with the
pushchair, I ought to say something useful myself. All I
could manage was a simple statement. The truth. 'I feel
trapped. I just don't know where to start.'

Penny picked up the sleeping Leda, leaving Mrs Walker
to bustle into the kitchen. Griff got up to follow, probably
to point out it was more than time the shop was open again.
Fishing out his noisy mobile, Morris looked at the display,
and stalked out to respond.

Penny brought Leda to sit opposite me. 'I was heading
for post-natal depression,' she said, out of the blue. 'Because
I could see all these things needing to be done – and done
by me. And I just didn't know where to start. Like you.
Then a friend dropped round and said, "You can't hope to
do everything. So prioritize. Choose one thing above everything else and that might shake things into perspective."'

I stared helplessly; the problems of a new mother weren't
much like those of a single girl sensing tigers everywhere.
But I nodded, as if she was making sense.

'Is there anything you can fix with a simple phone call?'
she began.

A simple solicitor's letter, maybe. On the other hand I'd rather speak to Habgood in person.

I shook my head.

'Come on – what about this Will who fancies you?'

'He has a friend who thinks I'm next best thing to a grave robber.'

'But you're not, and maybe you should tell Will you're not. And if he's as keen on you as Griff said . . .' She grinned. 'Not to mention your being keen on him.'

'He's a policeman,' I said dismissively. And then realized that saying that was a good reason not to trust him wasn't the most tactful thing in the world. I looked left and right. 'Just between the two of us, some antiques deals aren't always the straightest in the world. Or the dealers. Or do I mean the other way round? My last boyfriend was a dealer who turned out to be as crooked as a corkscrew. It made it really hard, being friends with Morris. But please, please, please keep that to yourself.'

'Are all your friends bent?' she exclaimed.

'Very few. But you can't have chunks of your life you mustn't talk about to someone you want to share your life with, can you?' I was talking about me and Morris; maybe she knew.

She shook her head. 'We're not talking about this Will being your life partner, Lina – we're talking about being nice to a guy you fancy and who might want to help you.'

I wrinkled my nose – only for a second, but she noticed.

'You know, Morris was right,' she laughed. 'You really are one of the most moral people on this earth, aren't you? How about a clergyman for a boyfriend? At least he'd just regard your shady cronies as sinners needing forgiveness.'

Was she just making a joke or had Morris mentioned what he saw as his rivalry with Robin?

'I do know a drop-dead gorgeous one,' I said cautiously, 'Adam's apple apart, that is. It bobbles dreadfully.'

'He's no good then,' she declared, starting to giggle. But she was soon serious again. 'If your Griff has been talking to Will already, I think you need to see him yourself, Lina. Really, truly. Seeing him could be the thing my friend suggested – the one that puts everything else into perspective.'

Wouldn't it be nice to have someone like her as a friend? But with Morris in the picture . . .

At this point he came back in, talking to Griff. He turned to me. 'We were talking about this Dilly Pargetter's pendant. Know what I'd do? I'd send her a receipt – only I'd make sure it got lost in the post. By not posting it, of course! You'll have a copy on your system, that way. And I've got your email on my system, printed off and dated, before you ask. It'll be a bait, Lina. But just make sure something too big doesn't try to swallow it.'

SEVENTEEN

At long last, we waved off our visitors. I didn't especially want to talk about them or their doings, so, attack being the best means of defence, I asked Griff what on earth he'd been doing in Kent Police HQ. 'I thought you'd gone down to Winchelsea to return Dilly's pendant,' I added. 'That was what I was really worried about.'

'At least we have expert advice on that matter,' Griff said. 'Not to mention a really good sale.'

He was better than I was at changing subjects. But I wouldn't bite. 'Whatever. But talking to Will? Why?'

'It occurred to me that a little friendly colloquy was in order after the way in which he and his colleague departed. Were told to depart,' he corrected himself. 'And I thought he might be too stiff-necked to call you.'

'Might have been me that was stubborn,' I admitted. 'I switched a call from him to voicemail and forgot to pick it up. Mind you, when I did get back to him, I had to leave a message he didn't respond to. Tit for tat.'

'So I was right to hie me to Maidstone. But a great shame we had time to exchange no more than pleasantries.'

Did I believe him for one minute? 'Hmm.'

'At least he had time to tell me he really needed to talk to you. Preferably over in Maidstone,' he added with less confidence.

'Police HQ!' The very thought made my hands sweat.

'While it reeks of security and officialdom, my love, it's not quite as bad as a police station. And Will did say I could come with you if you preferred. Not with any great enthusiasm, however, I admit.'

So next day, much as I'd have liked to hold his hand, I went on my own, to find Will waiting to escort me through all the checks. He kept blushing and stuttering, but then so did I. After all, we'd parted on pretty poor terms. There was an awful lot of after-you-ing, and, when we'd got to a room that looked horribly like the interview rooms where I'd spent a great deal of time when I was young, offers of tea and coffee and more comfortable chairs: anything not to get down to a proper conversation. I wasn't a hundred per cent surprised. He owed me a serious apology, or at least Winters did. But since I had something to offer I broke the ice.

'I know this isn't really your bag,' I began, 'but DC Winters and I didn't exactly hit it off, did we? So I didn't fancy calling him. The thing is, I may have remembered a bit more about the body I saw,' I said cautiously. There was no need to mention Morris's involvement. And especially not Titus'. 'I had to drive near the site the other day—'

He frowned. 'Had to?'

'My usual route from Hythe to Bossingham, where my father lives,' I said, with a nasty feeling the conversation might not flow after all. 'In any case,' I continued, with a great show of coming clean, 'I was puzzled when you said there wasn't a bridle path, just proper roads. I wanted to find why my memory had got it wrong. And I still don't know why, because a road is a road, even if it's a pretty narrow one.'

'Even if someone's put up a bogus road sign, which might have happened, I suppose. Look, give me five minutes. I could see you and Bernie weren't soul mates. I'll go and get the latest for you.'

'Not Winters – I really don't think I could be very polite to him.'

'Just an update. Promise. Will you stay here, please?'

'If I say no, you lock me in, right? OK, I can see you don't want folk wandering round getting lost,' I said, although I was seething.

'Quite. I could bring some coffee, too?' he added, suddenly reminding me of a dog hoping for walkies.

I nodded. Rules was rules, I suppose, and I'd much rather have him on my side than not.

I didn't have to wait very long. He'd actually got proper cups instead of the paper ones I'd expected.

'Not quite up to your and Griff's standards,' he said,

mopping some of the coffee he'd spilt on a cardboard file he'd brought along. 'Look, I never worked out why Griff came to see me yesterday. He was oozing fury. Then he checked his calls and disappeared. Just like that. Weird.'

I decided to answer the second point he made. 'An old friend turned up out of the blue. DI Morris, of the Fine Arts Squad, actually. Wanted to buy his new wife a ring. I'm sorry if Griff was rude.'

'Not so much rude as confusing. But at least he passed on the message that you wanted to talk to me.'

Did he, indeed? What message, Griff?

'Well, now I have. About the road signs?'

'They were swapped – at least that's what my colleagues on that case assume. Certainly the forensic team told them that someone had tampered with the signpost. They've no idea why at this stage.' By now he could manage a cautious smile.

'And I've no idea why what happened next happened,' I said, knowing that Griff would have winced at the ugly sentence. I did myself, come to think of it. 'Suddenly, out of nowhere, this 4x4 appeared, and seemed to object to my being there. He tailgated me all the way to Six Mile Garage.'

A couple of lines appeared between his eyebrows. 'I thought you were heading for Bossingham.'

'After a couple of hundred yards of that treatment I wanted to go somewhere with people and CCTV,' I said. 'Just in case.'

'Makes sense. So you pulled over—'

'Suddenly, without signalling. Nearly hit their little postbox. And he shot past, and turned towards Canterbury, also fast and without signalling.'

The lines deepened. 'So he could just have been a bad driver.'

'A bad driver with a profile that seemed awfully familiar.' I fished out my mobile phone and flashed the original photo I'd taken.

After all those frowns, he managed a grin. 'I can do better than that. We had the image enhanced by experts.' At last he opened the folder.

I know I was meant to be impressed, but actually it wasn't

much better than the version I'd downloaded on to our computer. Since we were supposed to be enjoying a truce, I'd better make some sort of intelligent comment. 'Are those his footprints or someone else's?' I asked, pointing.

'According to Forensics, they might be his. Look, you can see a pattern on the sole of that shoe. It seems to match that track there.'

'Sorry. It was a pretty stupid question. If he walked there, it had to be his, didn't it?'

'But if someone else carried him, he might have worn the same type of shoe,' he pointed out.

'Unlikely for two people to be cavorting round the countryside in footwear and clothes very much designed for the town. I mean, that suit looked pretty good . . .' When he raised his eyebrows sharply, I explained. 'Griff's partner – other sense – always wears terrific clothes. Something to do with the cut and the cloth?'

'And the money you spend on both.' Will tugged a jacket I'd seen in M and S – washable. Still, I suppose if you were a cop investigating crime scenes you might just want to pop things in the machine at the end of the day. 'Now look at this image,' he said, leafing through his file and passing me an A4 print. 'See, they've made his face look as if it's facing us, not the sky. And here's another giving just what you were talking about – profiles.'

'Wow! This is clever. Just like real life police mug shots,' I added grimly.

'Precisely. Now, without thinking too hard about it, does the profile still seem familiar?'

'You've got a rabbit you're dying to pull out of your hat, haven't you?' This time I managed a grin.

'Something like that. A computerized facial recognition system that picks out possible suspects from faces we've got on record.'

'But that would only work if he'd been in trouble.'

'True. But it came up with these people – none an exact match, unfortunately.' He passed me two pages covered in photos. 'See what you think.' He really wanted me to pick one out, didn't he?

I'd have loved to, and peered at each new face with hope. In the end I had to shake my head. 'None I could swear to. I'm sorry.'

'Between you and me they were long shots. But if you saw someone with this face driving round the Kentish countryside, then it'd rule him out anyway.'

'Not able to drive around anywhere? Inside? OK. Well, I suppose you don't get bits of DNA lying round in a field?' I said, trying to be helpful.

'There are all sorts of clever techniques for lifting information from all sorts of surfaces. I don't begin to understand how. But you need some evidence of a death. A few bones, for instance,' he added, grinning again. 'Which is more my area.'

I felt this huge blush coming up from my navel. I tried to hold on to it a bit longer. 'Winters mentioned an ulna.' That might have been pretty mature and measured. Pity the next bit wasn't. 'Will, you're going to kill me, but I actually went for a walk through those woods. I know, I know – but they are public footpaths, and I didn't cross your tape, honestly, or try to break into that archaeological site. I promise. But I did see something . . . I told myself it was only roots in a badger's sett.' At least Titus told me, but I'd keep him – and the coin he'd found – out of this. 'But I have the most awful feeling it was – the bones of a hand. It's probably my imagination. But you ought to know.'

He looked at me with a mixture of anger and something like approval. 'Take me there? Now?'

I looked down at the neat trousers and top I was wearing. My jacket was my better one, too – not my pushing through thorns and mud one. 'I've got some wellies in the van,' I said, trying to sound keen on the adventure.

'And I'm sure I can lay hands on a paper suit to protect your clothes.'

This time leaving the van where I'd parked it, I travelled in style, Will rather showing off his driving skills. Praying there was no sign of the wellies Titus had wanged into the hedges, I pointed out where I'd parked. Like me, Will kept two wheels on the road.

'You look like a snowman!' I crowed, as he pulled on the suit.

'And you!'

Blow me if we weren't both singing the Aled Jones song. So we seemed to be getting on at last. But we didn't hold hands and there was no floating through the air.

I didn't have Titus' knack of detecting invisible tracks, but set off slowly along one that looked right. There was no sign of any badger activity and at last I stopped dead.

'The ground was all lumpy, like a miniature moonscape,' I said. 'I didn't think it was this far. Oh, dear.' I surveyed the unappetizing spot.

'There was that path sixty yards back . . .' Will said doubtfully. 'Maybe I should have brought a dog handler – you know there are some specially trained to find corpses. Dogs, I mean.'

My shudder was genuine. What if Titus' patterans came to light? I fell in behind him as we marched back. The path he'd seen was more of a track – but then, that was exactly the sort of thing Titus had chosen. So I set off hopefully. It didn't take long to realize I'd got us hopelessly lost.

'You said you'd not crossed our lines, or got into the site. Did you see the hand before or after?' Will asked, in the tone of a man just about keeping his temper.

'Before. I think. Yes, before. Definitely.' I crammed all thoughts of Titus' weird behaviour into the back of my memory, and hoped that not even his name would pop out. 'Walked along; saw the setts; saw the bones or roots; headed fast to the police tape.'

'All very intuitive,' he said dryly.

'All very panicky! I wasn't staying near the bones, not for anything.'

'You didn't think of turning tail and running back.'

I lifted my chin. 'I'm not as good at running away as I ought to be.' Chew on that.

We pressed on, and at last I pointed. 'There – that's the track. All oozy and yucky.' And fortunately with a lot of confused footprints, not just two sets. 'Let's see – the road's over there. On our left. So we need to turn right.'

Only about thirty yards away was the sett. 'A bit further on. Slow down . . . Shine your torch over there. No. Look, give it to me.' Just as Titus had done I played the beam backwards and forwards, and then, recognizing where Titus had found his coin, shone it directly into the sett mouth. And although it was dead repetitious, I screamed again.

And lost my coffee in a nearby bush.

So there I was, stuck in the middle of nowhere with a gorgeous bloke who was so busy trying to get a signal for his mobile phone I might not have existed. Eventually it dawned on him that my teeth were chattering so hard I couldn't speak. What I needed was a good comforting hug. What I got was a suggestion that I went back to his car, but there was no way I was wandering about on my own. Not that I could say so. After all, officially I'd done exactly that a couple of days back.

I turned my head to a tree trunk and sobbed.

At last when he'd established that a team would come out, he turned and put an arm round me. 'I'd suggest we both went back now, but I'd never find it again. Here, what are you doing?'

Tears still dripping down my face, I was trying to tear little shreds off my paper overall. I hung a couple on bushes. 'Making patterans,' I managed. 'Leaving a trail.

'Come on, Lina,' he said, as if it was just dawning on him that something was wrong. 'Here.' He burrowed in a pocket and produced a packet of tissues. 'This isn't like you.'

I was so taken aback I asked, 'What isn't like me?'

'You're so feisty, so gutsy—'

'So guilty! I saw this man alive and did nothing. It was my fault he died and rotted in an animal's lair. Hell, I could have saved him if I'd had any guts at all. I left him lying in a wet field and . . . and . . .' I pointed to the bones.

He turned towards the road. We could hear emergency vehicles. Several of them.

'Could you do your patteran thing and go back and send them over?'

'Me?'

'I'd better stay here.'

'Couldn't you do your radio thing and guide them over?'

'You really are freaked out, aren't you?' He sounded more disgusted than anything – like Griff when one of his TV cricketers misses an easy catch or gets run out.

'And you wouldn't be?' In my anger I plucked at a fistful of paper overall. He wanted patterans, he'd get bloody patterans. But it wouldn't tear and I was left impotently tugging at the stuff.

'Hello, there!' The voices calling us sounded so everyday, so ordinary you'd have thought they dealt with bodies every day. It was only when I saw the first very businesslike cases and other gear that I realized they did. It seemed they even had someone in the team to deal with wimps like me, and before I knew it I was back in a warm car heading back to Maidstone.

One of the things that bothered me was the amount of explaining I'd have to do to Griff. It was one thing to persuade Will that I'd been wandering round on my own in the woods, but another to convince Griff. But the truth, that I was in the company of Titus, would be even less to his taste.

I phoned him from Maidstone to explain. And got, thank goodness, his voicemail. It was reasonably easy to lie, and say that Will and I were having a bite of lunch. Finding a skeleton wasn't the sort of thing you could leave a message about.

As a sergeant, Will was much too important to take my statement, which was fine by me. In any case, he was only a man for old bones, not new ones. Much as I'd liked him at first, he'd slipped so far down in my estimation that I didn't want to see him again. Except for one thing. As I signed where I was told, I said to the woman I'd dictated everything to, 'Before I go, I need to see DS Kinnersley again.'

'It doesn't quite work like that,' she objected.

'On a personal matter,' I said, looking straight at her with my still puffy and bloodshot eyes.

I was lying, of course. Technically.

She managed what might have been a sympathetic nod, and slipped out of the room. I didn't bother checking to see if I was locked in or not.

After about twenty minutes, during which I repaired my make-up as best I could, and practised what I wanted to say, in came Will, looking so apprehensive I nearly laughed. I didn't. Stern-faced, I got to my feet and said, 'I know you've got plenty of other things to worry about. But I really think it's time you returned my property to me, Will. Unless it's an essential part of your enquiry, of course.'

'Property? Oh, the rings.' He pulled a face. 'They're still bagged up as evidence, as far as I know.'

'Evidence? Against whom?' I remembered to add the *m* right at the last moment.

'Well, I suppose it was against you. But the receipts and everything were kosher, so you should be getting them back. Unless you want me to find a collection for them to go in?'

'If I decide they should go to a museum, I shall choose it myself, thanks. So do I sit and wait?' I plonked myself down again.

'Er . . . Look, as you said, I'm rushed off my feet now. Can I drop them round later? May have to be tomorrow. Perhaps we could have a curry or something?'

Damn, when I should have been saying that that wasn't quick enough, I took the curry bait. 'In Bredeham?' I squeaked in spite of myself. As far as I knew there was only one decent place to get a curry in the whole of Kent, and that was the Gurkha-run restaurant in Folkestone. What I ought to have done was tell him in no uncertain terms where to go. And I promised myself I would, the moment the rings were back in my hands.

EIGHTEEN

I spent the journey home rehearsing the version of the truth that Griff was most likely to swallow. I wouldn't lie, but there had to be a plausible explanation for my visit to the woods. And then I realized I had a trump card – Will not handing over my rings. That should get him so annoyed he'd forget to question me too closely about anything else.

There was a very nice car parked outside our cottage. Had Griff's partner Aidan come up with a new model? No. He was a Mercedes man, and this was a BMW. Whoever the driver was, he was just turning away from our front door, looking fed up. I pulled up behind him and gave a light toot. And then a smile and a wave. Our visitor was Harvey Sanditon, no less.

Even if you don't fancy a man, to have someone's face light up like that does your ego no end of good. So does having someone run to open your van door for you, as if you were minor royalty getting out of a Rolls. And though I'm no delicate flower, having a hand to support you as you wriggle out is quite nice too. So suddenly Harvey was flavour of the month, and I gave him one of my more welcoming smiles. Only to find I was being kissed, not the cheeks, one-two, either side, but full on my lips

'How wonderful! I thought I'd been so foolish, calling in on the off-chance, and here you are!'

'Yes, I've just got back,' I said, stating the obvious. 'And Griff's not in?'

'I was just going round to the shop to see if he was there. But it was you I wanted to see.'

'Another casualty?'

'You don't think I might just want to see you?'

Not on the basis of that dinner we had together, I thought, but didn't say aloud. Well, I couldn't think of anything to say aloud, as it happened. So I blushed (not something under my control) and gave a half smile. And then I thought of something. 'Well, me and a lady you might want to see even more,' I said. 'Let me just lock the van in the yard and I'll introduce you.'

'Lady in a Swing!' he said, turning the étui gently. 'Perfect? Or did you have to help her?'

'I had to wash her hair and give her a bit of a facial,' I admitted. 'But nothing involving the glue pot, I promise.'

'And she's for sale?'

'I did want to keep her for myself,' I admitted, more or less truthfully. 'And then I thought about the V and A – they have a collection of Gouyn's stuff, don't they?' Thank goodness that breakfast coaching session had stuck in my mind.

He put the étui down very carefully. 'But something held you back – my goodness, I can't believe you thought of me!'

When a man smiles at you like that, it's hard not to smile back. And then get kissed, quite seriously this time. Well, it was better than staring at a skeletal hand, that was for sure. Stupid woman, thinking about that. I stepped back.

'Have I done something wrong?' No wonder the poor man was confused.

'No! It's me. Something that happened earlier today.' Hell, this was not the moment for bursting into tears. But I was very close to it.

'Tell me. Or can I get you a drink?' He looked wildly around, as if he might find a drinks cabinet in our office.

'Let's have a cup of tea,' I said, with a horrible unromantic sniff. I grabbed some tissues. 'Oh dear, that sounds like something from one of those daytime war movies Griff watches if he has a cold.' But I led the way into the kitchen. 'Green or builder's?'

We agreed on Lapsang Souchong, and I dug in the cake tin. He watched while I laid a tray – some of my favourite old but damaged china – but insisted on carrying it through to the living room.

He sat me down and fussed almost as well as Griff did. But there was an altogether different feel from Griff's hand as he held mine and asked me to tell him what was wrong. And then he did exactly what Will should have done: he pulled me to him so I could bury my face in his shoulder. Shame about his suit. But maybe the fine cloth would deal with mascara and tears.

At this point Griff let himself in through the back door and came sailing into the living room.

'Harvey, how nice to – But Lina! My dear one!' He sat the other side of me, and took the spare hand.

'She was saying something about finding a body!' Harvey explained.

Letting go of both hands, and gesturing for a bit of breathing space, I explained the background to Harvey, then gave them both a believable version of the day's events. 'Will told me about the archaeological dig, and I'd never seen one, except on *Time Team*, so he said he'd take me. We came across this badger's sett and what I thought were roots turned out to be a man's hand. Oh, Griff, if only I'd stopped that day!'

Harvey grasped my hand again. 'This body was moved from where it lay to where it was found? My God, Lina, if you'd gone to investigate you might have ended up as a skeleton in a sett too! It doesn't bear thinking about!'

I stared. 'I was afraid they'd rob me and steal the van. I never thought of any other sort of danger.' Dabbing my eyes with a hankie that Griff handed me showed how much eye make-up I'd lost. There's a difference between tears and mascara streaks, so I excused myself as soon as was tactful. I wouldn't change. Just repair the face. A few minutes to clear my thoughts. That was what I needed. Time to ponder how much Griff had bought of my story, and time to ponder why Harvey was here. I'd been right about his reaction to the étui. How would he react to the price?

The answer to the second question was simple. He shoved his plastic into the terminal and tapped. Then he asked both Griff and me for dinner, but Griff swiftly said he was already booked.

I'd bet any money that he'd just nip off to Tenterden to spend at least the evening with Aidan. It meant, of course, that he'd given me his tacit blessing for anything that might develop.

Harvey booked us into the Silent Woman, another Bredeham restaurant. It was less formal than the Two Bays, and the menu less pretentious.

With no vase sharing the table with us, conversation rattled along. In fact, although we'd arrived pretty early in the evening, by the time we got round to leaving, we were amongst the last there. We walked back slowly, hand in hand. All that developed was a pretty nice snog. After a while, Harvey said goodnight, and nipped off to the Two Bays, where he was booked in. But he'd made an interesting suggestion, which got those dratted antennae (see! I could still remember the word!) working again. There was an upmarket auction at a minor stately home the next day, and he thought it might be nice for us to combine business and pleasure and go together.

It would, now I came to think of it. I suppose. Actually, at a sale like that, there wouldn't be much that Tripp and Townend would want, which is why it wasn't in our diary. The booze I'd sunk told me it'd be really pleasant to spend a day with a guy who was nothing to do with bones. Lovely.

And then I wondered how long it would be before he asked me to pull my divvying trick. If he did, it would be curtains for him. If he didn't – well, we would see.

I didn't scream but I only just stopped myself. I was trapped in my van by a fully grown lion, which kept prowling round, trying the doors and shaking the whole thing and its load of valuable china. I don't know whether I was more scared of the lion or by the insurance claim. I knew it was a dream and that you didn't get lions in Bredeham, but when its huge paw changed before my eyes into a skeletal hand, I thought it was time to wake up properly. Eventually Tim the Bear told me it was quite safe for me to drop off again; after all, he said, I needed my beauty sleep to look good for my trip.

*   *   *

Since our van held more than his car, we went in that, with
me at the wheel. Having come to Kent specially for the
sale, he'd already cased the joint and knew what he wanted
to bid for. As you'd expect, he'd also got a top limit for
each item. Unlike the house sales we go to, all the bidders
were well turned out, as if it was a social event, not a matter
of hard business. People were also bidding online and via
phone links. All very impressive. Possibly intimidating.

I always have a chip ready to pop on to my shoulder.
But if I'd let it out this time, it would have spoiled the day,
and I might have missed things I ought to be bidding for
– within a tighter budget than Harvey's, of course. So I told
myself that Bossingham Hall was altogether more impressive as a building than this, and the contents of the main
part of the building were decidedly superior to many of the
objets d'art here. But for a piece of paper I might be Lady
Evelina, or at least an honourable. I'd never asked my father
to explain about titles, for some reason. Anyway, I held my
head up high.

I wasn't even on the starting blocks for most of the
items but didn't mind watching other people push prices
far too high – Harvey included. But my antennae gave a
dreadful twitch as he plunged in after a perfect Chelsea
gold anchor piece, two mythological characters sharing
a plinth, guide price twenty thousand pounds. I gripped
his hand tightly and, as he looked at me in alarm, wrote
NO on my catalogue.

Up and up the bids went.

He pressed his mouth to my ear. 'Why not?'

I returned the compliment. 'I don't know. But I wouldn't
touch it at half the price. And certainly not – my goodness,
twenty-five thousand pounds! And still rising!'

Since it would be a couple of hours before the next items
he wanted came up, he guided me on to the terrace.

'What was all that about? I had a buyer ready!' I wasn't
sure if he was amused or angry. Perhaps he wasn't either.
He looked at me closely. 'Do you know something I don't?'

'I don't know anything. I just . . .'

Could he have been about to get angry? No, he reached out a finger and stroked my cheek, much as he'd stroked the étui's, come to think of it. 'Are you sure? I felt you tremble – for a moment I was afraid memories of yesterday had recurred.'

Recurred. Griff would have liked that. He always gets so worked up when someone says *reoccurred*. He did explain once, but I still don't quite get it.

I hadn't wanted to do this, but perhaps I must.

I looked him straight in the eye. 'Harvey, did you know I'm a divvy?'

He took a step back. 'You're what? You mean, you can—?' He dropped his voice, looking around him.

'You're sure you didn't know? Because I can think of any number of dealers who'd give their teeth to take me to an auction like this.'

'I genuinely didn't. I promise you.' He grinned. 'But if you are, I'd like to join that list of possible escorts! Lina, you're full of surprises and I love you more every instant. Let's forget all this and go and have a nice lunch somewhere.'

A man like Harvey use the L word! And throw up a chance to get some really nice pieces with astonishingly low guide prices. I must keep my head. I made a little rocking gesture. 'A nice lunch and then back here? There's something you haven't marked in your catalogue but I think you might want to bid for after all. And there are a few things at the fag end that might just suit Tripp and Townend.'

'All sorts of things fetch up in kitchens and attics,' I said, as we paid for our purchases at the end of the day. 'Things that in less grand houses would be in display cabinets. Those Coalport plates I bought, for instance. I suppose one got chipped and Her Ladyship decided it was time for a nice new set. And that so-called sauce boat – why are folk so mealy mouthed?'

'Because ladies aren't supposed to want to pee, Lina. Oh, what a delight today has been.'

I thought he was going to kiss me there and then, but he

didn't. The man who'd paid twenty-eight thousand pounds for the Chelsea group had come up behind us, and was mocking him for having dropped out of the running so early.

Harvey responded with the sort of Mona Lisa smile that always irritates people.

He waited till we'd taken our purchases to the van. 'What exactly was wrong with the Chelsea, by the way? The provenance looked good enough.'

'I don't know. Not exactly. But . . .' I closed my eyes to see it again. 'One of the arms was the wrong colour. Not by much. But enough to make me think someone like me had been at work.'

A sudden frown. 'Not you?'

'You know my policy. And if it had been my work I'd have leapt up and protested – like someone saying a wedding shouldn't take place.' I pulled a face. 'Wouldn't I have been popular!'

'In both situations, actually. So it wasn't just your divining instinct?'

'I honestly don't know how much is that and how much common or garden observation,' I said. 'I only know I have to go with it. And I also know it never works to order. So I'm not going to make a million on Lotto. And it doesn't work with people.' Perhaps my voice was more sombre than I meant it to be.

He didn't say anything, but took me in his arms, and gave me a wonderful, Hollywood kiss.

As if it were comedy, not romance, my mobile rang. He set me upright and waited while I scanned the display. Will. I despatched him straight to voicemail.

I checked what he'd said a few minutes later as we got into the van: 'Lina, there's a bit of a problem. Could you pop over and I'll explain?'

Harvey raised an eyebrow. 'Important?'

'Could be. Would you mind if I returned the call? It's the policeman I was with when I found the skeleton.'

But it wasn't that that Will wanted to talk about. 'I'd rather talk face to face, Lina, if you don't mind. Any chance you could come round? Now?'

'That sounds serious,' I fished.

'I'll explain when I see you,' he said, and cut the call.

'Problem?' asked Harvey, who'd been kissing each finger of my spare hand.

'Will – that's the sergeant who admired your vase – wants me to pop into police headquarters to discuss something,' I said. That sounded as if I might be snubbing him. 'I don't know what.' That was better. 'It's pretty well on the way home, so I'd really like to drop in. If you don't mind. Won't take long.'

'So long as I can take you out to supper tonight. To celebrate not buying the Chelsea piece.'

'You're on. I'll tell you what I suspect it's about as I drive . . .'

'You're prepared to give something to the nation, Lina? That's very laudable of you.'

'I didn't say *give* the rings, Harvey. I said *offer on permanent loan*. Or sell. Once I can get my hands on them, of course. But I have a funny twitch about my antennae. The sort I get when I'm about to divvy something.'

'You don't sound very happy about it.' He squeezed my hand as I changed gear, but let it go the moment I needed to return it to the wheel.

'I'm not. It's a very bad vibe. Very bad indeed. Harvey, I have this terrible feeling that something's happened to those rings.'

NINETEEN

I was surprised when Harvey suggested he should stay in the car, but didn't argue when he explained. 'From what I saw of him last time, young Will is so full of testosterone he might arrest me simply for looking at you.' That was news to me. So was the next sentence. 'And I have to say, I couldn't be in the same room as you without looking at you. If I stay here, I can keep an eye on our purchases.'

How should I react? Perhaps the sun had got to us both. But being on the receiving end of a bit of adoration didn't seem a big thing. So although Will wasn't there to greet me – he sent a silent underling – I could have sung and danced my way through the security checks. I was arriving at a time when far more people were going home than going into the building, so I saw a lot of faces coming towards me, atop a variety of clothes, from garments that looked like rejects from a charity shop to really snappy suits. If I glanced sideways, I got a lot of profiles. Obvious really.

It might to a stranger seem that the only people I knew were policemen. And I did know three or four pretty well. But apart from Will I didn't know anyone working in Kent Police HQ. So why did I do a double take on one of those faces, whose owner might have been dressed by my father's expensive tailor, heading quickly for the front door? I must have stopped in my tracks, because my escort sighed quite loudly – maybe he was due to leave too and resented every minute wasted guarding me – and nearly grabbed my arm to move me on. He remembered his manners in time, and soon I was in not an anonymous interview room but Will's office, which was as untidy as some of the rooms in Bossingham Hall, complete with tottering piles of cardboard boxes gathering dust. I was surprised he could find anything on that desk.

Will was in mid phone call when I arrived. I shrugged.

Why not finish what he needed to say? Meanwhile, I could peer at the photos on the right hand wall; that seemed a lot more tactful than looking at the maps on the others, with pins and arrows suggesting sites subject to Will's scrutiny.

I was looking at a snap of a lovely torc, similar to some I'd seen in the British Museum the day Sir Douggie started all this off, when Will finally cut his call.

'If anything should be in a museum for everyone to see, this should.' I touched the photo. 'Did someone really steal this?'

'They did. And tried to have it melted down for bullion.'

I sat down hard. 'Something as lovely as that?'

'Not just lovely, but unique. But there was a happy ending.' After a cheerful smile, he face slipped into something much more sober.

'But you didn't invite me here to talk about happy endings,' I prompted him, sitting down hard. 'That skeleton?'

'Funnily enough, it wasn't to talk about that. It's not my bag. I'm just a witness, like you. But I gather it's still awaiting the attentions of the pathologist. By the way, you won't talk to the press or anyone else about it, will you?'

Was he being furtive or official?

'It's a bit late to tell me that,' I said, truthfully. 'Griff knows, and so does another friend of mine. I was a bit upset all round, and they both wanted to know why. But I never mentioned it to the press when I saw it first time round, and I don't suppose I will now. So why am I here?'

He got up and looked out of the window. 'The problem is . . . well, I can't pretend it's not serious.' He turned to face me but had trouble meeting my eye. 'Lina, I'm very much afraid we've lost the rings.'

It took me moments to manage to say, '*My* rings?' I wanted to say lots of other things, more, but I managed to sit on my hands and take a few breaths. That was what the therapist had said. Well, it didn't take long to work out that I was angry. Disbelief was in there somewhere too. And for some reason I actually wanted to laugh. But I think that might have been to do with anger, too. I said slowly,

'The rings that are so important to our heritage that Sir Douggie tried to have me arrested for having them. The ones that made Winters hysterical – yes, he was, you know. The ones I was prepared to give to the nation if they were important enough. They fetch up in police headquarters – and they get lost?' I managed not to squeak; I also managed not to swear.

'That's just about it,' he said. 'An investigation is under way. And of course, our insurance—'

'Don't even start about insurance. Investigate. And find the person who stole them. Nail him.' I got to my feet. 'For God's sake, it shouldn't need me to tell you that.'

'It didn't . . . I just thought . . . you know, the value . . .'

'Can't be measured in money. In any case, I don't want the money value. I want those rings. The exact ones. Is that clear?'

'Absolutely. Look, would you like to talk to the person in charge of the investigation?'

'Not particularly,' I said. 'But I'd like you to tell me how I can make a formal complaint.'

He went white, then scarlet. 'But we might find them—'

'You can find them tomorrow, but I shall still want to know how to complain.'

I was through the door and halfway down the corridor when I realized I didn't have a minder. Tough. I'd just find my own way out. If anyone stopped me – the visitor badge hanging round my neck was a bit of a giveaway – then they could do the honours. I stomped on.

At last I heard feet running fast behind me. Turn? Not me. Not even when a voice called, 'Mrs Townsend? Mrs Townsend!' I didn't know the voice and the voice didn't know my name, so tough.

At last a breathless woman in a good suit overtook me and came to a halt. She'd be about Harvey's age, maybe a bit younger, with flaming red hair and the porcelain skin you'd expect. 'Mrs Townsend? I'm DCI Webb.'

'It's Townend,' I said firmly, pressing on. 'And I'm single.'

'I'm so sorry: *Miss Townend*. I'm one of Will Kinnersley's colleagues. I think you're owed an explanation.'

'*Ms*. And I'm owed my rings,' I said, coming to a halt.

'I know. I think you should know that we haven't lost them. We believe they were stolen. They were in a locked evidence store. We took every precaution: they were bar-coded and logged in on a database—'

'And still got stolen. I'm glad our firm's security's better than yours.'

'It's an inside job. Believe me, we want to find the perpet-rator. Almost as much as you want us to. But this complaint business – is it really necessary?'

I wanted something better than a bald *yes*. What would Harvey say? Flipping her my business card, I said, 'It gets more necessary by the minute.'

Something else got more necessary by the minute. Where the hell was the door? I bolted for it. I got as far as the immaculate front steps and spewed up my guts.

Which wasn't an expression that Griff or Aidan would have used. Maybe not even Harvey.

Harvey looked at me oddly when I asked him to drive, but said nothing, in a tactful, not uninterested, sort of way.

He got us out of the car park, but pulled over as soon as he could. 'I guess you wanted to get away from there quickly. But you don't look well . . .' He tailed off, still not asking a direct question.

I stared at my hands, which seemed to have taken on a life of their own, they were shaking so much. 'You know the expression *you make me sick*. Well, now I know what it means. Not you, of course, not you. Will. He says they've lost my rings. His boss says they've been stolen. And I got sick with rage and forgot to say something really import-ant. To Will. His boss. Whoever.'

He took my hands – they both fitted into one of his. 'Do you want to go back? I'm happy to come with you – and say anything you want me to say. But please, have a sip of this first.' He produced the bottled water I always keep in the side pocket.

That felt better. So did some of the rather soft chocolate lurking in the glove compartment.

'Divine,' I said with what felt like a rather stiff smile. 'Try some. Nice thing is,' I said, pointing to the wrapper, 'it's Fair Trade. So you can feed your face and know you're helping some other poor sod.'

'Excellent.' For some reason he started talking about cocoa solids and Christian Aid and all sorts of stuff. At last he stopped. 'Feeling better?'

'Much.'

'Ready to go back?'

I shook my head. 'There's more than one way of skinning a cat, isn't there? Would you mind if I made a phone call?'

'I'll leave you to it.' He got out of the van and strolled round to look at the delights of Maidstone's roads.

Titus answered third ring. 'Not a good time, doll.'

'One question. D'you know what Dilly's partner does?'

'Apart from beating her up? This is the bad bit, doll, why I never ever have anything to do with her – right? The bastard's in the filth.' He cut the call.

I got out of the van to join Harvey, who smiled me such welcome that I reached up to kiss him. 'One more favour: would you mind forgetting I ever made the call?'

'What call?'

Back in Bredeham, Griff was there to greet us and lock the gates behind us.

Harvey read the situation as if it was a large print book. 'We've bought quite a lot,' he said, getting out and coming round to my side to help me out. That gave him a mound of brownie points in Griff's reckoning, at least. 'I'd really welcome your opinion on some of it. Not that Lina would have let me buy any wrong 'uns.'

'I'll clear the table,' Griff said, bustling indoors.

'Bless you. I'll sneak off to apply some slap. And I'll choose my moment to tell him about the rings,' I whispered, opening the van and reaching out the first of the plastic boxes.

By the time I looked perky enough to put Griff off the scent a bit, the other boxes were on the kitchen floor. Like

Griff and me at Christmas we reached out, unwrapped and admired. Obviously Harvey's haul was far more impressive than mine, but Griff was pleased with what I'd found, especially the Coalport. In fact, he pulled some bubbly out of the fridge.

Which suddenly raised an issue which ought to have been on my mind before. When would Harvey have to leave?

For some reason Griff insisted on cooking for us, so any moments of snogging had to be snatched, and there was no chance of things going further. Despite that, we had the best of evenings, which only ended at midnight – well, it would, wouldn't it? – not when our riches turned to rags, but when Harvey blinked in disbelief at the pretty Georgian bracket clock that Griff simply couldn't bear to sell, even though it was perfect and would have been profitable, as it struck the hour. He was on his feet in an instant.

'And I've got a meeting in Marlborough tomorrow morning! I promised myself I'd be on the road by seven.'

'I can open our gates for you at six fifty five,' I said, 'so you can load your haul straight into your boot.'

Griff smiled. 'Make it seven fifteen and I'll have breakfast ready for you here.' But he didn't budge from the room, so Harvey and I had to say our goodnights like lovesick kids in the hallway.

TWENTY

'Don't think I didn't notice you popping painkillers this morning,' I told Griff as we locked the gates after waving Harvey goodbye. 'And your face looks quite swollen.'

'Just a pang, my love. Nothing a bit of that toothpaste for sensitive teeth won't cure. And how about your pangs, at seeing Harvey depart?'

Just the opening I hoped for. 'Nothing to the pangs at losing my rings,' I said, hooking my hand into his arm and steering him gently back into the warmth of the kitchen.

He stopped short, one foot inside, the other on the step. 'Your rings? The—?'

'Come and have some more coffee and I'll tell you all about it . . .'

When I'd finished, he sat and stared. 'My dear one, have you edited the story to spare my ears? Because if you spoke as assertively as that, without a single expletive, you did extremely well.'

I slammed my fists on the table. 'Just shut the fuck up about my bad language!' I bit my lip. I shouldn't be taking my temper out on him. But I still sounded angry as I continued, 'What matters is that some slimy toad of a policeman has stolen my rings from what's supposed to be a secure area. They've gone. Just like that. And you know what, it's not that I've lost something that worries me. It's – well, I just fancied having my name in the British Museum, after all your dear friend Sir Douggie did to us. It'd be a nice rude gesture that only the three of us would understand.' With a grim smile, I looked at him expecting him to return the smile. But his face stayed miserable, as if he didn't dare move it. 'Come on, that tooth's bad, isn't it? Let me phone the dentist now.'

'Please don't fuss. You know how I hate dentists. Let's give it a couple of days. Please.'

'Till tomorrow. OK?' And then I realized he might be
pale for another reason. If I couldn't bear leaving Griff,
how did he feel about me having a boyfriend who lived so
far away? Tooth apart, had he had any sleep? I kissed the
top of his head. 'Now, you always swear by cloves, don't
you?' I ran my finger along the spice rack; he insisted on
grouping them not in alphabetical order but by the recipes
that needed them. 'Here you are.' I shook a couple into my
palm. 'Pop them in. And I'll make you some soup for lunch
while I wait for a phone call from the police.'

He managed a wan smile. 'A phone call? I'd expect a whole
squad of them round here, all on their bended knees . . .'

Peeling the carrots for his favourite soup (carrot and
coriander, with fresh coriander on top) gave me a bit too
much opportunity to ponder. It was one thing to think I
recognized someone, but quite another to prove it. I knew
from personal experience how damaging false allegations
could be, and one thing that still niggled was that the source
of the rumours was none other than someone who as my
possible grandfather should have done everything to protect
my reputation. However, I didn't owe Dilly Pargetter's
partner anything. On the other hand, I couldn't prove he'd
tailed me aggressively – and if he had it was hardly a crime.
And if I could, where would it get me? A policeman seeing
someone with a reputation for handling stolen goods near
a valuable site: it was almost his duty to warn me off.

But there was something else. He beat his wife – someone
ought to dob him in for that alone. And he'd beaten his
wife when she'd sold me the second ring. That didn't necessarily mean anything. As a child I'd seen that domestic
abuse could be sparked by anything or nothing.

I really needed to chew this over with someone. Since
Griff didn't know about most of my conversations with
Titus, it couldn't be him. Mrs Walker was hardly a good
listener. Morris had made it pretty clear he didn't want to
be involved in my life again, and I liked Penny too much
to argue with that. Actually, I liked her enough to wish I
could talk to her, and not bother Morris.

And then a huge great smile formed on my face. I could talk to Harvey. But Harvey was on the M4, and even though he had a hands-free system, I didn't want to disturb his concentration.

And the smile disappeared. Not because I was worried about his driving. Because he'd never once mentioned that we'd be seeing each other again – let alone when.

A Toby jug featuring Kitchener's face never was going to be a joy to repair. For some reason I've never been turned on one scrap by Toby jugs, and having to touch up the beak of the man who sent all those young men to their deaths brought back all the terrors of my nightmares in broad daylight. I couldn't keep my hand steady.

'Dear one, what's wrong?' Griff asked, bringing me a cup of green tea.

'*Your country needs you!*' I said mockingly. 'Oh, Griff! All the dreadful things he did.'

'My dear, yours, to parody another quotation, is not to wonder why, but simply complete the commission. I've always disapproved of ivory, but that doesn't stop us selling netsuke. And take my word for it, if you don't finish it today, it'll be harder to start on it tomorrow. Ah! The phone! It's certain to be the police, my love.'

I went down to the office more slowly than I ought, but I was trying to gather my thoughts so I could string nice formal sentences. So I was really taken aback to hear my father's voice.

'Lina? That you? Running a bit short of casseroles and things, you know. And I'm quite out of that tea of yours.'

'I'm bang in the middle of a really shitty job—'

'Now, my girl, I can't help agreeing with that old queer of yours – not the sort of expression a young lady should use. So I'll see you this afternoon, shall I? You can bring him too if you like.'

'He's got toothache.'

'Do him good, a bit of fresh air.'

'And the casseroles won't be home-made.'

'Get some frozen ones. Won't tell anyone.'

'Tomorrow morning at the earliest,' I said at last. Griff was right about that jug. If I didn't finish today it'd go right to the back of the queue and offend a valued customer who had at least another thirty of the dratted things on her shelves.

Griff had looked quite cunning as I put the idea to him; at a guess, he saw a chance of dodging the dentist one more day. And he actually cooked a couple of curries and a casserole for my father, so I could get on with the dratted jug. I had no interruptions, either from the police or from Harvey. I didn't care about the one, but was getting quite upset about the other. All the same, I'd always worked on the principle that if you have a lovely day, like the one I had yesterday, you often have to pay for it with a really bad one. So I bit my lip and concentrated on Kitchener's face.

I was just washing my hands before supper when two things happened at once. The phone rang. There was also a knock on the front door. I chose the phone, taking the call in the privacy of the office.

Harvey!

'Darling Lina! I'm so sorry! I haven't had a moment to call you all day. A crash on the M4; meeting; endless lunch; meeting. And someone who really did not like my valuation and tried to tell me – well, you know what they're like, when they think they've got a swan and it's hardly even a goose. Now, tell me about your day.'

It didn't sound any more exciting when I recounted it than it did while I was living it. 'But it'll be fun going over to Bossingham Hall tomorrow,' I said, trying to sound upbeat.

'Bossingham Hall? Rings a bell somewhere.'

I gave him a text book description of the place, without going too much into my personal connections.

'No, it's not its architectural merits,' he mused. 'Something else. It's dancing round the back of my mind . . . But it won't replace you . . .' From that point the conversation was the sort that's nice for the people taking part but either boring or embarrassing for anyone else.

Eventually, hugging a huge smile to me, I wandered into the living room. To find Will Kinnersley occupying the sofa. To be honest he looked no more pleased to see me than I was to see him. But he stood up politely, so I nodded politely. When I sat, he did too.

'This is a strictly unofficial visit, Lina. I'd get into ten types of shit if anyone found out. But I thought you ought to know that the skeleton wasn't that of your body. So you shouldn't be beating yourself up about not doing anything that could have led to the death of whoever it was. Or maybe not his death, since we've still not found his corpse. If you see what I mean.'

I felt dizzy with relief. 'So whose bones were they?'

'Almost certainly a woman's and probably a thousand years old, give or take.' He continued anxiously, 'Not that this should make any difference to your calling in the rubber heel brigade.'

'The what?'

'Well, there are two things you could do. Complain to the IPCC – and their website tells you how to do that. Or you could complain specifically about me or someone to a senior officer, and that's where our own Professional Standards people come in. Though only if there's obvious wrongdoing by someone you can point to.'

'Which isn't you, Will. You don't run the Evidence Store, do you?'

'No, thank the Lord. I can think of only one thing worse – being a custody sergeant on a Friday night.'

'But someone does. And has messed up big time. Or,' I added, more charitably, 'someone has messed up for him. Fancy a coffee?'

'I'm not supposed to be here. Under new guidelines I'm supposed to be chaperoned if I come and see you. Well, not just you. Any female.'

'Griff's in the kitchen. Come on through.'

More painkillers! Caught in the act. But though I gave him a hard look, I didn't say anything. Will updated him while I got the kettle on.

By the time it was boiling, however, Griff had produced some wine. 'Since this isn't an official visit, have a sip.'

'Not on an empty stomach, thanks – especially since I'm driving.'

'The emptiness of the stomach can easily be remedied. I have food here for an army – or more to the point, for Lina's father. I'm sure he can spare some.'

Will looked anguished. I would have done in his position – Griff's chicken dopiaza is to die for.

'Will, you think you came to bring me some news. I think you came because I asked you. You and no one else. There's something the police should know about, and there's no way I'm talking to Winters. OK? I've seen someone who looks remarkably like the body. And the guy in the 4x4 who tailed me.' To cheer him up a bit, I added, 'And it's thanks to those clever computer thingies you showed me. Why don't I call your mobile now, so you have the call on record?' Without waiting for a reply, I speed dialled him. Then stopped. 'Will they be able to tell we were in the same room? Go and drive for ten minutes, just to work up an appetite, and I'll call you . . .'

'And meanwhile,' I added to Griff, 'if you're popping those tablets, no wine for you. At all. I don't want you to wake up and find you're dead. Understand?'

This time when Will arrived, he brought in his laptop. Had he really left it in his car before? What an idiot. And we'd already tried his standard set of mug shots and found no one on it, facial recognition system or no facial recognition system.

He put it on the kitchen table, which Griff was just laying for supper, caught Griff's eye, and took it off again. 'Your office?'

'I wouldn't bother even opening it,' I said flatly. 'The thing is, Will, I'm dead sure he won't be on there. Not unless you can access your Human Resources database. The man I recognized is one of your colleagues. A policeman.'

Griff raised a hand. 'Only she'd better not have said that until after supper, or I'm sure you'll be on the phone to your superior and have to go hungry.'

*　　*　　*

While we ate, Will demolished my theory just as I'd done myself. Even the half glass of wine he allowed himself with the cheese and bikkies didn't shake his conviction that I must be wrong.

'It isn't as if you had a name,' he protested.

'I might just have one, actually. But this is pure speculation, and I don't want to slander anyone. I know how mud sticks, remember.'

Griff said, 'I wonder if this isn't the time to call one of your superiors, Will. An accusation against a fellow officer's a lot for a young man to deal with. Is there someone you can trust? Really trust? No, don't start to bluster. We don't know who this policeman is – he could be your boss, even.'

'Not if she's DCI Webb – it wasn't her,' I said.

Griff tutted: I must have made a grammar mistake. 'It could be *her* boss even,' Griff said. 'If a man has killed once, he can kill twice. And, if she fingers him – I believe that's the correct term? – Lina is likely to be his next target.'

TWENTY-ONE

Will pushed his glass away and sat, elbows on the table, pressing his temples with his fingertips. 'Hang on. There's something weird going on I can't get my head round. Lina sees a body, which disappears. She then sees a live person, who chases her. Finally she sees another live person, and you're afraid this person will now be after her. Forgive me, Griff, but have I missed something?'

'My assumption, of course, is that the body wasn't dead. The media, our only source of information, never made anything of it, as I assume they would have done – unless there was some sort of news blackout? Come to think of it, there's been nothing about Lina's skeleton, either. My deduction, for what it's worth, is that you're trying to protect the archaeological site she says is nearby. Would that be the case, Will?'

'It would. If we had found a body, then things would have had to be done differently. If it's still a crime scene, I don't know why. Maybe someone's just forgotten to take away the tape.'

'So it could be that someone's made a good recovery and has got up and is driving a 4x4 and walking round Police Headquarters . . . I suppose that's what my fog of a mind was trying to work out all along,' I said. 'Or maybe I dimly thought there might be twins. I don't know.' I hung my head in shame. Woolly thinking. Griff had worked so hard on my brain, and this was all he got.

'The thing is, none of us followed it through, Lina,' Will said. 'My case load is so huge I can't see across my in tray – well, you saw, didn't you?'

Now he was contrite, I could be generous. 'Your job is chasing history, Will, not following up present-day cases.'

'Well, actually, Bernie's on sick leave. Some virus.'

'But he must have a boss, the equivalent of DCI Webb. Someone who's in charge of "my" case.' I took a deep breath. 'Do you know an officer called Pargetter?' I caught Griff's eye.

He nodded, wincing as the movement joggled his tooth. Dentist or die tomorrow for him.

Meanwhile, Will was shaking his head emphatically. 'But then,' he conceded, 'I can't know everyone in the service. Do you want me to ask around?'

'Absolutely not. You could find out very discreetly.'

'You might tell me why.'

'I gave you a copy of the receipt for one of those rings.'

'Dilly Pargetter.' His memory made me even more ashamed of my own.

'Her husband beats her. He's a policeman, which might explain why he gets away with it. He beat her after she sold me that ring. Am I making too many connections?'

Will went pale. 'I'm out of my depth here.'

'You and me both. But if it's not your job to chase wife-beating coppers, it's certainly not mine. Especially as I have to get Griff to the dentist first thing in the morning.'

Will took the hint and got up, thanking Griff for the meal. Griff tried to wave away my suggestion, but Will peered at his swollen jaw. 'Abscess, I should think. My dad's a dentist,' he explained with a flicker of a smile. 'I'll be in touch the moment I have anything to report.'

I'd just seen him out when something ambled into my brain. I turned to Griff, slapping my forehead but only very lightly. Just like anyone would, really. 'Pargetter. What if Dilly uses her own name, not her husband's?'

Griff said, 'I'm sure the lad's got plenty of sense. And so have you, my love. I think I must be down in the village when the dentist's surgery opens, don't you?'

To my amazement, the receptionist found a cancellation for Griff. Equally surprising, he emerged, clutching a yellow prescription form, before I'd done more than skim one of the old glossy mags. I wanted to look a little more closely at some of the photos, but that's not exactly why you go to the dentist's. Leaving him in the van, I nipped into the pharmacy. At least I'd get to read the instructions that way – and sure enough, the label on the antibiotic tablets said AVOID ALCOHOL in big red letters. Well, I'd better take notice for him, because I knew he'd manage not to see even a warning like that.

He insisted he was well enough to come to Bossingham Hall with me, probably because he wanted to bask in the glory of having done all the cooking. I took the precaution of taking fizzy water and some elderflower cordial, which can make a nice fake drink. I might even get my father to try some.

Just as we were about to set out – Griff was already in the van – our fax rang and hummed into life, churning out a message from Harvey I quickly pocketed and a sheet with several photos on it. According to the more public part of his message, spurred into action by our conversation, he'd gone hunting in the box full of his great aunt's memorabilia that he'd never quite got round to sorting out properly. He'd found these photos. Each had the letters BH pencilled on the back, with thirty-seven, thirty-eight or thirty-nine alongside, he said. Could these refer to Bossingham Hall?

The quality was very poor – old photos, a dirty scanner and our ageing fax paper. But they turned me hot and cold. Could that little boy with the outsize cricket bat really be my father? I put them in a folder and joined Griff, who forgot to be in pain and shoved his reading glasses on.

'Uh, uh. Driving glasses for you. I need to text Harvey a few questions,' I said. 'Like the name of his great aunt.'

'That's just one,' Griff objected, but he swapped places with me anyway, and drove while I tapped away, losing all sense of time. He stopped at the foot of the track to my father's wing. 'If you want this van up there, you drive,' he said firmly. 'As for me, I'd rather walk, thank you very much.'

Despite the potholes I got there first. Why hadn't Harvey responded to my texts? By now I had the most dreadful feeling I couldn't voice to Griff that maybe the only reason

Harvey had taken me up was my connection with Lord
Elham. He'd sworn he hadn't known I was a divvy, but had
taken me along to a sale; he'd sworn that Bossingham Hall
had only rung a bell. Another man using me. I felt like . . .
But I didn't accelerate as hard as I could and run the van
into the side of the building. I parked as carefully as I
always do, reached out the boxes of food and managed a
mocking smile as Griff eventually joined me.

It turned out that Lord Elham had been watching a TV
programme about antibiotics, and, having checked the name
on Griff's pills absolutely refused to let him so much as
taste any champagne. He might have been watching another
programme too, because he condescended to taste the brew
I'd brought. He didn't add it to the list of essentials I was
to bring next time though.

As usual, he took Griff into his living room, so I could
have a root round. He was happy enough for Griff to see
my spoils, and even value them, but he seemed to like to
keep my little hunts a family matter. Talk about skewed
logic.

Griff turned over the Wedgwood plates I produced, nodding
as I told my father how much champagne they should bring
in.

'Good girl.' Then he dropped his voice, leaning confi-
dentially towards Griff. 'Trustees get a whiff of any of this
stuff, they'll want it, the sniffling weaselly bastards. Look
at the state of that drive – will they put their hands in their
pockets and have it resurfaced? Will they buggery!'

The two chewed over the pothole situation for longer
than I thought possible.

At last, when they'd talked the subject to death, I screwed
up my courage. 'Have you made any progress tracing Nanny
Baird's descendants?' My voice was a bit funny. I hoped
they wouldn't notice.

He pulled a face. 'I've let that slide a bit, to be honest.'
What a surprise. 'What would I say to anyone if those
chappies found them? "Some woman who died sixty years

ago, years before any of you were born, was kind to me, and you lot, to whom she meant not a snap of the fingers, should have some loot." *Some* loot. You mark my words, as soon as they got their paws on *some*, they'd want *more*. And I'm not having that.' He pointed to a brown envelope near the TV zapper. 'That's what I've got so far. Nothing and a big bill. Just a trace of someone in Australia who may be her second cousin. Go on, open it.'

He was right. I was tempted to say nothing about the photos Harvey had sent. On the other hand, Harvey was a living person who would value a memento. Possibly. What would a trinket mean to a man with the latest Beamer? But then, of course, I could hardly describe a Cartier watch as a trinket.

I had a feeling my father was watching me, and when Griff drifted off to the loo he raised a finger. 'Griff's the one with the toothache, but you've got a long face too. Don't think I don't notice these things, Lina, because I do. And don't tell me you're just worried about him, because I can tell you that those antibiotics'll knock that abscess of his on the head, he'll have a nice little root-canal filling and be as right as nine pence within a week.'

Goodness knows what programme he'd been watching. Daytime dentistry? I knew there was a pub channel but I'd never found that.

I managed a smile. 'Where are your reading glasses? I've got something you should look at.' I patted the folder with Harvey's fax.

'Let's see.'

'I was wondering if these were pictures of you,' I said baldly. 'With Nanny Baird.'

'Why on earth should you think that?'

'Right years. And the photos have the letters BH on the back. And they were sent to me by someone who thinks he might have a connection with Bossingham Hall.'

He peered, holding the paper this way and that. 'You'll be telling me I need to get my eyes tested,' he grumbled.

'Griff goes to a very nice lady in Canterbury,' I said, glad of the diversion – I think. 'Do you want me to make you an appointment? We could get you some new leather slippers at that men's outfitters you like. And get you that mobile that takes photos you've been hankering after.'

He picked up the fax and looked again. And then he did something he never did. He took my hand and held it. 'I really can't tell, Lina. But I promise you this. Even if the person who sent this lot turns out to be Nanny Baird's first born son, he's never going to mean to me what you do. Understand?'

Apparently Griff and my father had decided we should stay to lunch. No point in arguing, especially as we'd brought so much. I was just heating some of Griff's wonderful creamy soup when a text arrived for me. Harvey. His great aunt had been a Florence Nugent. But he understood she'd got into trouble, and might even have pretended to be married. No one knew what had happened to the child, assuming it had survived.

Heavens, his thumb must have been getting tired by this point, despite all the abbreviations he'd used and which I expanded when I wrote it all down so my father could read it. I didn't add the lots of love and the kisses.

Before I could respond, another text came through. He'd have the photos digitally enhanced and email the results as and when. That was it.

We'd eaten and I'd washed up. Griff had retired to the loo, so my father was on his own when I told him about the text message. He stared at my handwritten trans . . . transp . . . translation? Near enough, maybe.

'Florence? Flo? Flossie? I've no idea. She was only ever Nanny to me. And I'd have thought she was a bit old for "getting into trouble". It was always tweenies and gatekeepers' daughters who got in the club when I was a kid.' He gave me a lopsided grin. 'At least I had better taste than that with your ma.' He looked at the photos again. 'Digitally enhanced? Does that mean a spot of fakery? Not having that.'

I explained, and promised to print them off and bring

over the results. It was time for us to leave – my father had
a programme he had to watch.

So where was Griff? I went into the hallway and shouted.
No response. My father must have heard the panic in my
voice. Emerging from the living room he strode off towards
the loo. When there was no response to his rattle at the
door, he reached on to the lintel, producing a filthy key.

Griff was standing at the wash basin, staring at his arms
and hands, which were covered in a bright pink rash. 'My
legs are like this too,' he said, in a thin little voice. 'And I
feel very strange. Do you think you could get me home,
sweet one?'

TWENTY-TWO

Our GP dismissed the rash as 'only an allergic re-action', and scribbled a couple of items on a prescription. Then it was back to the dentist's for a yellow prescription for a different antibiotic, which for some reason the GP couldn't prescribe, and then to the chemist's.

Despite all three lots of pills he kept scratching his poor palms, even though there wasn't any rash on them. But at last something seemed to have some effect. Even his face started to go down a little. He looked hopefully at the brandy bottle. I pointed a finger on one of the packs, which had the familiar message, AVOID ALCOHOL. I added, in red felt pen, AND THAT MEANS YOU!

The next day we were due at an antiques fair, just outside Ashford. There was no way I'd let him go, but on the other hand I didn't relish being on my own if accusations about that pendant were going to fly about. I'd written a receipt for it, and a nice covering note to Dilly, as Morris had suggested, printed them off, and binned them. At least if anyone wanted to go to the trouble of scanning the computer, they'd find the original. All the same, I still had that teth-ered goat feeling.

The only solution was to ask Mrs Walker to come with me. I might have offered her a day trip to heaven. Working late tonight to pack what we needed would be no problem. An early start tomorrow would be no problem. A late return would be no problem. The same for Sunday. Bliss!

Griff made a token protest, but Mrs Walker out-talked him. If, and only if, he felt well enough, she declared, than he could always mind the shop. There. So I settled him down in front of the TV with the zapper, a lot of water and a test match in a nice warm dry country for company.

* * *

As Mrs Walker busied herself unpacking and passing me items to place on the display stand, for the first time I had a glimpse of the woman she must once have been – efficient, purposeful, happy. Especially happy. The exercise and the buzz of the place – only two or three large rooms in a soulless modern hotel, not at all exciting for old hands like me – brought colour to her cheeks and brightness to her eyes. She knew the price codes by heart, of course, and had been known to haggle successfully in the shop. In fact, since she didn't keep drifting off to talk to old friends and ending up in the bar, she was a pretty good replacement for Griff. She was imaginative with the lights, too, and told me off in the nicest way for not displaying Dilly's pendant, which I personally wished at the bottom of the nearest bin, at the top of the display cabinet. I moved it.

She was pretty well shooing me off to look round the rest of the rooms, and promising to summon me for help if necessary, when she patted a new, very upmarket mobile phone, every function of which she wanted to show and explain to me. It had taken weeks to find my way about my own phone, so I was punch drunk after half an hour, not to mention amazed at her knowledge. And only then could I go for my prowl.

This was far too lowly an event for someone like Harvey, and probably too far for Habgood to come for what would probably be fairly meagre pickings. But it was just the place where I could buy cheap to sell on at a profit later. And there was Dilly Pargetter setting up in a distant corner.

Yes, of course I should have gone and spoken to her. Asked her about her latest bruises, spoken about her partner. But she was still ferrying in her boxes, now wasn't the moment, especially as the big guy in the hoodie I'd seen with her before was helping her. Shades? On a day as dull as this? Who the hell did he think he was? More to the point, who the hell was he?

The one person who'd know for certain, Titus, might or might not slink into a gig like this, but only when the place was crowded with punters so he could merge. And he'd only talk to people he wanted to talk to.

Mrs Walker was enjoying herself so much I stayed in the background unless we were busy. She recognized and called over customers she knew from the shop, sold them items she picked out especially for them, knowing their tastes, and had our terminal whirring quite happily. One man had clearly come to talk to her; she blushed a most becoming shade of pink. Why wasn't I surprised when, having wrapped a miniature Royal Worcester loving cup, and waved him on his way, she came over to me. 'I was wondering if I might just slip out for a sandwich and cup of coffee? I could bring you something back?'

I was a romantic at heart, of course. 'Take as long as you like,' I said – largely because everyone else seemed to have had the same idea, so the rooms were almost empty. And with her out of the way, Titus might slip over, assuming, of course, that he was here.

If he was, he didn't. But a few new punters drifted in, including a young couple who fell for Dilly's pendant – hook, line and sinker. I wrote a very careful receipt, pressing very hard to give two clear carbon copies, including information I never give, such as the fact I was selling it for another dealer. Neither Pretty Lady, the name Dilly operated under, nor Dilly's own name seemed to mean anything to them. I gave automatic discount for cash – how many people flash five hundred pounds in tenners? – equipped them with one of our pretty boxes for the pendant, and waved them on their way. In a trice, I had one of the two duplicates of the receipt in a jiffy bag, plus the cash. Phew. All I had to do was walk past Dilly and slip the bag into her hand. She took it like one of those relay runners Griff likes watching on TV, without looking but grasping it firmly. And without missing a beat she continued her spiel to the customer worrying about the ethics of a butterfly-wing brooch.

I could have sung and danced my way round the rooms. Twice. All that fuss and it had fizzled out. I was free! Yes! I'd have loved to phone Morris and tell him, but on a Saturday he'd more then likely be at home.

Actually, I'd better get back on duty because Mrs Walker

had taken me at my word, and there was still no sign of her.

Her first words as she eventually bustled back were, 'Next Tuesday. You know it's always a quiet day in the shop. I was wondering if I might close an hour early. Not if it's a problem, of course.'

'Of course it isn't.'

'Only I was hoping I could get my hair done. And sometimes Maureen in the village has slots late in the afternoon.'

I could contain my big grin no longer. 'He's asked you out, hasn't he? That nice guy who always looks so disappointed if he finds me in the shop, not you!'

'Mr Banner. Paul. Lina, do you think it's all right? I mean – oh, there's a customer!'

I headed off. But I had an idea she picked up her new mobile again. Middle-aged love must be as bad as the young version.

It wasn't just one punter, but three, bunched together, trying to pick things up and examine them right at the far end of the stall. They were all men, in their thirties. Often that meant one of them was trying to pocket something. I headed over. But for some reason, Mrs Walker didn't back me up: she was playing with that phone of hers. Perhaps she hadn't worked out how to switch to voicemail. All the same . . . If I took my eyes of this lot, something would disappear. Surely she could tell something was up!

At last, one shoved an ironstone plate I'd always disliked under my nose. 'How much?'

I checked underneath and doubled the price.

'Trade?'

'But you're not trade.'

'And how do you know that? Don't know everything, do you? Why not ask your boss? The old lady? She'd give me discount.'

The others loudly agreed.

'You give me your business card, I give you trade discount.'

Without a word, he put the plate down, and hunched away. So did the others, melting into the crowd.

What was all that about? And where was Mrs Walker? Still pithering with that damned mobile of hers, right the other side of the stall, that's where. In fact, nowhere near the stall. She was talking nineteen to the dozen – did she talk any other way? – to that miniature collector. Paul Banner.

He fished his phone out; they both peered at it; they exchanged smug smiles.

And I had acquired an extra item on their side of the stall. Not just any extra item. A lovely Lowestoft tea bowl. About five hundred pounds' worth, at a glance. I was just about to pick it up to check.

My thought processes always were slow. I knew that. But I could almost feel each clunk as I worked out what had happened. The punters hadn't wanted to buy anything. Well, I knew that. They had wanted to distract me. Yes, I knew that too. But they hadn't wanted to steal, either. They wanted to frame me. And as soon as I picked up that tea bowl, they'd have my prints on it and they'd have me.

And here it came. A bored looking security guard, dragged along by someone I didn't think I recognized. Drat my shaky memory!

'That's mine! She's stolen it! She's stolen it.' He spoke with a local accent.

Before I knew it the Law turned up. Only a Community Support Officer, but the Law. There was total chaos. People milled round the stall as if I was about to give stuff away.

I found my voice. 'I'm happy to answer any questions, officer. But please, get people away from the china. All of it. We're talking hundreds of pounds here. I don't want anything broken.' All the time I kept my hands in the air. I had an idea Mrs Walker was on the phone yet again.

The CSO did his best, I have to admit. And eventually Mrs Walker turned her attention to what she should have been doing in the first place, and her friend Mr Banner joined her. Maybe they'd manage to save the stock.

Before I knew it, I was having a camera thrust into my face. Wonderful. This could really finish Tripp and Townend.

Was I being robbed or framed? Just when I'd thought I

was safe, it was both giant lizards and tigers that were after me, while I was safely staked to the CSO. I only knew one thing. I must not, absolutely must not, touch that tea bowl. In fact, I'd have been really grateful if the CSO had decided to handcuff me. At least our insurance covered us for theft, even if it'd take a bit of doing to explain the circumstances.

Soon a couple of fully fledged police constables turned up. They took in some of the situation at a glance, and herded away the people milling round, leaving the CSO to guard either me or the stall. I couldn't tell which. At least if they arrested me and shoved me in the police car I could draw breath. When and if they started to ask sensible questions, I could try to answer them. Sensibly. Jabbering about being a goat wouldn't work, would it? I thought of Morris, even Will, and the sort of language they'd approve of. I even gave a passing thought to Farfrae: I'd trusted him but he hadn't even responded to my email. My damned lower lip started to wobble. I bit it hard to stop it.

To my surprise the cogs in my head started to move again. If I wasn't under arrest, I could use my phone. Morris? I brought up his numbers, both at home and at work. But either way I didn't want to upset things between him and Penny. And in any case, the pendant wasn't the problem.

So it had better be Will, even though this was nothing to do with ancient artefacts and everything to do with saving my skin.

Voicemail. I managed a bit of a hesitant message.

Griff? Absolutely not. Nor my father.

Harvey? What could he do, long-distance hugs apart?

Seemed I was on my own.

Where had I seen that tea bowl before? I knew it from somewhere. The blue design – the Good Cross Chapel – mocked me, daring me to pick it up. The more I thought about it, the more I suspected I'd not seen it on my morning round. I'd have clocked it as a desirable item even though it was slightly early for us to handle. And who on earth was my accuser? I'd never seen him before either. At a small fair like this you knew everyone, and the sisters, cousins and aunts who regularly helped out.

If I could make only one call, in a situation like this, it wasn't to any of the people I'd thought of before, but to Titus. And hope he'd choose to pick up. Not to mention, when he heard the hubbub in the background, deigning to speak to me at all before he cut the call again.

The last was the biggest if.

I took a deep breath and dialled.

TWENTY-THREE

I should have known better. There was no response. I didn't even bother leaving a message, since the CSO was now paying me a lot more attention.

'Am I under arrest?' I asked.

'Not yet. But I wouldn't advise you to do anything you might regret, miss. Such as running away.'

'And leave hundreds of pounds' worth of my stock behind? Not to mention five hundred pounds' worth of someone else's? I don't think so, officer.' I tacked on the last word to make it sound a bit less insolent.

I'd have sworn his ears pricked, like a dog's. 'You admit it's not yours, miss?'

'I'll go further,' I said, trying to think like Griff. 'I actually insist it's not mine. I've never seen it before in my life, so far as I know. My theory is,' I said, lying in my teeth, 'that a punter saw it on someone else's stall, fancied it, picked it up and just forgot to put it down. And then he panicked, and realized what he'd done, and dumped it here. I'm not saying he wanted me to take the blame. Just that he wanted to be rid of it.' No, I didn't believe a word of it, but it sounded better than claiming I'd been framed, which might just sound para . . . paranormal? Paranoid! 'Why not ask the guy who owns it if he saw anyone lurking? I had three shifty characters over here just a few minutes ago. Someone must have seen them,' I added. If Mrs Walker hadn't still been fiddling with that damned phone of hers, she'd have been able to support me.

One of the constables mooched over. Everything was happening so slowly. Didn't they realize that every minute this was going on, my professional reputation was shrivelling? I tried telling them just that.

'But it's a very serious allegation, miss,' the constable said. 'And I gather it's not the first time, either.'

Talk about that thing Griff talked about, something you'd
already seen. Day-something view. My eyes narrowed. Two
people in the Kent Police with the same idea. Two too many.
'Would you like to tell me what you're talking about?'
'You've handled stolen silver, haven't you?'
'Tell your informant that if I hear that once more I shall
sue. And you'd better check your facts. Here.' I brought up
Morris's home number on my mobile: I told myself a fellow
officer asking questions wasn't the same as me badgering
him. 'Try talking to DI Morris.' I pressed the dial button
and passed it to him. 'He's in the Met,' I added, praying
he wasn't switched to voicemail. 'And make sure you tell
him I managed to sell the pendant and gave the cash to the
person concerned. That's really, really important.'

As soon as he started talking he moved right away from
me so I couldn't listen in. The CSO saw me trying to drift
nearer, and plonked himself between us.

'I told you, I'm not going anywhere – especially without
my mobile. But it'd be nice if you could tear your colleague
away from my assistant—'

'Who?'

'Mrs Walker. The lady with your colleague and another
man.'

'Isn't she the boss?'

'I'm Townend and Tripp's at home with toothache,' I
said. 'What he ought to be doing is checking for the three
yobs. I know there are hardly any CCTV cameras in the
place, but they ought to be on record somewhere.' Trying
not to sound sarcastic – after all, I was the one who needed
to think, and it had taken all this time for the idea to struggle
up from the depths of my brain – I added, 'You might even
see whoever put the tea bowl on my stall. He seems to have
disappeared, doesn't he?'

He stared. 'You're serious, aren't you?'

'Dead serious. Especially about the fact he's vanished
without trace.'

The other young man looked almost relieved to be
summoned. Mrs Walker stuck to him for a while, but Mr
Banner held her back.

Before Constable Two reached us, however, Constable One returned, my phone in his hand. He might have been chewing on a very sour lime.

'So who do you think's responsible for all this?' he asked.

I held out my hand for the mobile. 'I gather DI Morris convinced you that I was more likely to be innocent than not?'

'He said something about someone trying to incriminate you.'

'Yes. I've got there. But who and why? And more to the point,' I added, looking at the people still looking sideways at me and whispering behind their hands, 'what are you going to tell that lot?'

They agreed to go with the theory I'd spun them – that someone wanted to buy the bowl, and put it down absentmindedly in the wrong place, then panicked and accused me. They made an official announcement over a husky PA system and put out flyers saying that I was absolutely innocent. So far so good. But there was a lot more to find out, as I pointed out to Constable Two – the other and the CSO had disappeared, with the tea bowl in an evidence bag – over a cup of really evil coffee. I insisted we drank it in front of my stall, and asked him to smile a lot for the benefit of any punters who might still have doubts. He obliged. When he did, he looked quite nice, despite the close-cropped hair that made him look as if he could head butt me as soon as blink. He'd be about thirty and his name was Steve – but never Chalky – White.

'We'll run through the CCTV – it's a pretty poor system,' he said. 'But I gather your boss – I mean, your assistant – has some useful photos on her phone. They don't put you automatically in the clear, but do confirm what you said about the yobs. And there's a picture of you at the stall which doesn't seem to show the bowl, although we need to have it digitally enhanced to make sure. And another with the bowl in place. She told us all about how she'd taken them, and how she'd sent them to Mr Banner, just to make sure.'

Any other time, I'd have cracked a joke about her – the young man was certainly inviting me to – but it seemed that all the time I'd thought she was letting me down she was saving my bacon. 'Do you think she'll make a good witness?' I said, as a compromise, but also as a nudge back to the fact we were dealing with a serious matter.

'You think it'll come to that?'

'I certainly hope so. You see, I think your colleagues will find something interesting when they examine that bowl. Or rather, not find. They won't find my prints, for a start. I made sure I never touched it. And I'd be surprised if they find a price label. Because I don't think that it came off any of the stalls here. I'd have noticed something like that. I think the idea of accusing me of stealing another item fell flat, so they had to rush in with another one.'

'That'd be the pendant your friend DI Morris was talking about. The one you said you'd sold and given the money to the rightful owner.'

'Right. Here's the receipt. As you can see, it's a bit more detailed than you might expect. Belt and braces.'

Steve looked at me with narrowed eyes, but more as if he was sympathizing with me than accusing me. 'And hands in pockets, I'd say. So the person I have to speak to is whoever runs Pretty Lady. No? What have I said?'

The obvious, really. 'Just make sure no one else is around when you do. I think her husband beats her . . .'

'I'll get a woman colleague on to it. Very discreetly. What's her name?'

'Dilly Pargetter. But she specializes in jewellery, not china.' My protest was feeble. I wanted it to be overridden.

'Which makes it all the more likely that if she or anyone else connected with her planted that bowl, it was a deliberate act. And if it wasn't one of her contacts, it puts her in the clear.'

I took several deep breaths, not because I was afraid of going wild with my fists, but because I was looking for a bit of bravery lurking somewhere inside. 'What if I had a word and got her to – well, come to you people and confess? If there's anything to confess, of course.'

'Can you fix it so I can overhear?'

I shook my head. 'Seems too much like spying. I'm not

a cop, remember. Just an acquaintance. In any case, the usual place women for women to have their heart to hearts is the ladies' loo.'

Josie, the woman who had the stall next to Dilly's, and who dealt with any would-be customers, was an old friend of mine. Each time I saw her she'd shrunk a little more; each time she insisted that this was her last fair. Frowning, she said she'd not seen Dilly for half an hour or more, when she slipped off to get a coffee. As far as she knew she'd gone on her own.

'And with that husband of hers, she wouldn't dare do anything different. Great thug. Poor child pretends she's walked into doors or fallen down the stairs. I tell her, get the law on him. But then, he is the law, isn't he?'

'I've never met him,' I said. 'What's he like?'

'A total sweetie, you'd think. Butter wouldn't melt. And can he turn on the charm? He'd have all the ducks off the water before you can say orange sauce. You can see why she won't leave him.'

'Has she tried?'

'Three or four times. But she always goes back. They do, you know.'

'But she should report him to the police—'

'D'you suppose they'd take any notice? Look after their own, don't they? Now, where's young Griff . . .'

I explained, trying not to upset her by edging away too quickly. But at last I came straight out with it. 'I'm worried about Dilly, you know. I'll go and have a look for her. And if he's hurt her, I might just dob in PC Pargetter myself.'

'PC . . . Oh, you mean the inspector. And he's not called Pargetter. She's really Mrs . . . now what is it? Mrs Mason, that's it. And you want to be careful not to make things worse, luvvie. He's a big bloke.'

So he was big. 'Does he have a hoodie and pair of shades in his wardrobe?'

'Not exactly in his wardrobe, silly – not when he's wearing them!'

*   *   *

There was no sign of anyone in the rather overblown ladies' cloakroom, which had gone wild with a rose motif – wallpaper, carpet, even the tissues and hand towels. But one of the doors was shut. Shut but not locked from inside. Not that I could budge it much. And then I realized one of the huge pink roses was redder than it should have been.

Jabbing 999 on my mobile, I ran outside and screamed for help. The emergency switchboard responded more quickly than the people milling round – perhaps they thought I'd cried wolf earlier. When at last people started to take notice, Steve was the first to come running. I dodged back inside. There were no gaps under the cubicle walls I could crawl under, and I was too short to see over the walls, let alone scale them. All the time the blood stained the roses more deeply.

It seemed hours before they came, but soon the room was full of emergency workers, and for once I was happy to be jostled to the back. In fact, I actually retreated, quite fast, to use my phone. 'Will? What does the name Mason mean to you? Inspector Mason? Because some time soon someone's going to tell him his wife's badly hurt. Only it might not be news to him, if you see what I mean.'

'Slow down, Lina. I need to get this right. OK?' Little by little Will extracted the information he needed. Soon I was talking to his boss, DCI Webb.

'Is there any way,' I asked, 'that I can see his photo before anyone tells him about his wife?'

'He's not rostered for this weekend. He could be anywhere. But I can get a car over to collect you so you can look at his photo on file.'

'I've had your people crawling all over my stand this afternoon.' I explained. 'My reputation's in shreds.'

'You've lost the immortal part of yourself, have you?'

It was only because of Griff's evenings with me reading plays aloud that I dimly recognized the quotation. There was something else, about being bestial, but I couldn't recall it accurately. I just said, 'I can't go whizzing off in another police car. I won't have a business left.'

'OK. I'll come out myself. If this Dilly's been assaulted,

then there'll be a police presence anyway. And I'll be in plain clothes. It's very unfortunate that it had to be you that found her. Actually I bet there's a nice fat rumour around that it's you who did it.'

'That's not funny,' I said.

'It's not a joke.'

TWENTY-FOUR

I looked at the photo DCI Webb laid on the display cabinet in front of me.

Wearing a fleece and jeans, she'd arrived as unobtrusively as a woman with her hair could be expected to arrive, and had done an impressively slow circuit, as if she was a genuine punter checking out each stall. She'd come to a halt in front of my stall, and was pretending to be attracted by a piece of Crown Derby that clashed something shocking with that hair. At least, I hoped she really was only pretending. It was a very vulgar piece.

'The face in that photo could well be the face of the man I thought was lying dead in that field, and then thought was tailgating me,' I said slowly. 'But I suppose it's not against the law to lie in a field or to chase a slo-mo motorist. Beating your wife's a different matter though. Allegedly beating,' I corrected myself before DCI Webb could open her mouth. 'Or are you saying she injured herself? Whichever, there was an awful lot of blood,' I mused.

A frown appeared between her eyebrows – she'd done her best to tone down the orange with a brown pencil. The shutters came down. DCI Webb was not an officer I could pump, was she?

'If you want someone to pack away her stall, I'd suggest Josie, that tiny woman who's next to her. Everyone knows she's as honest as the day. She'll be a mine of information too.' I added bitterly, 'This time I'm not offering my own services.'

Nodding, she didn't even need to make a note. 'It'll have to be done under supervision, because we'll want to make a list of every single item on the stall. I'll get one of the uniform lads to have a word with her.' A quick mobile call and she focused on me again. 'DI Morris tells me you're in a very awkward position, Ms Townend.'

I was impressed: there was no need to correct her this time. I smiled. 'Lina. Short for Evelina. Those rings have brought nothing but bad luck, Ms Webb – if I believed in such a thing. But I'm not superstitious. I'm not very bright, and I've no education worth speaking of, but I can see humans at work here, not chance. Someone wants to destroy my reputation, and that way destroy my business – which took my partner years to build up.'

Webb was staring at me. 'Sit down. You need a coffee.' She looked over her shoulder as a genuine punter drifted closer. 'Don't you have an assistant?'

'Yes. She's a witness. She's busy talking to one of your colleagues about the strange appearance of a tea bowl on my stand.'

'Ah, that witness. OK, I'll come back and think about this,' she added loudly, touching the Derby and drifting away.

'No Griff?' It was one of our regulars, who collected spectacle cases. She looked at me more closely. 'Are you sure you're all right, Lina?'

'A bit shaken. Someone was ill in the loo. I found her.'

'I can see that would explain the ambulance but why all those police?'

'Another incident.' But that wasn't good enough for someone who'd spent so much money with us. She deserved the truth. 'You'll hear soon enough. Someone accused me of nicking a bit of china and trying to sell it.'

'You're joking! They should have tried accusing someone else – everyone knows you're as honest as the day, you and Griff.' Suddenly she stopped talking and gathered me up in a big hug. As she let me go, she added, 'And so I shall tell anyone who says different. Now, I was looking for a little something for a sixtieth birthday present . . .'

I phoned Griff to say I'd be late home because I'd been the one who'd found Dilly and the police wanted to take a statement. I was a bit vague about the timescale so he wouldn't start asking questions. As for things I might want to ask him, they could wait.

Since Mrs Walker was still presumably bending the ears
of her interviewers, I packed away myself. It was hard,
because I was still trembling, despite Webb's strong coffee,
or perhaps because of it. She hadn't managed to find a
better brew, but maybe it was she who produced a welcome
sight – Will Kinnersley, who appeared by my side as I knelt
by one of our plastic crates.

'Here, leave that to me,' he said, grabbing a pretty Spode
plate as it slipped from my shaking hand.

'Thanks.'

'I thought you could leave stuff *in situ*. Plenty of security guards, after all.'

'I want to make sure the best stuff's safe with me. And
I want to make sure I get my stuff and not someone else's.'

'Yes. I heard. At least the lads did their best to put that
right.' He pointed to a flyer someone had trodden on.

'What's the news of Dilly?'

'Not too good. Intensive care.'

I sat back on my heels. 'Did she self-harm or was someone
else involved?'

He didn't answer; perhaps he didn't need to. He looked
at me with narrowed eyes. 'I heard about that business with
the pendant, too. And the call to Morris. It was he who got
on to me, actually. He says you need looking after.'

In the police or the personal sense? 'Did he, now?'

'He didn't have time to explain – I gather his baby wanted
to use the phone too.'

I managed a smile. 'There, I think that's all. The rest can
stay put.'

He put out a hand to yank me to my feet. There was a
long silence, then he said, all of a rush. 'There's a warrant
out for Chris Mason.'

'For wife beating? Or whatever the legal term is? And
anything else?'

'I can't tell you any more than that.'

'Where does he work?' I asked, trying to sound innocent, but obviously not succeeding.

'He's in CID.'

I had another try. 'You didn't answer my question about

Dilly. If she dies, will you be – how do they out it on TV
– looking for anyone else in connection with her death?'

'I'm just an artefacts man – I'm not involved in the
enquiry.'

I might have smashed him over the head with a willow
pattern plate if DCI Webb hadn't arrived. 'You might want
to look at some CCTV pictures,' she said.

'I thought you were here in connection with the Dilly
business,' I replied. 'And the not-body in the field.'

'Female multitasking,' she said with a smile that looked
friendly. 'Let's get your things out of here, then security
will take over here in the hall.' She even picked up the box
I'd packed. Will took our computer terminal, and I had my
bag, an arrangement that felt all wrong. 'I suggest these
stay with you until someone can bring your van round.'

'What about Mrs Walker? Though maybe she should see
the CCTV footage.'

'She's already given us a great deal of help,' Webb said.
'And I've suggested that Mr Banner takes her home. This
way, please.'

She led us to the back of the hotel, where, in a pokey
little room, someone had set up a few chairs and a video
player. 'What I propose is that I run the sets of CCTV
footage without comment. You should interrupt if you see
anything useful. Will, can you find a pot of tea? I can't
stand any more of that vile brew pretending to be coffee.
Unless you'd rather he didn't sit in?' she added, as he left.

'Fine by me. Does it mean all this ties in with his heritage
work?'

'It means I think you could do with some company.'

'Is there any news of his friend, by the way? Colleague.
Whatever. Bernie Winters. Will said he wasn't well.'

'Bernie Winters?'

'I'm not winding you up. He's got a proper name, only
it's gone.' I pressed fingers to my head as if to massage my
brain into action. At this point Will came in with a tea tray.
Alongside some really unforgivable crock mugs was a pot
of thick brown tea. Fortunately there was also a jug of hot
water so I made myself some green tea with one of the

bags I always had with me so there'd be no excuse for Griff
to fall off the wagon. It also made me feel as if Griff wasn't
so far away.

Webb turned away to take a call.

'Will,' I began, 'that guy Winters – the one who interviewed
me.' Griff would have spotted that as a . . . a yew-something
or other. Something ending with *ism*?

Will grinned. 'He doesn't always lose it like that, Lina.'

'I should hope not. I was just wondering how he was.'

'Still off sick. Do you want me to send him your love?'

'Hardly. He just seemed – unbalanced? As well as looking
sick.'

'Where's this going?' He wasn't grinning any more.

'OK,' Webb said, so I didn't have to respond. 'To work.
This footage here.'

Had they already looked through it? Were they trying to
make me incriminate myself? I was so proud of myself for
getting the word right first time that I didn't realize that
this time the mobile phone singing away was mine.

Blushing, I checked. 'I'd like to take this, if you don't
mind.' I stepped outside. 'Harvey?'

'Darling, are you all right? You sound a little rattled.'

Darling! But then, I was used to Griff's thespian friends
who used the word all the time. 'It's been a bad day. Oh,
an antiques fair near Ashford. Someone tried to top herself
and I found her. And there was another problem, involving
me and a stolen bowl.'

'In that case, I'm on my way. I should be with you by
midnight if I put my foot down.'

I glowed. But then I had to say, 'You don't know how
much I'd love to see you. But I'm on duty here tomorrow at
this fair. Griff's poorly and I couldn't ask Mrs Walker—'

'Indeed not. But if it's just one day – surely you could
just pack up and forget it.'

'It's not as simple as that. If people see me scuttle off,
they'll believe the allegations. It could ruin our business.
So I have to be here, whether I want to or not.'

'But—'

'Please don't try to persuade me, Harvey. I'd give my

teeth to see you, but I just must be here. And now the police want to talk to me,' I lied, so he wouldn't hear the tears in my voice. 'I must go.'

If Webb noticed how upset I was, she said nothing.

The footage was as grainy and jerky as you'd expect, but it didn't take me long to see someone I'd love to have identified. 'There. That guy in the hoodie and shades. He was helping Dilly set up. There you are – he's got a box of her stuff.'

Will stopped the tape. 'Why does he look away from the camera each time he passes one?'

'Because he knows exactly where each one is,' I said tartly. 'Hell, what a crude system. Ours is far more sophisticated than this. Better definition cameras and some that you wouldn't know were there.' I stopped grumbling and asked, 'But how does he know where each one is? Has be been here before?' And then something else occurred to me. 'I take it Dilly's too ill to ask who her muscle is? Oh, dear. But Josie suggested it was none other than her husband. I'm sure she'd confirm it. Question mark shaped lady,' I added, but Webb didn't look as if she needed the prompt.

'I'll get on to it.' At least, she must have got a minion on to it, because she was back in the room in a flash, gesturing Will to press on.

People came and went, people I knew well by sight and others I wouldn't know from Adam. I had to shake my head. 'Sorry. Nothing.'

'Plenty of other footage. On you go, Will. What about the room Lina was in?'

I thought I might have glimpsed Titus, but couldn't be sure, because Titus always managed to look so ordinary and behave so naturally there was nothing to latch on to. But there were some genuine punters who'd stopped at my stall, which was unfortunately out of shot. At last I pointed. 'Those three men. They were part of the bowl scam. Look, they're heading out of the picture now. And while they were talking, someone slipped the bowl on the stall the far end.'

'As Mrs Walker's photos confirm,' Webb agreed.

'And soon after someone came charging over and said it was his. Middle-aged. Thickset. Accent from round here. If only we could find him and you could get a still to Josie. Yes . . . no . . . Yes! There. The man with his hands in his pockets.'

Will froze the frame. 'We can get that printed off, ma'am.'

'God, in a broom cupboard like this, I'm Freya. And to you, too, Lina. Yes, we need that. Lina? Are you all right?'

'Shhh. Just a minute.' I sat with my eyes closed. I saw dogs and beeswaxed oak. 'I know where I've seen the bowl before. Before you ask, it's only just come to me because I see a lot of bowls, and you forget where . . . But I know where I saw that one. Mattock Farm. It's not far from Dover. It belongs to a couple called Broad-Ticeman. They wanted me to handle it,' I breathed. 'She kept stopping beside gorgeous items and willing me to pick them up. And there was a camera on every single one.'

'Did you touch any of them?' Freya asked quickly.

'Normally I would have.'

'But not this time?'

I shook my head. 'There was something wrong with the whole visit.' I explained. 'But that didn't stop them trying, did it? All I had to do was pick it up when it appeared on my stall and bingo, prints and DNA all over it.'

'Have the Broad-Ticemans any reason to bear you a grudge?'

'Heavens, no. He's a big international fine art dealer, way, way out of our league. I've never even met him. Just his wife, who was really nice to me when we first met. But the second time I saw her she treated me like a leper. No reason for either.'

'Look at the man again. Are you sure you don't know him?'

'Sure. If he was a genuine stall holder, his details would be kept on record, wouldn't they? By the organizers? And by the hotel?'

'So I'll show them this frame too.'

'Slow down, Will. You're Heritage Man. Anyone can do the day-to-day routine. You're only here to keep us company, remember? Now, one more set of CCTV footage to look at, and you two can push off.'

I waved Will goodnight – for some reason neither of us suggested a meal together might be nice, not in the future but there and then – and set off for home. It was only a step, or I might have gone for our emergency option, staying for the night at the hotel. We always carried emergency bags in case of winter weather or a breakdown. Unfortunately my pack didn't include Tim the Bear or Griff, so home it was. At least Mr Banner was dealing with Mrs Walker, so I didn't have to deal with her chatter.

I drove slowly, something fluttering round my brain. It wouldn't get close enough to the surface to be called an idea, however – it just niggled away like Griff's tooth must have done, before it went really bad. The thought of him sitting there worrying brought my foot harder on to the accelerator, and it wasn't long before I was in his arms being fussed and given a reviving glass of wine.

TWENTY-FIVE

A t some time after two, or it might have been three, in the morning, Tim the Bear sighed and said the best chance I had of ever getting to sleep was to make a list of the things going round my mind. When I'd got to the end, I should fasten the pad with a rubber band, tuck the pencil in it, and put them both at the bottom of a drawer. Where he'd got that from, I don't know, but it sounded very much like what my therapist once said.

Griff. (Yes, I underlined the heading.) I was worried about him. Definitely. But his face was much less swollen and the itching bearable. He'd taken his book to the shop, had a couple of sales, and was now sleeping deeply – occasionally I'd catch the sound of his snores.

Me. Who would hate me enough to persecute me like this? Goodness knows I'd hurt and offended enough people when I was younger, but not the sort of person who could go in for subtle revenge – they've have been much more likely to use their fists. The only people I could think of were the dodgy ex-boyfriend, now stuck out in the Falklands, and Lady Petronella Cordingly. She was now in jail, and hadn't liked me much before. But was either of them in a position to hurt me?

Tim looked at me unblinking. I wasn't getting very far, was I?

Arthur Habgood. He'd been spreading gossip about me, enough to come to the ears of the police, and I still couldn't understand how a man claiming me as flesh and blood should want to spoil my reputation, especially as he'd no doubt want to involve me in his crumby little business if he could prove we were related. The seedy man at today's fair had spread it, too; at least if the police ever ran him to earth they could ask him for me.

Bernie Winters. He'd sounded really vindictive when he'd

thought I was involved with night hawks. And <u>Sir Douglas Nelson</u> had looked at me in much the same way as <u>Mrs Broad-Ticeman</u> had, second time round. (All this underlining made it look very official.) Griff and he were supposed to be friends, so perhaps he didn't approve of me for that reason and wanted to separate us. Except something niggled, didn't it, Tim? Griff had called him Dear Douglas, but had been very vague about their relationship. *We've known each other forever*, he'd said, when I asked. So could this really be just an attempt to separate me from Griff? I didn't think so. On the other hand, someone else, apart from Habgood, that is, had tried to split Griff and me up. <u>Harvey.</u> What if all Harvey's sweet words had been another way of separating us? No, I couldn't go there, not yet.

I tried another tack. <u>When did all this start?</u> When I found the body? Or when I found one ring and bought another? Or when we showed the rings to someone – that was the first time the police got interested, and when the rings went into police hands. From where they had now disappeared.

At one point Griff had said that anyone attacking me attacked him.

I put the pencil down and stared at Tim, who solemnly held my gaze.

Could that really be what was happening? Did it all start with Sir Douggie and Griff? Really? We'd have to have a very long conversation tomorrow.

I stowed the pad, as I'd been told, at the bottom of a drawer. It joined the photo of my grandmother. Had Harvey sent those digitally enhanced photos through yet? I'd never even looked in the office when I'd got home, let alone switched on the computer and checked my emails – I knew Griff wouldn't have opened anything addressed to me from Harvey. If I tiptoed down I might not wake him. In any case, the biscuit tin was calling pretty loudly and might wake him if I didn't open it.

The photos looked pretty good, but if I printed them off tonight – this morning – the noise of the printer might well interrupt those snores. So I saved them and headed for the kitchen. Milk and biscuits. Chocolate ones. And the big *Times*

crossword. No, not the proper one. The easy one. Griff and
I usually made a point of doing it together every Saturday
evening, but the grid was still blank. Would he mind if I put
in the word CAUTION, which must be the answer to seven
down? Ten down might be BULLDOG. I munched, the noise
amazingly loud, and sipped and pencilled in. And then I found
my head nodding hard enough to hit the table. Tim the Bear
would be really fed up if I went to sleep down here.

As I tiptoed back upstairs, I heard the sound of a car
slowing to a halt by our cottage. In a village like this, with
no street lights and very little traffic, the noise was alarming.
I might tell myself that if anyone approached the house,
they'd have their photo taken; if they tried to get in, first
there'd be another mugshot, then a seriously loud alarm. But
what if someone threw a petrol bomb? They'd tried a lot of
other things, but that might just get us if the thatch caught.

I switched on the security monitor, and toggled round till
I found what I was looking for. The car was parked right
outside our door, with the lights off. There was someone
inside, but whoever it was simply hunched down in the driver's
seat, only moving in the way you would if you were trying
to get your head comfortable. On the other hand, in a car
like that it'd be a damned sight easier than in our van. A
car like that? The car outside was a BMW. Harvey's BMW!

He'd ignored my protests and driven all that way to see
me. To stop me going to the fair? Well, he wouldn't manage
that, would he? Cold and forlorn as he looked, Harvey had
just moved himself up to be number one suspect.

Maybe.

On the other hand, he might just have driven all that way
just to see me. Full stop.

'Lina! Ah, there you are – oh! I do beg your pardon.'

Gorgeous in his dressing gown, Griff had burst into the
living room, flinging open curtains, singing cheerful songs
and generally being the sort of damn nuisance anyone would
be rousing you when you'd had about three hours' sleep but
knew they were right to disturb you since you had to be
showered, changed and on the road in half an hour flat.

It wasn't just me he was waking, however. I'd had to fetch Harvey in, hadn't I? And feed him biscuits and a glass of one of Griff's single malts? Had to. We'd snuggled up romantically together on the sofa, and managed to ignore Griff's clock striking every hour by falling deeply asleep in each other's arms. Harvey kept rubbing his neck, and I had pins and needles in both arms and both feet. The bloody clock struck nine.

Griff put on an expression of suppressed urgency. 'Harvey, you will find a spare razor in the bathroom. Pull the red cord to switch on the shower, which is set at a moderate temperature. And are you an English breakfast man?'

'Toast and black coffee, please. My bag's in the car.'

Griff waited till he'd gone out and come back in again, taking the stairs – riskily – two at a time before he turned to me. 'And might I ask—?'

'Ask away. I couldn't sleep. I couldn't manage the cross-word without you. I found him asleep in his car. And toast and tea for me, please.'

As I came down, showered and dressed, I could hear Harvey giving his version of last night's events. 'I tried to persuade her to abandon the fair and take some time out. OK, time out with me. But when she said that doing that might ruin your business – and on reflection I had to agree with her—'

Griff nodded. '*He that filches from me my good name robs me of that which not enriches him, and makes me poor indeed . . .*'

I'd have to introduce him to Freya Webb.

'Exactly! So I decided to come up anyway and join her on her stand. That's if she'll have me, and you'll agree,' Harvey added, suddenly a good deal less assured.

What sort of face was Griff pulling? He was very good at pretending to be a Victorian father, but we'd agreed that interrogating each other about our love lives was forbidden.

'You mean, you hope by the simple fact of your presence to redeem her reputation in the eyes of the *cognoscenti*?'

'I wouldn't presume . . . I just thought that it might be nice for her to have someone to stand shoulder to shoulder with if you were still unwell.' He sounded much shiftier than he had earlier this morning.

'She has Mrs Walker.'

I'd have liked to hang around to hear how the conversation progressed, but didn't have time. 'And Mrs Walker has Mr Banner,' I said, 'and could have prevented some of yesterday's problems if she'd been more concerned with preventing what went on than recording it on her phone.'

'But the phone evidence might be crucial,' Griff began.

'It might not have been necessary if she'd stopped whoever it was dumping the Broad-Ticeman's tea bowl on our stall in the first place.' On three hours' sleep I didn't feel forgiving. 'Sure, it's nice to have the incident on CCTV, but all those people heard his accusations! And he couldn't have made them if he hadn't put the bowl down.'

'Are we talking about a sacking offence, my love?'

'Of course not. Once she's over the first throes of love she'll be fine.'

Harvey gave a crack of laughter. 'You sound as if your ages were reversed.'

I sent him a smile over my toast, irritating Griff by catching the crumbs on my hand, not on a plate. 'She's actually a terrific worker—'

'But can talk the hind legs off a donkey, as I recall. I shall try to be discreet and silent. If you're not too unhappy with the situation, Griff?' He put his plate back on the table and downed his coffee.

Griff gave a reluctant smile. 'Your presence will not go unremarked by those who know about the trade.'

'May I take that as a yes? And Lina, we might talk about the Broad-Ticemans as we go. Your van or my car?'

'The stuff's still locked in my van. Give me two minutes to print off the photos you sent. We may have to pay a visit to my father on the way back, Griff.'

'I shall delay supper until your safe return,' he said, with a bow.

But the old bugger had done it again, hadn't he? He'd ensured I was chaperoned for the evening.

TWENTY-SIX

I n not much more than the time it had taken Harvey to shave and shower, I'd enlarged the photos as much as I could and printed them off in highest definition. They were now in a folder, ready to show my father. But was I introducing Harvey to him just as a possible heir to Nanny Baird, or as my current squeeze? That sounded horribly as if I might be asking for his approval, which was something I wouldn't even ask Griff for.

Once I was in the van I felt shy. Curling up with a man not because we couldn't keep our hands off each other but because we couldn't keep our eyes open was one thing; facing him with Griff as an interested spectator had been quite another. And now having to talk to him about everyday things was different again.

'Tell me about Arthur Habgood,' I said, all businesslike, waving to Griff as he locked the yard gates behind us.

'And how nice it is to see you, too,' he said, leaning over to stroke my hair, still damp from the shower. 'Have your feet got warm yet? I must say, I've never seen slippers like those you were wearing last night.'

They were like baby pink Ugg boots, with a fringe of fleece where the tops met the soles and another fringe like a cuff. 'A Christmas present from Griff. He said they were ironic. I don't understand the irony myself. They're very cosy, although I suppose they do make my feet look like giant paws.'

'Therein lies the irony, I fancy. But they weren't doing their job very well.'

'That's because I spent about four hours roaming round while they sat beside my bed. Didn't even think to put my dressing gown on. I was a bit stressed, to be honest.'

'You don't say. So what's the first worry I can help get rid of?'

I took a big breath and plunged in. 'I don't know that you can get rid of it. But you might help me understand something. Why should Arthur Habgood be so vic . . . vin . . . vindictive? How well do you know him? He's based in Cullompton, after all, not so far from you.'

'Sure. We run into each other at house sales. But as you know, we're not competing for the same lots, which is fortunate, because he really does not like being outbid. He bears grudges. If anyone annoys him, he bad-mouths them. A while back he was saying all sorts of unpleasant things about a woman who'd rejected him. When someone ran into his van—'

So he had form. Was that reassuring? 'Does he accuse everyone who crosses him of handling stolen goods?'

'No, because they're not all libelled – or near enough – in the trade press. That Cordingly woman did you a lot of harm. Tried to,' he added hurriedly. 'Not as much as she came to herself, of course. But people and their friends have long memories.'

'Are you saying that this hate campaign is down to her?'

'I wish I knew.'

'You're taking a hell of a gamble to be seen with me,' I said bluntly.

He touched my hair again. 'Your reputation has possibly taken a knock at the bottom end of the market – the sort of fair we're going to now, amongst people who will think there's no smoke without fire. But believe me, amongst people wanting restoration of the highest order done, your reputation's embarrassingly good. Not just for your skill, but for your probity.'

That sounded a really good word. Did I dare ask him what it meant? Why not? He might as well learn about my problem sooner rather than later, and preferably from me. 'Harvey, you may not know about my childhood. After my mother had died, that is. I ran wild. Had so many foster parents I lost count. More schools than I can remember. And very little education. Griff's done his best.'

'And a very good best it is,' he said obligingly.

'Well, it might be now, because he's taught me as much

as he can about everything from music to cooking and books. But my memory for a lot of things is still poorer than I like. My vocabulary's so bad I actually have a book to write long and unusual words in to help me memorize them. And I'm afraid that one isn't in it. Could you repeat it and spell it so at least I can try to remember it, even if I can't write it down just yet.'

More embarrassed than I was, I think, he did as I asked. 'And it means?'

He explained. Then he said, 'To hear you no one would know you were an autodidact . . . That's—'

'I know that one! But I told you, I'm not self-taught so much as Griff-taught. And it was he who taught me my . . . probity. How to be . . . I don't suppose there's a describing word, an adj-whatever-it-is, from probity? Probous?'

He put his head back and laughed. 'If there is, I don't know it. And I was educated at Eton and Oxford. Lina, do you tell everyone so much about yourself?'

'Only people I like and trust. I don't want them to like me on false pretences. My false pretences, not theirs, I mean. You're taking a risk for me. I'm taking a risk trusting you with all this. *Quid pro quo,*' I ended triumphantly.

'You see that lay-by there? Just pull over, will you?'

I did as he asked. 'Why?'

'Because, darling Lina, since nine o'clock this morning I've wanted to kiss you, and I can wait no longer.'

There was a lot of police activity round the hotel, and when I found the ladies' loos still cordoned off I drew the logical conclusion – whatever injury poor Dilly had suffered it was probably not self-inflicted. As if I'd ever believed it might have been . . .

Harvey put his arm round me and pulled me close, dropping a comforting kiss on my head. 'It's about time the police updated you,' he said, as we made our way to the Tripp and Townend display.

As if on cue, Freya Webb bounded over, stopping short as she saw Harvey. I introduced them formally. 'Harvey thought that after my name was so impugned yesterday,

I might need some support,' I added, my chin raised a little. I was quite pleased to have remembered that nice word *impugned*, too.

He nodded. 'Accusations like that can ruin the purest reputation. It's an honour to stand shoulder to shoulder with her.'

She looked as if she suspected that more than shoulders were involved, but smiled. While Harvey looked at all the pieces for sale, nodding occasionally to himself, I asked, 'What's the latest on Dilly? Not to mention Chris Mason?'

'They're still hoping she'll make it. But she lost a lost of blood, as you saw.'

'Is selling a ring enough to make anyone want to kill someone? Let alone your wife?'

'As I'm sure your aware, domestic violence doesn't operate on the level of logic. Could I just ask you to explain that business of the pendant once more?'

'Might have been p . . . paranoia on my part. But I was worried about the secrecy she wanted. A lot of deals are confidential.' I flicked a smile at Harvey. 'But this was secretive. And involved cash and no receipts. That isn't how Griff and I function. Ever. Absolutely everything we do is logged.' X's contributions apart, of course. 'That's why I asked DI Morris for advice.'

'So you really expected someone to frame you?'

'Yes. So although the tea bowl business was a shock, it wasn't a surprise. If you see what I mean.' I added, for Harvey's benefit, 'Lowestoft, Good Cross Chapel. And I'd seen it before, at the Broad-Ticemans' place. Or its twin.' I'd never even thought of that. My poor blancmange brain! 'There must be others floating round in fairs like this. Bloody things. And why on earth should the B-Ts be in cahoots with Mason?'

She blinked. 'They needn't be. They could have simply had the same devious idea.'

'Bit of a coincidence,' I muttered.

'So you suspected it was a plant,' Freya said, making a little winding gesture to get the conversation back where she wanted it. 'That's why you didn't touch it?'

'Absolutely.'

Her smile was pretty bleak. 'You were right not to have done. It was clinically clean. More than just a polish-with-a-duster clean.'

I pulled a face. 'Wouldn't there be the odd bit of DNA on it?'

'Only a bit. A hair from the Community Support Officer. But nothing, repeat nothing else.'

Harvey joined in. 'I hope whoever got it that clean didn't damage the bowl in the process. If it was in good condition it was worth – what, five hundred pounds? Maybe more?'

'I didn't look all that closely, but yes. And it looked perfect. Have you run to earth the guy who planted it? I know the CCTV pictures weren't great, but—'

'He pops up, but again, not very clearly, on your Mrs Walker's camera pictures,' she said, pulling a face. She looked around. 'I take it you gave her the morning off?'

'No. No, actually I haven't spoken to her today. I assumed she was with her new boyfriend, Mr Banner. They may just have lost track of time. She's never let us down yet,' I added, a frown appearing of its own accord. 'Of course, she might just be caught in traffic.'

'On a Sunday?'

'And the doors aren't open to the public yet. This is her first fair – she might not know you should get in early.'

'Let me know if she doesn't come – say, within the next half hour. I can understand that you might not wish to disturb love's young dream, but I wouldn't have the slightest compunction.'

Another nice word. No time to worry about that now, however. 'Have you . . .' I searched for the police formula '. . . any reason to believe he's not kosher?'

She smiled grimly. 'Maybe I'm just paranoid too.'

I could have sworn she looked over my shoulder at Harvey. Perhaps he thought so too. He produced his card. 'You might want to check me out too. I don't know if it's relevant, but because I do some voluntary work, I've had to have a Criminal Record check too. Negative,' he added with a smile that didn't so much as flicker towards the smug end of the spectrum.

She nodded. 'As a matter of interest, Lina, do you happen to know where Mrs Walker met her new boyfriend?'

'He came into the shop,' I said slowly. 'And he was so pleased to see her here. Took her for a very long lunch. And then she came asking to have time off so she could have her hair done on Tuesday when they planned their first date.'

'Let's just hope their affair moved rather quicker than she expected, then,' she said, and turned to move away.

Not yet she couldn't. 'Freya, you never answered my question about Chris Mason. Did you run him to earth? No? And would you mind my asking if the five hundred pounds I gave Dilly just before the assault on her ever came to light?' She didn't need to answer either question. 'A man can get a long way with that much cash in his pocket.'

'True. He won't need a cash machine yet. And he may avoid using his mobile phone. But we've still got a few tricks up our sleeve, Lina – surveillance cameras. Number recognition cameras. We'll pick him up soon. Don't worry. Ah! The paying public.' She turned back for a moment, dropping her voice. 'We've put out a statement about the assault on Dilly, but haven't mentioned you at all. With luck, the other stall holders will be so irritated at having to traipse through the hotel for alternative loos you won't figure in any conversations at all. If they do, well, we'll just have to hope that having Mr Sanditon here will allay everyone's fears.'

If there'd been punters for everyone else and none for me, he might have had to. But there was hardly anyone around yet.

'Tell me about this Lowestoft tea bowl,' he said, 'and the Broad-Ticemans.'

I gave a quick resumé.

He nodded. 'You've seen that they've got a lot of money tied up in the property and in paintings?'

'They're rich,' I exploded. 'Bloody rich.'

'Only if they can sell their assets. The way the market is now they may actually be suffering cash poverty.'

'Poor things,' I said, not very sincerely, perhaps because I knew at first hand about the commoner sort of poverty. 'But why try to get at me? What had I ever done to them? We inhabit different worlds. No competition, no rivalry. She played with me like a cat playing with a pretty dim mouse.'

'First, you're pretty but not dim. Secondly, I've known bored young women like her do odd things simply because they have the power to do them. You might have been imagining the whole camera and DNA thing; she might just have wanted to show you things and have some company for lunch. And when you pulled out, she got miffed and decided to teach you a lesson. Or not. Simply behaved as she usually does, with no consideration.'

'Are they and Lady P best buddies?' Lady P sounded so much more grotesque than the name I'd really known her by, Nella.

'I've never seen them in each other's company. Nor am I likely to now. And not just because Lady Petronella's in prison. Afterwards, no one would want to be tarred with her brush. Knowingly fencing, forging provenances, ringing silverware . . . She's rather brought the whole profession into disrepute, hasn't she? And you can't rub shoulders with people like that without calling your own honesty into question.' As if to reassure me that that didn't apply to me, he put his arm round my shoulder and kissed me. What Griff, even my father, would have made of such public displays I dreaded to think.

Although we certainly didn't need Mary Walker to fight back the hordes descending on the stall, Webb's official anxiety was infectious, and I caught myself looking regularly at my watch.

'Why don't you simply phone the woman? You're her boss, after all.' Harvey changed the angle of a plate by a millimetre.

'I know I am. Mind you, everyone assumes it's the other way round. Funny, I can't get round to calling her Mary. She was a teacher,' I added. 'Retired and lost her husband almost immediately.'

'Did she talk him to death? Go on, phone her. No need to sound headmistressy.' He watched as I fished out my mobile. 'Now what are you doing?'

He might as well have the truth. 'I'm practising what I want to say, in case I have to leave a message.'

'Everyone I know leaves garbled messages.'

'I want to get them right.'

Sure enough, I was switched to voicemail. 'Good morning, Mrs Walker. Lina here. I'm just a bit worried that I haven't seen you today. It's not a problem if you can't make it – but just phone me back when you get this to say you're OK. Bye.'

'Very good. You could give lessons.' He was about to kiss me again when he said, 'Punter approaching from your left?' He stepped back and let me take centre stage.

It wasn't the man who'd left the tea bowl, but another, equally nondescript one. It wasn't a piece of china he held in his hand. It was a squeezy bottle. And it was pointing at me.

TWENTY-SEVEN

'Darling, it was a choice between my suit and your face. No contest. Now, are you sure he didn't get you?'

We were lying on the floor, me on my back and Harvey on top of me, in the cramped space behind the display area where he'd pushed me away from the jet of bleach. It was all too clear that in other circumstances he'd have enjoyed it very much indeed. Actually, I would too. At last he moved enough for me to roll away and on to all fours. On the other side of the display table there was a lot of yelling. I crawled beneath to see what was going on. Mistake. All I could see was feet, a lot of them: if I twitched the pleated fabric modesty panel, goodness knows how many pieces of china I would pull off.

At last, both of us picking our way round some splashes that were rapidly giving the carpet the clean of its life, we got to our feet. Harvey shed his jacket and sniffed.

Bleach. At least it wasn't acid. Meanwhile, the scuffle had moved from our stall to way down the room. Punters were pressed up against stalls – at least one man was trying to nick something from a display under cover of all the chaos.

Without stopping to think, I hurtled towards him. 'Stop, thief!'

That improved everything no end. Or not. By the time I got there the brooch or whatever was back where it should be, and everyone close by looked as if not even Benecol would melt in their mouths. At least the stall holder had time to lock the case – idiot, leaving it open in the first place. And I was close enough to see that under a pile of navy blue was the guy with the bleach bottle.

I assumed he'd have to stay there till he was cuffed. But somehow he was using the scrum to ease himself free.

In his dreams.

A great rococo brass candlestick found its way into my hand. As soon as I could get in there, his skull would feel it. With luck it'd be the last thing he'd ever feel. There was just that candlestick and his skull in the whole world.

Until someone grabbed my arm. A voice said, 'Don't be a bloody fool. We need him to talk, woman. Just behave yourself.'

I couldn't not. I was in an arm lock myself, and I knew from bitter experience that, bar fighting very dirty indeed, there was nothing I could do to free myself. But then the candlestick was gone, and my arm was my own again. Harvey was gathering me up and holding me tightly, but it was a hug, not a restraint. The police had the man I'd been ready to kill on his feet and there was a sudden silence.

'OK,' Freya yelled. 'Fun's over, everyone. Just carry on spending your money!'

Would they hell. Not with all that lot to talk over. What was really needed was someone with a bit of initiative printing off a load of T-shirts saying, *I SURVIVED THE BLEACH BOMBER*. I had a nasty feeling that Harvey and I were about to become the focus of everyone's attention. We couldn't even retreat to the quiet of our stall because it was suddenly an official crime scene. Where the white paper suit brigade had popped up from, and so promptly, too, I'd no idea.

So we had to act normal, even if neither of us felt like it. I turned to him with a smile. 'I didn't know you could do arm locks.'

'I can't. I don't. This guy suddenly appeared from nowhere, disarmed you, and then vanished. Weird. But thank God he did. What the hell were you thinking of, Lina?' There was an edge to his voice I'd never heard before.

I shook my head. 'It's what I do. You know there's this fight or flight hormone? In my case, it only operates one way. Fight. Has as long as I remember. I thought the therapy had sorted it out. Sorted *me* out. But sometimes . . .' I'd better tell him another thing he wouldn't like. 'Usually I turn my anger on myself. I self-harm. No, not with a razor.

I don't cut myself. I hit myself. Hardly ever these days. So if I had a row with Griff, say, a really bad one, I wouldn't punch him – oh, never, ever – but I might black my own eye.'

He managed a smile. 'So if we ever have a row, I must handcuff you first? For your sake, not mine?'

I kissed his cheek. 'Exactly. Now, what am I supposed to do with all this lot before one of the Scenes of Crime Officers knocks something over?'

He shook his head. 'Not you, Lina. Us. OK?'

Before I could say anything, one of the SOCOs reared up, like a polar bear clutching a pretty poor fish. 'This your mobile? 'Cos someone's trying to leave you a message and she's run out of time twice.'

I grabbed it and pressed the call button. Only it wasn't. It was the conference button. So now everyone in the hall heard poor Mary Walker's tearful confession that she'd got terrible cystitis and couldn't leave the loo. I managed to switch the bloody thing off just as she was explaining – in detail – what had caused it. Too much information all round. Even I was blushing.

Harvey, on the other hand, laughed, but kindly, I thought. 'Nice when the silver generation discovers the joys of sex all over again. For goodness' sake, Lina, don't be a prude.' He looked at me closely. 'Griff's got a partner – how do you deal with that?'

'I suppose,' I said slowly, 'because they're very discreet. Sure, Aidan spends time with both of us, but Griff goes to his place pretty often, and I don't ask any questions. Any more than Griff asks about my sex life,' I added, hoping he'd get the message.

'He might not ask, but he's mighty concerned,' he said. 'Isn't he? Does he like *any* of your suitors?'

'He quite likes Will.' It was only as I answered the question that I realized that he was saying something else. 'Why should you think he doesn't like you?'

Freya Webb appeared before Harvey could reply. The trouble was, I was now trying to work out the answer for myself.

'We're putting it about that your attacker is a loony making a random attack,' she said.

'In those precise non-PC words?' Harvey asked, with a twinkle. 'And are you saying it's the same loony as yesterday, or are the public to assume that Lina attracts loonies like blood attracts piranhas?'

'We're just keeping our cards close to our chests. I came to ask two things: have you had any news of Mary Walker yet?'

'Oh, the whole fair has had news of Mary Walker,' Harvey replied. 'Cystitis. Cystitis brought about by an excess of sex, to be precise. Lina's phone was on conference.'

'Shit! Oh, the poor woman.'

'That'll cure her of messing around with a bloke when she should have been working,' I said, though I couldn't quite tell whether I was joking or not. At least the other two laughed. So I must have been. And then I thought of Harvey and me, and I'll swear the blush came up all the way from my navel. 'What was the second question?' I asked.

'What do you want to do about your stall? Dismantle the whole thing and go off home?'

I couldn't believe what I was hearing. 'Why? Surely we can move the stock? I came here to sell antiques, Freya, not go into victim mode.'

Perhaps people took pity on Tripp and Townend, now looking as if they were operating in some table-top sale. It could have been worse, as Harvey pointed out. we could have had our own personal boot fair out in the car park. Anyway, we sold more than enough to cover the event fees, and Harvey declared he was proud of me. At one point we had a mini-tiff, because he didn't want me to put his ruined coat through our insurance.

'It's all a bit academic, anyway, isn't it?' he said at last. 'It's tucked away in an evidence bag for the duration. And remember, Lina, my jacket is disposable. Your eyes aren't. So no more arguments.'

What on earth will you tell your wife? No, I didn't let the words out, but they formed themselves in my head for no reason at all. That divvy thing? And they bumped round in there long enough to worry me. At last they settled down in a corner deep enough to be buried, but I didn't like the spiteful backward glance they gave as I left them to it.

Halfway through the afternoon he insisted on getting us some food. Almost as he left the room, my phone went. This time I made sure I was pressing the right button. Good job, too.

'Someone's got it in for you all right, eh, doll.'

'Any idea who?'

'Me if you try and crack anyone's skull. Bloody hell, talk about a street-fighter. I'm on to it, doll. Till I tell you different, watch your back. Don't trust no one.'

'That's a big help, Titus,' I told the dead phone. Had it been him who'd stopped me braining Domestos Man? Whoops. Had it been *he*?

Although our route home took us pretty near Bossingham Hall, Harvey didn't seem keen to go. In fact, he looked almost relieved when I got a call from Freya asking if I wanted an update. It meant going to Maidstone nick, but at least that didn't seem so bad with Harvey to hold my hand. This time he didn't argue about leaving the van unattended. Either he was reassured by a nice big CCTV camera that would peer at it every time it did a scan, or he thought my insurance would cover the van contents if it got nicked – after all, he'd bought hardly anything until the last ten minutes, when he'd alighted on a pretty Chinese famille rose plate without any help from me. There was a visible crack in it: I had the feeling that any time now I'd be asked to fix it.

I'd found nothing to buy the whole sale. Where my divvying gift had gone I'd no idea. Perhaps it thought that anyone who was prepared to kill someone just for squirting bleach at her didn't deserve any profitable treats.

'He's not talking,' Freya declared, by way of greeting. 'And he's not on our system, as far as we can tell. In fact, one of the lads has a theory that he's not a UK national.'

'You mean not talking at all? Not just saying *No comment* to everything?'

'I mean exactly that. He won't speak to us, or to the duty solicitor. Schtum. Zipped. Whatever. Of course, the fact that we've got him in custody, with lots of our people as witnesses, plus the CCTV footage, means we can charge him. There's even his DNA all over the bottle. His and absolutely no one else's,' she added looking me in the eye.

'You've probably got me on CCTV,' I added, 'threatening him with a brass candlestick.'

'So long as it was only a threat, Lina, we won't talk about that, if you don't mind.'

'What you can tell me,' I said, 'is who stopped me.'

'No, we can't. Not at the moment.'

For *can't*, read *won't*. Surely it wasn't Morris? It must be! My heart sang. Yes, that's right. *Sang*. Not *sank*. Though I suppose it would have been *sunk*, really. What would he make of Harvey? And what would he make of Harvey and me, not the Will of whom Griff had boasted?

To take my mind off it all, I said, 'I don't suppose anyone managed to check if the Broad-Ticemans had a tea bowl sitting under a spotlight? I think it was in a room near the dining room, where I was shown the damaged epergne.'

She shook her head. 'Apparently they're away on holiday.'

'I believe they left some staff to keep an eye on things. Couldn't someone check? I could, so long I was with you, couldn't I?'

'In your dreams, Lina. Give me a quick sketch map of where it should be and I'll get someone on to it. Tomorrow. It hasn't quite the same priority, I have to admit, as finding Mason.'

A quick look at her face confirmed the worst. 'Poor Dilly. And it was all my fault.'

'No it wasn't,' Harvey said. 'It was her killer's. His and his alone.'

'If I hadn't wanted to keep my hands so lily-white pure! If I'd made more effort . . .'

'Lina,' Harvey said very firmly, 'you made the effort. You got her the cash. You put it in her hand. Apart from tailing her to the loo, and everywhere else she went, what could you have done? You might even have had your throat cut or your brains knocked out or whatever.'

For a terrible moment I'd been afraid he'd reveal how she'd been killed and betray himself as the killer. Where had that come from? I really was worrying myself this afternoon.

'You know what,' I said, now horrifying myself by starting to cry, 'I just want to go home.'

What I meant was I wanted an evening's cosseting from Griff – reading a play aloud, perhaps, or watching the DVD of a play or movie he thought I should know. I didn't mean a polite evening with the three of us, all minding our manners and using the correct cutlery.

Although he looked tired, Griff probably wasn't as exhausted as either of us. But he took his role as chaperone very seriously indeed. He allowed us five minutes to say a nice kissy goodnight, and then started moving round in a way that said very clearly he wanted us out of the hallway so he could use the stairs.

Eventually Harvey took the hint. 'I'll see you tomorrow morning. After breakfast,' he said, with a little jerk of his head in Griff's direction. 'And then I suppose we beard your father in his den.'

Perhaps it was time to do a little bearding on my own account. I marched back into the living room. 'Griff,' I said, my heart breaking at the hardness of my voice, 'we have to talk. You have to talk. You have to tell me why you don't like Harvey. And, more importantly, you have to tell me why your so-called mate Douggie hates you enough to try to ruin you by attacking me.'

TWENTY-EIGHT

'It was something you said to me,' I said, allowing him a teaspoonful of brandy to swirl in a pretty Victorian balloon, as I sat him down in his favourite chair. I found I deserved another glass of wine and sat on mine. 'That anyone attacking me attacked you. I'm wondering if it's the other way round. And the only people I can think of are X, Douggie and Aidan. Aidan and I are never going to be best mates, but I respect him far too much to pop him on my list of suspects, which leaves X and Douggie. If you didn't pay enough booze money, X could kill you with a kitchen knife before dawn, so I don't think he'd need to be subtle. But Douggie and you go way back, and he put the police on to us. Not something you'd do to someone you liked.'

Griff's colour was returning. But he didn't speak, just nodding to encourage me.

'The police option didn't work, did it? So he needed an alternative. I would bet today's takings he knows the Broad-Ticemans. He's the sort of man who'd naturally delegate – wouldn't soil his hands with dirty work. And he's probably university educated – he'd know about DNA traces and stuff. And maybe, just maybe, he didn't want to have my name on a card in the British Museum.' And I did, very much indeed.

He bit his lip. I'd never seen him so frail and vulnerable. 'I never thought . . . I'm not a man to bear grudges. And you'd have thought that Douggie, since he's risen so far in the world, way above our good selves, would have had the grace to forgive and forget. It was way back in the days that being gay was illegal, my love. I was trying to pretend to be straight, as were so many like me. I flirted a great deal with the prettiest women in town, but obviously – let's just say, I wasn't the marrying sort. But one young lady I dallied with – I'm sorry to use such dated terms, but that was how we thought of women in those days – was supposed to be young Douggie's property. She wore his ring, after all. But she was a freer spirit than he, and preferred her jewellery to be more recent in origin than his choice. More recent and from Bond Street. I was certainly not offering a ring, but she saw an actor with a little money as a more attractive proposition than the underpaid and academic Douggie. Actually, she saw a lot of men as more attractive than Douggie. Somehow he'd got himself engaged to someone your generation would assuredly call a slag. You could say I did him a service.'

'And did you tell him that?'

'Possibly. In the heat of the moment. But he went on to marry – someone else – and I came out. And I assumed we were all adults. What I wonder, however, is if he thought you were my blood granddaughter. Which would, all these years later, have brought into question the plea of homosexuality I offered him in mitigation.'

'You actually told him you were gay? Wasn't that a bit of a risk?'

'A few years, a very few years, earlier it might have been. But by then we were well into the Sixties, and the 1967 Act was in sight. But to hold such a grudge . . . I can't imagine anyone doing so.'

'So would you rather blame X? I've always worried that you didn't pay him enough.'

'My love, X can't read or write. And with all the cheap booze he sinks I don't think he's well enough to make the sort of plans that have circled round you. I'd rather blame Arthur Habgood. Unless he really is your grandfather.'

'Harvey says when he can't get his way, he's vengeful. He may well have his knife into someone else by now. Hey, vengeful's a good word. I wonder where that popped up from. He doesn't move in the Broad-Ticeman sort of circle, and I bet Douggie does. And with their art exporting activities, the B-Ts would know all sorts of folk who didn't speak much English and would accept a dirty job as part of an immigration scam.'

He held up his hands. At least they weren't shaking any more. His eyes were as shrewd as ever. 'What's this about people who don't speak much English? And would do dirty jobs?'

My turn to bite my lip. 'You'll have noticed that Harvey wasn't wearing a jacket at supper time. It wasn't because he found the central heating too hot. It was because someone had doused it in bleach. Aimed for me. I wasn't going to tell you in case it upset you. And now it has.' I allowed a drop more brandy to fall into his glass.

'The police know?'

'Yes. And I'm afraid they're going to have to know about X and about Douggie.' But not, if I could help it, about Titus. 'I bet he doesn't like the fact that Douggie means something *so* not respectable on the streets.' I explained.

'At least you've found something to cheer me up,' he said, chortling.

'And at least you're not scratching and your face has gone down,' I said, 'so there are two more reasons to be cheerful. But there is just one more thing, Griff. What's Harvey done to get up your nose?' I waited. 'Do you know something I should know? Like he's married?'

He shook his head. 'I don't know anything, anything at all. But he's a good deal older than you and is clearly a man of the world, as we used to say. Most of all,' he added with a funny little smile, 'he wanted you to leave Tripp and Townend and join his firm.'

'And I told him – and you – right at the start that I wouldn't.'

'But that was before you started to fall in love with him.'

'And that was before I had this divvy thing,' I whispered, crouching beside him so I could bury my face in his shoulder. 'Not about a plate or a ring or anything. About Harvey. I heard this voice in my head, wondering what he'd tell his wife about the jacket. My divvy voice. I told myself it wasn't working, because it hadn't taken me to anything I should buy. But it was.'

'And have you asked him?'

I pulled away gently. 'Not yet. I'm waiting for the

moment. I don't think I'd want to be in his company too much if he is, because I really do fancy him and you know I don't do married men. Full stop. We're going to take those photos to Bossingham Hall tomorrow, remember, so I'll wait until that's out of the way.'

Griff nodded reflectively. 'It'll be interesting to see what Elham makes of him. He's an old soak, just like X, but, again, just like X, he does have these extraordinary moments of insight. And in his own weird way he loves you, my child.' He looked me straight in the eye. 'And that's another reason why you won't leave Kent, isn't it? Because you don't want to leave him.'

I kept him waiting a long time. Even that bloody clock struck. 'I certainly don't want to leave him to his own devices. Not halfway through my restoration project. He'd go back under within a week without someone to keep an eye on him. And I could scarcely ask you to.'

'You know, if I thought you were really happy with Harvey, in Devon or wherever, I just might. But he's not a project, loved one. He's your own flesh and blood.'

I helped him to his feet so I could hug him. 'He's not my family though, is he?'

There was no point in setting off very early to Bossingham Hall, so I called Freya and told her about Douggie. She heard me through, occasionally stopping to check a fact.

'And this all started then?'

'Assuming the non-body was a false start, yes. It was the day after our meeting with Sir Douggie that I attracted Will's notice.'

'And then you attracted it in a rather different way. OK, I don't suppose anyone ever died of a broken heart. So this Sir Douggie's top end of the market, and would know the Broad-Ticemans. Ought to be Broad-Ticemen, oughtn't it? As it happens, I've sent Will round to look at their place this morning, to check on that bowl. OK, it's fine art, not heritage, but what the hell . . . I shouldn't imagine he'll be long. Will you be on this number?'

'No. I shall be out on family business. And Griff will be at the dentist's. As for Mrs Walker, who knows?' We shared a laugh. 'But you can always try my mobile. Freya, I know you won't want to tell me, but have you run Mason to earth yet?'

'I don't, and we haven't.'

'Have you really, really hunted near the place where we found the body, Will and I? Because – I don't know why. All that ground cover, I suppose . . . Not a lot of CCTV cameras, either,' I said with more conviction. 'And maybe more treasure . . . And Freya, just one more thing. And this is really, really important. Get the latest on Bernie Winters' health. I know he's on sick leave, you see . . .'

'Any moment I'm going to have you down as one of those nutcases that phones in with helpful suggestions about where we can find Madeleine McCann,' she said.

'I know. But all the same.'

She covered the phone and spoke to someone.

'Any moment I will,' she said. 'But not quite yet.'

I'd phoned to warn my father that I should be bringing the digitally enhanced photos I'd promised, plus the man who owned the originals. I didn't mention the cake and biscuits Griff had provided, and didn't warn him about the Beamer, because I'd assumed I'd be driving our van. But if Harvey was prepared to risk his suspension on that track, who was I to argue?

'Does all this ring any bells, Harvey?' I asked, as he picked his way towards the house, the car making much less of a meal of the jolts than the van did.

'None at all. I was born and bred down in Devon and tend to regard Kent as outer darkness. And as for the photos, you've seen they're all taken too close to walls to get any idea of the building as a whole.' As the full glory of the house hit him, he gasped. 'This is lovely, isn't it? And it might be yours, one day?'

'Not a chance. It's all owned by trustees, even the part my father lives in. And when he dies, it will revert to them.'

'You don't get a bean, then. What a shame.'

'Thanks to Griff I've got a damn sight more beans than I had when I was a kid,' I said, not thinking I needed to tell him about the money in trust for all my father's offspring, not just me. 'And with the skills his friends taught me I can always earn more. So long as people keep breaking things. Do you want me to tackle the crack in that Famille Rose plate, by the way?'

'I was afraid you'd never ask. I'll leave it with you before I go back to Devon.'

So he did intend to keep in touch with me. Had he bought a damaged plate so he had a reason to? An excuse, if he had a wife? Damn that idea, for insisting on popping up, even as he was helping me out of the car and kissing my hand as he did so.

My father, standing on the front step, must have seen the gesture, but didn't remark on it. He was decidedly cleaner than usual, freshly shaved and wearing his London outfit. He was even reasonably sober.

'I've found some more photos to compare yours with,' he said, showing us into his living room. Already on the table were the trinkets he'd shown me before, minus the Cartier watch. Presumably he was keeping that on one side until he'd decided whether Harvey really was Nanny Baird's true heir. I passed him my magnifying glass, and wandered off to make tea, because, family reminiscences not being exactly my thing, I thought I'd feel a great deal more comfortable in the kitchen.

I was waiting for the kettle to boil and trying to decide what I felt when I had a phone call. 'Will?'

'Tell me exactly where I ought to find that tea bowl,' he said.

I did. He cut the call.

Now that was interesting.

At last I was ready to carry the tray back through, with the jasmine green tea that was my father's grudging favourite. My father liked good china cups – in fact he refused point blank to use a collection of thick mugs someone had long ago left in the kitchen – and I'd unearthed enough Minton plates to make the whole thing quite jolly. It'd get even more festive if the vintage champagne I'd spotted in the fridge was called for.

Another phone call. 'Are you sure that's where it should be?'
'Positive.'

'Interesting. Because all I've got is a ring of dust. Can't get the staff, can you?' End of call.

The two men were shaking hands warmly when I pushed the door open, but Harvey sprang away to take the tray from me.

'One thing I can't get hold of is this name of yours,' my father said, as if he'd not noticed my presence. 'Sanditon. What sort of name is that?'

'My real name's not very user-friendly. I was christened Ronald Harvey Biggs. And I think you'll find Ronnie Biggs isn't the best name to trade under. My mother was a Jane Austen freak. Hence Harvey Sanditon.'

'The unfinished novel, the one most concerned with trade,' I said.

'God, and you pretend you're uneducated!' he said with affectionate irritation. 'I wish she was *my* daughter, sir.'

Daughter! What sort of Freudian slip was that when it was at home?

'She's mine and I'm proud of her.' My father nodded with pride across the room. No, I mustn't expect a hug or anything like it.

'Do you have any daughters, Harvey?' I asked, my voice as even as I could make it.

Harvey went ivory white.

Even my father noticed and pushed a chair forward, not one he'd cleaned, unfortunately.

Harvey didn't sit, but gripped the back. 'Just a son. Very good at cricket.'

'You should talk to Griff about him. He's passionate about the game.' My lips were still working quite nicely. Perhaps I should be grateful for those bloody divvy's premonitions. 'So you are Nanny Baird's relative. What a weird coincidence.'

'No. Nothing's proved. You can't see the whole of the toddler's face in any of them. OK, it's likely. But it'd never convince a lawyer. And we've agreed neither of us needs convincing either way. It's just a nice theory.'

My phone again. Freya. 'There's been an interesting development or two. Care to come over?'

'I'd need a lift. I'm out in Bossingham, in Lord Elham's wing of Bossingham Hall. Not the main drive, up a little track off Mann's Hill.'

'Could you bear it if I asked Will to collect you?' She didn't wait for an answer.

'I could—' Harvey began.

'It could take forever,' I said. 'And I know you've got to tackle the dreaded A303.' Should I take a risk? 'If you want to drop off the plate at the shop I'll fix it for you. I can return it next time Griff and I are in Devon. Powderham or Matford?'

He nodded. 'I'd best be off, then.'

My father looked at the unused tea things, but said nothing. He heaved himself to his feet. 'We'll see you out.' He offered me his hooked arm, and we progressed to the front door together, standing on the bottom step to wave our guest goodbye.

When we were back in his living room, he said, quite huskily, 'That was a terrific performance, my girl. Stiff upper lip and all that.'

'How did you know?' I asked numbly.

'That old bugger Griff, of course. Saw this Ronnie Biggs' picture in some magazine at the dentist's. With his wife. Phoned me. But you knew anyway?'

'Inspired guess.'

He shook his head. 'More like what you do with the china. Talking of which, I could do with a bit more bubbly. Hang on, before you go walkabout, you should try this for size.' He dug in his pocket and produced a leather covered box. 'Was going to save it for your birthday, but you earned it today. No, I wouldn't have let anyone else have it even if he could have dotted all the i's and crossed all the t's. Here you are. What the bloody hell's that racket? The damned house isn't on fire, is it?'

Just Will, employing blues and twos. The walkabout would have to wait. But at least I managed to put my arms round my father's neck and give him a hug. He even patted my back lightly in return.

* * *

Not every one travels to a police station with a Cartier watch round her wrist. I pulled my sleeve down over it, in case anyone wanted to accuse me of nicking it. Will told me he was under instructions to say nothing of what was going on, but it was clear he was as pleased as I was to have found a spot that just fitted the tea bowl base. SOCOs were happily recording all their findings, according to Will.

Freya swept in to greet us both in a conference room, one with all those clever electronic screens showing what people should be looking at. 'How well do you know your Shakespeare, folks? Lina?'

What sort of question was that? It hadn't been a very easy day so far, and I was tempted to tell her where to put her stupid test. But she was clearly bubbling with something, and although the topmost file of the pile she'd dumped on a table clearly said BUDGET I didn't think it was with the joys of accounts.

'It depends which play,' I said without a smile.

'*Hamlet*. The bit where Claudius is talking about his wedding to whats-her-name?'

'Gertrude,' Will prompted. '. . . *The imperial jointress to this warlike state . . .*'

'Yes! That's the good thing about you graduate fast-tracked people, you know your stuff. *With an auspicious and a dropping eye*. Two conflicting emotions. Which is what we've got here.'

She waited while the room filled up with other officers, one or two of whom I recognized from the fair. Not PC Acne, and not Bernie Winters. 'Firstly, I have to give you all some bad news. PC Winters, known to a lot of you as Bernie, has died. He was suffering from liver cancer. But he didn't die of it. He killed himself. Because he'd committed a crime no police officer should ever commit. He'd killed someone. Chris Mason. We found both the bodies by the site near Ottinge that we've all been protecting because of its national importance. Mason was strangled; Bernie hanged himself.'

Someone asked, 'Why should he—?' But, covering his mouth, sprinted off without waiting for an answer.

Freya looked at me.

'Night hawking?' I suggested. 'Bernie loathed night hawks. Worse than just thieves, he said. They desecrated graves, like the one Will and I found by accident.'

'Female, ninth century,' Will put in, with a quick smile at me.

'And he must have been a bit careless about hiding his loot,' I continued, 'because his wife managed to sell a ring on her jewellery stall. To me. But he can't have had anything to do with the one I bought at auction.'

'Actually, it's a slightly different period,' Will put in again. 'If it's the one we found in Mason's lock up. Plus a whole lot of other stuff. You've heard of the Staffordshire hoard? This isn't as big – yet. But it could be just as important. And Mason had destroyed all sorts of vital evidence the archaeologists could have used.'

'Poor Bernie. The thing he hated most. And if you know you're dying, you might decide to take the law into your own hands,' I said quietly. Should I offer them our CCTV footage to show how unhinged he was? Perhaps later, in private.

'We think he'd tried it before,' Webb said. 'When you found your "body", Lina. But something must have interrupted him and he stopped. Mason could hardly complain, could he? Not without giving the game away.'

'Which of them switched the road sign around?'

'Who knows? Whoever it was was trying to deter other people from finding the site, I should imagine. As these people will all tell you, Lina, we tie up most of the ends, but sometimes not all.'

I smiled. And suddenly more Shakespeare came into my head. *'There's a divinity that shapes our ends, rough hew them how we will.'* I caught Freya's eye and straightened my shoulders. 'But what's the good news you promised, DCI Webb?' After all, she was very much on duty and might not appreciate my using her first name.

She smiled. 'That's about you, too, Lina. Sir Douglas Nelson and our friends the Broad-Ticemans. There is a connection. A very interesting one. But here we've had to consult with one of our colleagues from Met Fine Art Squad, ladies and gentleman, so he knows his onions.'

And in walked a familiar figure. 'Morris!' I gasped. Thank God there was a table between us, or despite everything I'd have run into his arms.

I've a nasty suspicion he might have held his arms open for me, too, from the way his colour came and went when he spotted me. But he confined himself to a curt nod, and kept his eyes away from me as he did the meet and greet stuff with his Kentish colleagues.

It seemed best for me to shut down any emotions I might have been feeling – there wasn't time for me to examine them as my therapist had told me. But I did recognize was a surge of anger, alongside – well, the desire to hug him. Hug! As if.

But he was already speaking, tapping the screen to bring up photos of the people and the places he was speaking about. I thought the technology had gone a bit OTT when a snap of the British Museum flew up. It was, come to think of it, like those rather random images they use on TV news stories, when they don't want to have a blank behind the presenter's head. If there's a health scare, they show pictures of hospital wards, and people looking busy – that sort of thing. Anyway, it was then replaced with a photo of a very haggard old-looking Sir Douggie that would have made Griff grin maliciously, and then by a set of official-looking snaps of ancient artefacts.

'A number of these items have surfaced in collections across the world – acquired, in general, by people not too fussy about provenance.' He couldn't resist a glance in my direction. I licked an index finger and marked a figure one in the air. 'In fact the provenance, had they seen it, would have been impeccable – from the BM's vaults. It was only when a bona fide collector was offered something he'd only seen in a textbook – one written, ironically, by Sir Douglas – and contacted his local force that we got involved. And then things started to get interesting.'

'Not for me,' I'd recovered enough to chime in. 'They got interesting for Griff and me when Sir Douggie accused us of stealing Saxon artefacts and put you lot on to us, Will.' If I'd had more panache, I'd have reached over to squeeze his hand. I didn't want to give the lie to Griff's claim that he and I were besotted with each other, after all. As it was, all I could manage was a warm smile.

Morris registered the smile, I was sure of that, but continued, 'Perhaps he thought that if he showed he was lily-white pure in the matter of stolen items it would throw up a smokescreen around his own activities. Stealing big time from the BM. But he's a Very Respectable Person.' You could almost see the capital letters. 'Not the sort of guy to know the sort of fences we usually deal with. So we needed to find a connection with someone whose business was international, who was used to sending expensive and very well packed items through Customs and Excise without the inconvenience of having them randomly opened and checked. It was something Lina Townend said that gave me the idea.'

Lina Townend, eh? How very official.

'I leafed through endless antiques and society magazines and found several pictures of him at the same gathering as one of your Kentish residents.'

Just as Griff had found pictures of Harvey and his wife. But Harvey was yesterday's news. Already.

'Which brings us on to Charles and Phoebe Broad-Ticeman. Why such a distinguished and hitherto irreproachable man should turn to crime I've yet to find out.'

'Cash flow problems,' I heard myself saying. 'He may be stinking rich by the standards of everyone here, but he's got to sell stuff or he doesn't have any cash. And the way the market is now . . .' I gave what I hoped was a worldly-wise shrug.

'So why should Broad-Ticeman want to mess up Lina's reputation?' Webb put in.

'I don't know. Yet.'

'Try this theory for size,' I said, suddenly enjoying the fact that I knew more than a lot of experts. 'Griff – that's my business partner and very dear friend,' I added, for the benefit of any officers who might not know him from Adam, 'offended Sir Douggie years back. Most other people forget grudges. Sir Douggie doesn't seem to be that type. So Griff's theory is that these attacks on my reputation have been ways at getting at him. So presumably he roped his posh mate in to help with the dirty work.'

'Presumably doesn't get convictions, unfortunately,' Webb observed. 'But we'll certainly put that to him. For corroboration, we'll ask the people who mounted the bowl and the bleach incidents. We've got good clear images of the people involved in the weekend's activities.'

'Any familiar faces?' Morris asked.

'Some of our local rent-a-villains – the sort of toerags who'll do anything for a couple of bob. I'm sure we'll pick them up soon and sort it all out.'

'What about the silent ones?' I asked, not knowing I shouldn't.

'We've an idea that the Borders Agency people might be interested in them – there's a suspicion that the big packing cases Broad-Ticeman sent abroad may not have come back empty.' She looked around the room. 'Anything else we should all know?'

Will said, 'Since the media are bound to get wind of the . . . the new crime scene, ma'am, English Heritage and the other archaeologists would like to go public. It's a major site, and will attract a lot of attention. There's talk of the local museums setting up a fund so that all the finds can be kept together.'

'In that case, they'd better have my ring too,' I said. 'Not that it is my ring, is it? For all I bought it honestly, it was stolen property, and not mine at all. Ever.'

'I'm afraid that's the law, Lina. I was wondering how to break it to you,' Morris said.

I wished he hadn't sounded so kind. Kindness always makes me want to cry. I stuck out my chin. 'Well, I've still got the other one. The one I accidentally bought at auction. Unless that was nicked too?'

'Don't worry – we're busy checking,' Will said. Which worried me all the more.

*   *   *

In the end, it was easier to donate the ring I'd bought at auction to Canterbury Museum, and let them sort it out. True, it ended up with a nice spotlight on it, and a little white card giving my name, but it wasn't quite the British Museum unveiling and champagne at the Savoy I'd secretly dreamed of. Tough.

Another ring I was more than interested in – my grandmother's – still lurked somewhere in Bossingham Hall, though my attempts to pick up its vibes consistently failed. On the other hand, I did find a nice rare piece of early Wedgwood under a bed, and an amazing Flemish mirror, tucked in the back of a wardrobe in my father's part of the attic. Not our area at all, of course, but it still brought in enough for a very great deal of champagne.

I was still celebrating that when I got a call from Freya Webb. They'd picked up the lowlife who they thought had popped the Broad-Ticemans' bowl on my stand, and would like me to ID him. It took me five seconds. He was quite happy to spill all he knew about the B-Ts, in return for whatever deal the police cut him. As were the illegal immigrant servants – the woman who was as scared of the dogs as I was, and her bleach-squirting husband.

The B-Ts' trial, and Sir Douggie's, will take place soon. A big affair. I'm not looking forward to going into the witness box, but I shall only be one of many. And there's something about justice being done in public that I like. These days, anyway. I know this view irritated Titus, but he was distinctly off me at the moment. My moment with the candlestick had profoundly disturbed him, since it broke his cardinal rule of never doing anything to attract the attention of the police.

Mrs Walker now sported an engagement ring. Mr Banner had decided not to buy one from us, for which, in view of what the world knew about his sexual prowess and endurance, I was very grateful. There was talk of me being her bridesmaid, but I continued to pray they'd have a very quiet register office wedding.

She'd been so contrite over what she called her dereliction of duty that she was ready to resign. But Griff's partner

Aidan broke an ankle, and Griff had to spend so much time in Tenterden that I had to swallow my immediate response and tell her I was happy for her to stay, with even more hours. Restoration work was flooding my way; maybe Harvey had put in a good word for me with his upmarket friends to salve his conscience. I saw him occasionally at fairs, or when he had something that needed my skills, but there was no more dashing round the country at unearthly hours to pick up the vase or whatever. I filed the occasional email he sent under E for Experience and didn't get round to replying. Likewise a couple Morris sent me after that meeting in Maidstone.

All those hopes Griff had of Will and me? Hard to tell. Will's on some long-term secondment, largely, I think, because his bosses don't want him to be romantically involved with a key witness. Or is that just a good excuse? We shall see. But a large box containing two wretched Toby jugs arrived this morning and if I worry about my own long face I shan't be able to tackle theirs.